Cast Me Not Away

Cast Me Not Away

Patricia Thomas

For Doug,
The real professor in my life.

Cast Me Not Away

This book is a work of fiction. Named locations are used fictitiously, and characters and incidents are the product of the author's imagination. Any resemblance to actual events or places or persons, living or dead, is entirely coincidental.

Published by
Lighthouse Christian Publishing
SAN 257-4330
5531 Dufferin Drive
Savage, Minnesota, 55378
United States of America

www.lighthousechristianpublishing.com

Prologue

No, not again! Only this time there were no gun shots, no screams of terror, yet the memory of his father's words supplied him comfort. *Once you start to run my son, do not stop and no matter what you hear behind you, remember Lot's wife and never, never look back. For they come by night, the darkness their friend. They will hunt you down, and when they catch you, my son, they will kill you. So, remember Lot's wife and never, never look back.*

She caught a glimpse of him from her dormitory window, a thin dark figure slipping between the bushes lining the building's foundation walls. The Headless Horsemen she thought, a smile lifting the corners of her mouth. Movement inside the sweatshirt hood signaled his fright and her body shivered in response.

"I know what it is to be afraid, to run with no place to go," she whispered, gently touching the glass with her fingertips.

And then she heard the sirens. Big red fire trucks lumbered up the cul-de-sac. Shielding her eyes from the piercing white light, she gently closed the heavy curtains hoping her roommate would stay asleep.

As the black smoke curled around the back door frame, he disappeared into the shadows. With his father's dying words driving him on, with the windows exploding and the fire fighters yelling he never looked back.

Chapter One – Monday

The Week of the Fire began innocuously enough. A bright Monday-morning sun arose in the east quickly erasing the thin layer of mid-October frost laid down the night before. Gray sidewalks crisscrossed the lush campus grass where sheep and cattle used to graze in the years before Phineas Barrett donated his farm in 1871 for an institution of higher education. One year later Miss Hannah Elizabeth Emerick founded the Quaker School for Women the only institution of its kind for hundreds of miles around.

The original brick walkway still runs between Frame Meetinghouse and Harvey Library forming the southern border of Emerick College. At the opposite end of campus a ruggedly handsome redhead took the front steps of Dalton Science Hall two at a time and disappeared inside the glass doors arriving just in time to deliver his eight o'clock lecture.

Ruthalice Michels parked her two-door lemon colored Focus in its designated spot and gathered her belongings. She pulled open the solid oak door to Frame Meetinghouse and walked down the dimly lit corridor. Stopping in front of the Office of Campus Ministry, she gave her green canvas bag a shake. "How is it possible to lose something that substantial?" she mumbled impatiently peering inside. "I know you're in there somewhere!" *unless, perish the thought, I've left my 'keys to the kingdom' at home on the kitchen counter.*

Her fingers sorted through the crumpled Kleenex, gum wrappers and assorted detritus at the bottom. "Aha!" she exclaimed as her middle finger snagged the bulky key ring. "Gotcha!" She flipped them over one at a time, located number 1749, and unlocked the office door. Having dealt efficiently with the first crisis of the day she stepped inside. Draping her russet colored cloak over the spindly clothes tree she picked a slender grey hair off the worsted fabric. The rough texture under her finger tips reminded her of saddle blankets which always brought with it the warm pungent smell of her best friend's horse barn *one of the most wonderful smells in the whole wide world!*

Ali stared at her reflection in the full-length mirror nailed to the back of the door. A woman with straight cut bangs and waist length thick braid stared back at her from light blue eyes. The woman placed a hand on each hip, sucked in her tummy, executed two quarter turns and ran an experienced eye down the length of the practical black cotton skirt double checking to make sure her slip wasn't showing. Satisfied she had passed muster, Ruthalice Michels was ready for whatever the world had in mind for the forty-eight year old Campus Minister of Emerick College. She recited in her best preacher voice, "*this* is the day which our Lord has made, let us rejoice and be glad in it. And," she added in a voice soft with gratitude, "thank you, God for trusting me with another day." Her week was off to a fantastic start.

With a sigh of satisfaction, Ruthalice surveyed her friendly headquarters. A surplus (though still serviceable) metal desk occupied most of the south wall. To her right floor-to-ceiling shelves were piled high with a haphazard collection of books. Miscellaneous trinkets picked up along life's journey were tucked between Bibles, volumes on spirituality and a variety of resource books. Bright red and blue squares of sticky paper covered with cryptic notes and to-do lists were stuck to the wall above her desk phone. Her seminary diploma in its polished mahogany frame though suitably plain still looked so handsome against the original off-white, bumpy plaster walls. Wetting a tissue with a cursory spit, Ruthalice bent and wiped a smudgy finger print off the glass. "Ruthalice Michels, Master of Divinity, I send you on your way today with this affirmation," her old mentor and spiritual guide intoned at the graduation ceremony. "You are a builder of bridges, and one day it will be said of you, well done my good and faithful servant." Mildly amused by her own frailties, Ruthalice chuckled softly. *Yours is such a lovely sentiment my dear Thomas, but oh how far short of its lofty goal I seem to be most of the time.*

She seized the frayed pull cord for the Venetian blinds and yanked them up. Outside the new day sparkled with possibility and promise. Sunlight reflected off the hand-painted sign of the Leaky Cup Coffee Café across Division Street and glinted off car windows passing by. Missy Springer, the proprietress of the café crossed the wide front porch and poured seed into a plastic bird feeder hanging from the rafters.

Having procrastinated as long as she dared, Ruthalice decided it was high time to make a sizeable dent in the number of unanswered messages confronting her. She scooted her spiffy new leather desk chair with it four sturdy little wheels across the wooden planked floor getting a tremendous kick out of knowing that if she really put her mind to it she could shoot clear across the office, down the hallway and end up in the classroom where she taught *Introduction to the Bible* every Monday, Wednesday and Friday at 10 o'clock. Two days after breaking her ankle and already tired of the cumbersome crutches, Ruthalice experimented with using her desk chair as a wheelchair. Careening into the classroom she narrowly missed barreling smack dab into the assistant professor of psychology who shrieked, leapt out of the way, and then demanded a ride. Captured by cell phone, a photo of the entire episode quickly texted its way across campus and much to the delight of those involved, ended up in the college year book.

Ali ripped the nearest post-it note off the wall and squinted. *It looks like 'call Becky re lunch'*. Intent on deciphering her scrawl the tentative knock on her door didn't register. The young woman tried again striking the door twice with her knuckles.

"Come on in, the door's open."

After a furtive glance down the hallway she stepped inside pulling the door shut behind her. Ruthalice spun around in her chair and broke into a grin.

"Rani, how nice to see you; haven't seen you all summer." Indicating the two overstuffed chairs on either side of a low coffee table she added, "Please have a seat."

Gathering her long denim skirt around her legs, Rani Brown chose the maroon and blue striped chair leaving Ali the frightfully gaudy orange alternative, a gift from the Lutheran Women's Tag Sale after no one hauled it away. Painfully aware that her extra-large purple blouse strewn with scarlet-red cherries clashed horribly with the chair's unfortunate fabric, the Campus Minister sat down and studied her visitor.

Regal; painfully shy and private, she seems more nervous than usual; braid now as long as mine but without the gray, about the age of Skylar.

Humming softly Ruthalice located the fire-starter under the coffee table and bent forward to light the lilac candle. Rani's coal black eyes studied her every move, *just like Skylar's after his dad died as though I might also disappear if he looked away for even an instant.* The gentle flickering invited sharing, but Rani's attention had turned to the small object in her right hand. As her long brown fingers relaxed their grip, a cluster of colorful little dolls appeared. Ruthalice leaned forward.

"Those are worry dolls aren't they?"

Rani's eyes filled with apprehension. Ruthalice slid the Kleenex box around the candle so it was within reach in case her visitor burst into tears. As her brain scrambled through its mental files searching for helpful tidbits of information about this particular student she frowned. *What was it? Oh, yes, the family had recently moved to Kingston to find work. Her dad's Kenyan and her mom's from Calcutta or some such terrible place!*

"I remember staying in your home about eight years ago when I was visiting Jamaican Friends. And your father was looking for a job," she added lamely.

"We moved from Port Antonio." Some hidden memory sent a shiver through Rani's slender body. "But now Papa manages *The Big Blue Mountain Coffee Shoppe* down by the harbor on Port Royal Street." Her eyes shone bright with pleasure.

"I love Blue Mountain Coffee! It's the best coffee in the entire Western Hemisphere!" Ali blurted out grinning broadly, her nose and tongue remembering the delicious smell and taste of Jamaica's famous coffee. "Maybe we can talk the Leaky Cup into serving Blue Mountain as one of their specialty coffees." An awkward silence fell between them. *So much for that great idea!*

As Rani pulled a pink tissue from the box and dabbed her eyes, Ruthalice grew uneasy. "Is there something wrong at home" she inquired gently. Rani shook her head. "And you and your roommate are getting along ok now, right?" This sparked a twinkle in her enormous eyes.

"Yes," she replied tenderly, "Sally and I are good friends."

God and seminary having adequately equipped her to accompany people on their personal and spiritual journeys, Ruthalice adjusted her glasses and quit guessing. She had learned from ten years of experience as campus minister that every person who appeared at her door bore the potential to expose the darker side of human nature and knock the day's best laid plans helter-skelter in the process.

"I heard two students in the bathroom," Rani began softly. "I wasn't trying to listen, but they were talking so loudly I could hear them over the running water." Her conscience cleared of any appearance of eavesdropping, her voice picked up strength and speed.

Ali watched the young woman turn and glance out the window at a brown squirrel darting up the maple tree. A large collie appeared out of nowhere. The dog jumped a few times, its paws bouncing off the trunk then lost interest and trotted across the street. She waited to the count of ten then tried again. "Rani, what were these women talking about?"

"A fire." Her fingers picked at the doll's embroidered face.

"A fire? What sort of fire?"

Rani shrugged. "One girl said, 'It's going to be enormous'. The other one said, 'That's fantastic 'cause then the whole town will know about us.'"

Ruthalice leaned forward and began to push the soft wax into the hot candle flame with her right index finger. "I'm a firm believer in woman's intuition, Rani. What's your own sense of what's going on here?"

Rani's jaw tightened as if to trap any words of speculation that might inadvertently slip out. Ali decided to take charge.

"Have you told your resident advisor what you heard?"

"Yes."

"And?"

"She thinks they were just talking about the homecoming bon fire."

"Hmm, that doesn't compute," Ali mused out loud stretching her legs in front of her in order to admire the shiny toes of her new black boots poking out from under the ankle-length skirt. "Homecoming was last Friday and it was all pretty tame by EC standards."

Ruthalice looked inquisitively across the coffee table. Rani's attention had slipped back to her little bundle. "You're not buying that either are you, Rani?" The dolls faces were in danger of being rubbed raw. "What else is going on?"

"I heard them again last night. They were whispering. I think they knew somebody was in, well, that I was in there."

"In the toilet stall?"

She hesitated. "Yes. The loud girl said she'd gathered all the ingredients and it was gonna be so awesome and the other girl said the house would never look the same again."

Down the hall a door opened and student voices checking cell phone messages and returning calls signaled the end of classes.

"Rani, I'm grateful you confided in me. I'll follow up with the Dean of Students after lunch, but right now I must go teach."

Rani stood up and dropped the worry dolls into the pocket of her denim skirt.

"One of them is Priscilla Brinkley," and with that she slipped into the stream of students flowing down the hallway.

Idly curious why that name seemed to ring a bell, Ali grabbed the textbook and annotated Bible and headed for class.

After lunch at the Leaky Cup Coffee Café, Ali carefully negotiated the uneven brick sidewalk between Frame Meetinghouse and Harvey Library. After collecting her mail from the Jones Student Center she had a quick exchange with the Dean of Students who assured her the staff was keeping its ears open for any fire rumors. The day invited a walk, so Ali meandered past the Reflection Pool to the administration building intending to have a chat with Mary Scott, trusty secretary to the academic dean. *You have an uncanny ability of knowing exactly when a confidential bit of info might help me perform my pastoral duties. Where in the world would we campus ministers be without the likes of informants like you, dear Mary?*

Opening the door to Fox Hall, Ruthalice spotted Theodore Cope slumped on the bench outside the

Academic Dean's office. Recalling Coach Stevens' recent comment that his starting goalkeeper had an attitude problem, Ali's internal antennae went on full alert: *attempting to disappear inside an Emerick hoodie; right pant leg cut to the knee to accommodate an ankle-length caste; wishing he were any place else.*

"Hey, Ted," she said lightly snapping back to the present. "Mind if I sit down?"

A disinterested shrug was his only acknowledgement.

"Saw your shutout Saturday night. That was a heck of a win for the Quakers!"

Undeterred by the lack of enthusiasm, Ruthalice settled herself on the bench aware of the light touch of their hips. The young man moved away a fraction of an inch.

"So what's up?"

Placing his hands on the bench he thrust his right leg out in front of her. One look at the spanking new snow white cast and Ruthalice was abruptly propelled back sixteen years.

"Ali, for god's sake pick up the phone!" Her mother's panic-stricken scream reached the back hallway where her daughter had just emerged from the bathroom. "Something's terribly wrong! Skylar can't stand up."

Driving like a woman possessed, her mind filling with unspeakable possibilities, Ruthalice could still feel the flood of relief she'd experienced that afternoon when she saw her laughing six-year old son being carried by her kid brother down the front porch steps. Firmly unwrapping his nephew's chubby arms from around his neck, Dexter carefully placed the child on the front seat of his beat-up sky blue Buick.

"Just a broken leg, Sis" her doctor-in-residence sibling assured her. "You can come along if you want to or wait and I'll give you a call when Skye's cast has set-up and he's ready to come home."

Ali jumped into the back seat and slammed the door. It was a no-brainer decision.

Listening to the mixture of voices floating down the hallways, Ruthalice sighed with relief for all the mothers whose sons had 'just a broken leg'. Suddenly remembering the young man slumped next to her, Ruthalice pictured the conclusion of Saturday's soccer match: ecstatic Emerick players converging and leaping into a heap of bodies on top of the goalie. Even though husband Cliff as an ex-football player viewed these victory pile-ups as a normal form of healthy male bonding, Ali remained convinced this victory ritual was a disaster waiting to happen.

"Oh man, how'd you do that?" she asked innocently thinking she might be spot on this time!

Ted leaned on his elbows, scowled at the floor and said nothing. Wary of sounding overbearingly parental, Ali waited him out.

"That Red Knights squad's got a bunch of damn sore losers." He glared at the far wall. "There was nothing cheap about my shut out! Is it my fault the ref didn't call the mid-fielder for a hand ball?"

It should have been whistled a hand ball Ruthalice thought remembering the controversial 'non-call' of Saturday's one-nothing win, but she sighed sympathetically and kept her opinion to herself.

"And..." Ted wrestled with just how much confession was good for his soul. "I kicked the gym locker and broke my foot!" He clenched both hands until the knuckles turned white. "Now I'm out for the friggin' rest of the season. It sucks!"

"It sucks all right," Ruthalice commented dryly adopting the 'I'm-with-you-on-this-one' approach. Ted favored her with an amused smile. "I broke my ankle three months before my wedding." She glanced at the bare toes sticking out the end of his caste. "I hobbled around on crutches for weeks. It was a real nuisance."

Ted shifted uncomfortably, his eyebrows raised slightly as if to say, "Yeah, so?" Ali tried again.

"Are you in academic difficulty?" Praying she wasn't about to overstep her bounds she added, "If not, surely Coach Stevens will let you sit on the bench with the team the rest of the season."

"The reason I came to EC was to play soccer." His voice grew sullen. "My dad's made it perfectly clear that if I don't play him and mom aren't spending any more money on college." Ted banged his head back against the wall with a thud. "The old man's quick to remind me it's my mom's hair brained idea that her first born needs a college education in order to make something of himself."

"So are your parents coming to get you?"

"I haven't actually told them." Ted shifted uncomfortably avoiding eye contact. "Student insurance paid for the cast and trip to BCMH so I didn't call them." Ted's eyes hardened. "I'm dropping out and beating dad to the punch."

The office door swung open.

"Evelyn Feller will see you now, Theodore."

Ted reached under the bench and retrieved his crutches. Mary Scott waited while he lumbered to his feet and awkwardly maneuvered himself into the outer office. As Ali gathered her thoughts and bent to collect the mail which had slipped off the bench into a disorderly pile on the floor, Mary stepped through the doorway and strode briskly down the corridor. For an instant Ali thought about bounding after her but decided she was just too pooped and besides Miss Scott had already disappeared up the stairs. With no more to be gained by remaining, Ruthalice stood up and headed back across the parking lot. By the time she reached her office every internal voice was yammering for her attention. *You're not taking this fire stuff seriously enough. Maybe not but what more can I do? So you're going to play it safe and do nothing?*

"Man oh man, Rani's angst is getting to me."

Settling into the gaudy orange chair Ali closed her eyes and waited for the chattering to cease, but like the voice of St. Luke's persistent widow before the hard-hearted judge, Rani's fears continued to pester her. Realizing she had to do something, Ali turned on her computer and pulled up the student directory.

"Barton, Beasley..." she read running her index finger down the screen. "Bosner, Bradley, Brinkley. Ah, Brinkley, Priscilla – D104. We'll just pop by her room and see if we get lucky," she said out loud hoping to satisfy all sides of the on-going internal debate. "If I strike out then at least I've done something."

She passed the backside of Harvey Library then paused outside Douglas Hall. Sorting through her 'keys to the kingdom', she located the handy-dandy skeleton key the facilities director had reluctantly entrusted to her care and let herself into the lobby. Bruce Springsteen's voice, unhampered by the 6 inch plaster walls, sang her down the hallway to Room 104.

"Someone's home," she surmised wryly pounding on the door with her fist. Ali was about to try again when

Bruce was cut off in mid chorus, and the door swung open.

"What." The disembodied word lay somewhere between a bored question and a disinterested statement.

"I'd like to talk with you, Priscilla. May I come in?"

The young woman shrugged, moved out of the way and dropped down in the middle of a beautifully made bed. Stepping through the doorway Ali felt as though she'd just fallen down the rabbit hole and landed smack dab on the cover of *Better Homes and Gardens*! Pale green draperies secured with gold tasseled tie-backs hung gracefully on either side of the metal-framed window. Bedspreads, throw rugs and pillows in bright contemporary colors and patterns complemented the light blue cinderblock walls. Two framed posters of castles somewhere in the mountains of Europe hung between two matching walnut desks. Except for a ratty brown terrycloth bathrobe tossed on the other bed, this dormitory room was ready for inspection by the fussiest boarding school matron.

My, my, Ruthalice thought surveying the immaculate room. *My mama done told me when it comes to interior decorating, nothing beats good taste and a whole lot of money!*

"Priscilla, I had no idea a college room could look this good. You've worked a miracle and created a veritable oasis in here!"

"My mom's a frustrated interior decorator." It sounded like a curse, the suffering daughter's cross to bear. "So, she takes it out on my rooms."

Having failed to ease the resentment emanating from the blue-blooded young woman lounging on the bed, Ruthalice decided to go for broke.

"I understand you're planning a spectacular fire."

Priscilla blinked. "A fire?"

"Someone was concerned enough to report a conversation she overheard in the bathroom."

Priscilla frowned. "Oh yeah, now I remember. I was just bragging about how awesome the homecoming bon fire was going to be." Her eyes moved to the framed photo of a black-haired cheerleader holding a navy and white pompom in each hand, arms stretched high over her head. "I'm captain of the spirit squad," she added as though that explained everything.

"The bonfire? That's it?" Ali asked refusing to be side tracked

"Yup, that's it."

Running a hand over the polished dresser top Ruthalice looked at her fingertips and smiled. "I'm impressed, Priscilla. You pass the white glove test for good housekeeping."

Priscilla yawned, a let's-humor-the-grown-up expression on her face. Ruthalice walked to the center of the room enjoying the feel of plush carpet under her boots.

"So, tell me about last night's conversation."

"Holy cow, your little eavesdropper's been busy. What's she trying to prove?"

"You are reported to have said you had all the ingredients and that the house would never look the same, or words to that effect."

Priscilla's stare hardened. "Give me a break! " She spit the words out.

Ali remained standing content to wait.

"If you must know we were talking about decorations for a twenty-first birthday party for one of the girls in the house." Priscilla crossed her arms. "That's allowed on this campus isn't it?"

"Who's the lucky girl?"

"Regina Faulkner."

"Oh, Regina's in my Bible class. I'll be sure to wish her the best."

Forcing a note of relief into her voice, Ali stepped back and stood beside the dresser.

"Thank you for clearing this up for me, Priscilla. Regina strikes me as a woman who will be very appreciative."

With her hand on the doorknob Ali added, "Is it a surprise party?"

"Not really." Priscilla seemed to have already turned her attention to other things.

Knowing she'd gotten as much information as she could for now, Ruthalice pulled the door closed behind her, crossed the leaf-strewn campus, grabbed her canvas bag and headed for home. Forty-five minutes later she bounced up the tree-lined lane of Horsefeathers Farm in her bright lemon two-door Focus.

A large UPS box leaned against the front door. *Cool our new blanket's here.* Ali closed the garage door, walked around the side of the house and climbed the porch steps. Holding the screen door open with one foot, she grasped the bulky box with both hands then stepped into the tiled entryway, the very spot from which she first surveyed this lovely old living room as a newlywed nearly a year ago.

"You know something, Cliff," she said as he bowed from the waist before formally escorting her across the threshold, "There'd by no M&Ms today if Drew hadn't suffered that heart attack and Paulette hadn't gotten fed-up with playing second fiddle to your passion for hunting mollusks 24-7!"

She set the blanket box on the floor and tromped down the hallway into the kitchen whose only nod to the 21st century was a Lowe's floor model, high-efficiency refrigerator and a micro-wave left over from Cliff's fifteen years of bachelorhood. Ali dumped her canvas bag on the counter and began rummaging through the pantry cupboard. Twenty-five minutes later a car door slammed, and Cliff materialized in the mudroom. Kicking off his Western boots he stepped sock-footed into the kitchen.

"What's for supper?" He gave both Ali and the wooden spoon an enormous hug before dropping his keys into the basket on the window sill. Cliff inhaled deeply. "Ah chili!" he exclaimed answering his own question.

Across the kitchen in three strides, Cliff yanked the snack drawer open.

"Can't eat chili without crackers."

He winced as Ali plopped a large spoonful of rice into her bowl before burying it under chili. Though a bona fide malacologist with a PhD from The Ohio State University, Clifford P. Mowry remained a farm boy from the top of his curly-red hair to the bottoms of his size 12 feet. Rice though a passable side dish if dowsed with sufficient soy sauce, most certainly did not belong under chili!

The newly weds clasped hands, offered a silent blessing and began to eat. After five minutes of contented chewing, Cliff led off the nightly ritual of catching up on each other's day.

"So, what fires did the Campus Minister extinguish today?"

Ali bent her head and grabbed the plaid napkin off her lap as a coughing fit seized her.

"Oh dear, excuse me." She shook her head and dabbed at her watering eyes. "It's just that you couldn't have picked a more apt metaphor, my dear Watson."

Cliff gave her a puzzled look.

"Fires – you asked about extinguishing fires."

Reaching for the crackers he dumped another handful on the chili residue in the bottom of the bowl and picked up his spoon. "Go on."

"Rani Brown our Jamaican student came to my office this morning really quite distressed because of a conversation she overheard in the women's bathroom. Apparently Priscilla Brinkley and another student were talking about a spectacular fire." Ali poured half a glass of milk. "I touched all the bases I could today – Babs has her student leaders on alert for any rumors – so we'll see if anything further comes of it."

Ali picked up the glass and emptied it, then rubbed any tomato sauce or milk mustache off her lips. "Students dribbled in all afternoon with various lame excuses for missing the scheduled Bible test! I had to keep reminding myself I'm not their mother let alone some Universal Voice of Conscience."

Cliff chuckled sympathetically.

"A parent called asking why we allow anti-war protestors to hold signs and pass out literature on campus and to inform me the letter-to-the-editor I wrote last Wednesday was patently unpatriotic! So, I patiently explained our Quaker Peace Testimony that we strive to live a life which 'takes away the occasion of all war'. At least he didn't slam the phone down when he hung up on me."

She slipped the two inch gold hoop out of her left ear and massaged the lobe with her thumb and middle finger.

"And you, dear heart? What transpired in the hallowed halls of Dalton Science Building?"

"You'll never guess who showed up expecting me to solve her enormous problem!"

"OK, I'll bite. Who was it?"

"Your Mom's old buddy Mrs. H! She proceeded to inform me she's being absolutely inundated with disgusting things – her term by the way - and pontificated on how these creatures are consuming her mums at an alarming rate! After five minutes of rapid-fire scientifically vague and thus useless rambling, I agreed to look at a sample if she would bring one in. Well, that was my first mistake! She shrieked, 'There's no way on God's green earth I'm touching one of those slimy nasty things,' and reminded me in no uncertain terms that because I'm the scientist here not her, I'm the one who's used to handling all sorts of creatures no civilized person would even mention in polite company."

Cliff rolled his eyes.

"There's more?"

"There's more. 'You only teach two classes and a lab so how busy can you possibly be anyway? Surely you can spare a half-hour and come with me to the garden and investigate!"

Ali regarded him fondly.

"I offered to come by this weekend and take a look," he added feebly.

Ali burst out laughing. "Fat chance of that, right? When Suzanne Matilda Polk Henson has an emergency it's a crisis of biblical proportion."

Cliff fiddled with his spoon, turning it over and over between his thumb and forefinger.

"Quickly ascertaining there'd be no peace in heaven or on earth until I relented, I proceeded directly to Henson's Formal Gardens collection jar in hand."

"So pray tell, what IS this dreadful creature busily consuming Suzy's mums?"

"Actually, it's the not so common Limax maximus!"

"Limax whoimus?"

"The leopard slug, a rather impressive little critter actually. Limax maximus are wrinkled and grayish yellow with four tentacles. Usually nocturnal they will sometimes come out when it rains. Oh, and they leave a lovely long cushion of mucus slime."

"I love it!" Ali leaned back, clasped her hands and rested them on her stomach. "Suzy the Doozy certainly came to the right man for the job. Who needs Ghostbusters?"

"You know my motto: *Malacologists to the Rescue!"*

"Let's see if I can remember." Ali tilted her head back and gazed at the ceiling as if the definition were written beside the light fixture. "'Malacology, the branch of zoology dealing with mollusks, the second largest phylum of animals in terms of described species.'"

"Give that woman an 'A'." Cliff placed both elbows on the table and pointed an imaginary piece of chalk in her direction. "Now tell me young lady, how many existing species of mollusks have been identified?"

"One hundred thousand!" she pronounced sitting up straight and returning his mischievous grin.

"Furthermore, because Ohio boasts an unusual number of species of fresh water clams, The Nature Conservancy has designated our fair state, quote, a hot spot for clam biodiversity, unquote."

"Well done, my dear, well done!"

Cliff stretched his legs under the table and rested his knee against her leg. Ali picked at a blob of red wax stuck in the weave of her placemat.

"Actually I never heard of a leopard slug," she admitted resting her head against the high cushioned back of the dining nook bench. "I assume it has spots."

"Indeed. Four inches in length, loves mushrooms, even eats the occasional slug." Cliff gave a pensive sigh. "However in the interest of academic honesty I was forced to admit it's highly unlikely the leopard slug is her culprit. I did suggest that by importing toads and turtles she could reduce the number of Limax maximus in her garden, but Ms H. gave me the distinct impression my findings as well as my latest helpful hint left something to be desired." He smiled ruefully. "But that's often the way of much scientific inquiry."

Ali lifted the forest green shawl she'd discarded on the bench at breakfast and pulled it her over her shoulders.

"Moses didn't really part the Red Sea you know."

"Really. How so?"

"After our quiz this morning, a kid produced a story from the *LA Times* explaining the entire episode as a natural event using wind speed, the moon's gravitational pull and the depth of the water."

"I won't tell if you don't."

Cliff set his dessert bowl in front of him and put an enormous spoonful of butterscotch pudding in his mouth.

"Sometimes I wonder at our human need to explain everything scientifically." Ali broke her sugar cookie into two pieces. "I'm content with the occasional miracle now and again."

After supper they sat in the living room and read as darkness slowly closed down the view of the meadow between the house and Fair Ridge Road. Finding nothing of interest in the *Boone County Bugle*, Ali folded the newspaper and waited until Cliff looked up from his book.

"Do you have Ted Cope in class?"

"Not this semester. He's the soccer goalie who broke his foot at the end of that game we saw Saturday."

Cliff slipped the torn envelope he was using as a bookmark between the pages and laid The Rustlers of Pecos County, first edition Zane Grey, on the end table.

"Word has it he's dropping out of school." Seeing Ali's scowl he added, "Am I to deduce you're involved in this somehow?"

"That's what Ted told me when I bumped into him outside Evelyn's office." She removed her glasses and rubbed the bridge of her nose. "Apparently papa's going to be royally fried."

"Is 'fried' a theological term?" Cliff grinned and squeezed her hand.

Ali chose to ignore him.

"Ted said going to college is his mom's idea, and I surmised from our conversion that as soon as Mr. Cope learns about the broken foot, he'll tell Ted to get his fanny back to the farm and quit wasting his time in college, so young Ted is heading him off at the pass."

Ali inhaled sharply then shook her head.

"Geez, poor Ted can't win for loosing can he? He can't run the combine; no more soccer; unable to stack hay!" She put her wire-rimmed glasses back on and turned to Cliff. "I've never met his dad, but I hear that Oakes Quarry's finest have escorted his mercurial Uncle Sidney from many a Little League game for yelling obscenities at the refs."

Ali gently extracted her hand from Cliff's, slipped her thick silver-flecked braid over her shoulder and began brushing its soft, fluffy tip along her cheek.

"Just remember, honey, Ted's dad Roger has lived his entire life as Sidney Cope's kid brother. After inheriting his half of the farm from their dad, Sid Cope made a killing selling off the frontage. Old Sid thinks rather highly of himself, and most folks around here see him as an impetuous but shrewd wheeler-dealer."

Cliff yawned and stood up.

"I don't know a soul in Boone County who doesn't have great sympathy for Roger Cope! I actually feel kind of sorry for that son of his." He leaned over, grasped Ali's hands and pulled her up. "Theodore's bright enough to make it in college and with some encouragement will make a competent seed salesman even if he doesn't want to farm. But his Uncle Sidney's the proverbial bull in the china shop throwing his weight around whenever it works to his advantage. That's a difficult shadow for his one and only nephew to get out from under."

They headed down the hallway turning off lights as they went. Ten minutes later Ali lay in bed listening to Cliff's gentle snoring. *Ted ...Priscilla...Ted...Priscilla* his breathing seemed to intone. Rolling over on her left side, Ali draped an arm over Cliff's chest. Up and down, in and out. *Ted...Priscilla. What was it about those two? The hot-headed farm boy and the bored little rich girl both angry and alone, fighting personal demons in their own way.*

Hoping to mollify the tension in her jaw, Ali rested her left cheek against Cliff's upper arm. The firm muscle just under the warm, tanned skin was strangely reassuring.

"Which of our human frailties have you unearthed today, Ms. Rani Sequoia Brown?" she murmured.

Staring out the east-facing window at the rising moon, Ruthalice began to pray as she did every single night.

"Dear God, I surrender the world and all the hurting people to your loving care. And please," she added closing her eyes, "don't let there be a latent arsonist in our midst, ok? Amen."

Chapter Two - Tuesday

"Oh what a beautiful morning, oh what a beautiful day!" Ruthalice sang lustily as she gazed through the thick wavy window glass above the kitchen sink. The hackberry trees rippled gently as if under water. A Cardinal-red blur flitted into a cedar on the edge of the yard as the morning sun touched the west edge of the pasture with yellow-orange light.

When she and Cliff exchanged wedding vows six months, four days and 18 hours ago, Ruthalice Michels eagerly moved into his family's Centennial Farm House eight miles east of town. Quickly growing to love the late summer hum of cicadas, uninterrupted view of spacious corn fields and the canopy of stars at night, she forgot what had always seemed so exciting about city life. Which one of her girl friends would have predicted that Ali Michels, the heavier-than-she'd-like-to-be campus minister, would fall in love with Clifford Philip Mowry, a forty-six year old bachelor and professor of biology who not only owned a farm but relished the challenge of teaching? But the real miracle of all miracles was his eagerness to take up housekeeping with the forty-eight year old, widowed mother of a twenty-two year old son!

So after two years of on-and-off dating, they joined in marriage in a traditional Quaker ceremony and enthusiastically combined furniture, pets and personality quirks to create their own dynamic duo. Delighted that she had the proverbial cake – the Campus Ministry position at her beloved Emerick College and wife of the most eligible bachelor in town, Ruthalice greeted each day as if she were eating it too.

Straightening pillows and magazines as she went, Ali sashayed across the living room into the spacious master bedroom at the south end of the farmhouse. Flipping on the light in the enormous walk-in closet Cliff's mother had built, she stepped in and began sorting through an impressive collection of oversized shirts.

When Ali was in the sixth grade, Suzy Henson instructed her on the proper way to get dressed. *Always begin with the blouse* she insisted as she poured another cup of coffee and assumed her accustomed seat on the bar stool. *Coordinate your clothing by starting at the top and working your way down to the shoes.*

Thirty-six years later, Ali was still following her advice. Selecting her favorite blouse, the one with lemon and tangerine hibiscus blossoms strewn across white linen, she pulled it off the plastic hanger. She tugged her black skirt over her head smoothing the soft wool over her tummy, slipped gold hoops through her ears, added five matching bracelets of varying widths and voila! With low black boots, her ensemble was complete. *Lose twenty-five pounds and you're one elegant woman!*

"Easier said than done," she reminded her reflection. "You're conveniently forgetting our predilection for all things chocolate!"

Ten minutes later she backed Lemon Drop out of the two-car garage, coasted down the hill and headed west into town. Clumps of Queen Anne's lace, chicory, goldenrod and ironweed dotted the brown hillsides with clusters of white, pale blue, deep gold and purple.

"I've got a wonderful feeling, everything's going my way!"

Her strong contralto voice drifted out the half-opened window as she pulled into the spot designated Campus Minister. Setting both feet firmly on the pavement she hauled herself out of the car. Her boots made a satisfying click-click in the cool dimly-lit corridor of Frame Meetinghouse. Each eight foot solid oak door had a glass transom at the top, a left-over from pre-air conditioning days. Ali loved the old fashioned black door knobs and half-inch thick metal bolts which secured each office. Hers was second on the right between the coat closet, now holding the janitorial supplies, and Room 6, the larger of the two classrooms. Except on days when the building bustled with students, Ruthalice had the place to herself. Raccoon Creek Friends Meeting held unprogrammed meeting for worship every Sunday morning in the large worship room at the south end of the building.

Ruthalice unlocked her office door and wandered to her desk, gently touching the face of Professor Clifford Mowry smiling at her from a green bamboo frame. Resplendent in brown rubber wading boots, khaki broad-rimmed hat cocked at a rakish angle, her hubby stood hip deep in the waters of the Little Miami River.

"Reliable rumor has it, Dr. Mowry you were much happier sloshing around in rivers and streams than behind the wheel of a tractor." She tapped the Start Key on her computer and sat down to wait for all the icons to finish appearing. She typed off a short note, hit Send and sighed contentedly. "I hope your day is off to a great start, my darling Clifford."

Cliff had arrived on campus at 7:30, shoved a copy of *Science* magazine into the outer pocket of his briefcase and jumped out of the black Ford pickup. In denim jeans, deep logan v-neck sweater and pin-striped Oxford shirt (all LL Bean of course), Cliff still looked every bit the rugged outdoorsman. His lanky 6'2" frame easily carried the twenty pounds gained since graduate school. Envious male colleagues periodically reminded him that every coed on campus was madly in love with his curly red hair, booming laugh, and simply ADORED the fact that Clifford Mowry wears hand-tooled Western boots!

"Good Lord, they'd faint dead away if word got out you have eight pairs in our closet!" Ali teased one noon after two attractive coeds pointedly starred at his feet.

Adroitly skirting a sodden pile of brown leaves clogging the street drain, Cliff strode the short distance to Dalton Science Hall. From the moment he set foot on campus five years out of grad school, it was love at first sight. As was his wont, Cliff paused to admire the exquisite workmanship. Massive beige foundation blocks supported the stately brick building each stone having been dug, cut and then hauled by teams of horses from the Old Oakes Quarry three miles southwest of town. Heavy leaded windows and a green copper roof added to Dalton's strength of character. Named in honor of the mid-19th century Quaker chemist John Dalton, the Hall was built in 1882, the last of the original buildings dubbed The Three Sisters.

Cliff bounded up the stairs, walked down the hall into his office, snatched the glass coffee pot from the window sill, ducked into the men's room and filled it with water. His start-up routine complete, Professor Mowry donned a white lab coat, passed out biology exams and proctored the next hour by devouring an article on "The Habitat Requirements for the Host Fish of Freshwater Mussels." Only two students interrupted his reading to ask for clarification of an essay question.

At precisely 8:55am Professor Hopkins left his office on the second floor of Fox Hall and using his sleeve, polished the bronze plaque affixed to the door: ***Charles E. Hopkins, Faculty Emeritus.*** An overstuffed accordion file clutched securely under his right arm, Charles marched purposefully across campus. *Been the sole instructor in EC's History Department for sixty odd years, and all I've got to show for it is a plate with my name on it! Aye, but I'll show them what Charles E. Hopkins is made of for I intend to lecture until the day my voice gives out or my brain withers away, whichever comes first.*

Letting himself into Cliff's office Charles assumed his customary seat in the well-worn visitor's chair and waited impatiently for his chum's arrival.

"Sorry, Mate," Charles sputtered pulling his well-worn brogues under the chair. "Didn't mean to trip you."

Regaining his balance, Cliff dropped 23 bluebooks on his desk and smiled fondly at his colleague.

"So, who's the latest addition to the upcoming book this week, my friend?" Cliff crossed his legs and assumed his role as friendly sounding board.

"Bishop Swithum, humble advocate for the poor and sick."

"Ah, the beloved bishop whose shrine drew thousands of pilgrims from all over England and the Continent."

"Precisely, travelers who established what would later be known as The Pilgrim's Way between Winchester and Canterbury made famous in literature by Geoffrey Chaucer." Curly sighed contentedly. "My school mates and I slogged our way through that god-awful olde English with its quaint spelling and cumbersome poetic lines eager to reach the naughty bits we'd heard so much about!"

An avid researcher with a healthy dose of skepticism for any source other than primary, Charles Hopkins, single, cranky and solitary, passed his weekends sequestered in the same library carrel he'd occupied since joining the EC faculty more than fifty years ago.

Charles winked mischievously. "There's more to this tale than meets the eye, old bean and I reveal all the twists and turns in my fifth book The Political Impact of Religious Pilgrims on the British Isles!"

The Red-winged blackbird on the Audubon clock above Cliff's door chirped ten o'clock signaling the end of Tuesday's weekly ritual. Curly rocked his 260-pound frame up and out of the creaking chair, and with a hearty "cherrio!" wandered back to Fox Hall taking with him Cliff's last excuse for avoiding the stack of newly minted exams.

It was nearly four o'clock before Ali went searching for Coach Stevens. She wandered behind the two brick dorms, turned left on Wood Avenue and followed the shouts and whistles of fall practice sessions to the athletics compound. Bob Stevens, whistle clenched between his teeth, stood at mid field watching the players execute their passing drills. Ruthalice leaned against the chain link fence enjoying the choreographed dance of bodies and legs accompanied by the thump of feet striking leather balls. Coach Stevens turned the players loose for a scrimmage game and headed to the sidelines.

"Hi, Ruthalice, are you looking for me?" She nodded and he joined her at the edge of the field.

"I had a troubling exchange with your keeper yesterday, Bob. He told me he intends to drop out of school."

The coach looked at her intently.

"What exactly did Ted tell you?"

"That he came to Emerick to play soccer and now that he can't play out the season he's withdrawing before his dad gets on him to come back to the farm." Ali hesitated. "However, I've got that feeling there's more to this story."

Coach Stevens removed his ball cap and scratched his head letting his hair fall forward across his face. Replacing his cap he smoothed out some seen-only-by-him lumps in the playing field with his right foot. Apparently satisfied he raised his head.

"I put him on probation for his behavior after Saturday's game."

"For kicking his locker and breaking his foot?" Ali's sense of overkill spilled out, but Bob cut in before she could back tract.

"Is that what he told you?"

"Yes."

Bob crossed his arms and scowled at something over her left shoulder.

"Some of the team went to Slippery Sue's after the game to celebrate our shut-out, and as it turns out some of the Red Knights were there as well. The boys got into a shoving match outside the bar." Bob smoothed out more lumps in the grass. "By the time the cops got there, two Knights had bloody faces and Ted Cope had broken his right foot. I spent Saturday night in the waiting room so I could bring him back to Gurney Dorm." Bob sighed. "As you can imagine, I'm not a happy camper about all this. I just wanted to keep the whole thing under wraps and in-house."

"Well, I can assure you it's not in house any more." Ali let her fingers bounce lightly along the chain fence as they walked. "OK, so you put Ted on probation so he can't play soccer anymore this fall, but why drop out of school?"

"I suspect he's furious at me, and this is his way of evening the score."

They shared the weary smile of veterans who had weathered many a student's emotional outburst.

"Have you heard from Roger Cope yet?"

"Not yet." Bob stopped walking. "I checked with Dean Ev this morning. She's encouraged Ted to back off a bit and give himself the week to think about his decision. She told him to come back next Monday if he still wants to drop out and she can terminate him then."

"Good, that gives him time to simmer down, and hopefully realize dropping out of college doesn't solve his problem."

"I hope that's where he ends up, but Ted flies by the seat of his pants and tends to make rash decisions which is the reason he's one of the best goal keepers I've had in fifteen years of coaching."

Ruthalice chuckled appreciatively. "I'll say he's good, three shutouts already this fall. You'd have to go back a ways to beat that record!"

"To tell you the truth, Ruthalice, I'm much more concerned about Ted's Uncle Sidney than I am about his dad. Talk about flying off the handle. Whew!" Bob smiled then pointed at the sky. "Please put a word in with the Big Guy for me, will ya? I sure could use all the help I can get."

"I'll see what I can do. And please call me if there's anything more I ought to know." Turning to go she added, "I'm assuming Ted's still on campus."

"He was as of this noon." Bob blew his whistle and the team sprinted over to collect their athletic bags. Ali heard the clatter of cleats on the asphalt drive as they trotted back to the locker room. Then a car door slammed.

"Stevens! Stevens! I need to talk to you," Sidney Cope hollered as he lumbered toward the soccer field his coat askew.

Ruthalice watched as Uncle Sid flung the gate open, stormed through it and positioned himself squarely in front of the coach. *My gosh, he's the schoolyard bully who's got you cornered in the locker room.*"

She inhaled deeply. "God, it would be really good if you would protect Bob Stevens right now so he doesn't get punched out! Please grant him tons of courage and patience." Ali paused then added in a whisper, "And may both men find words to express their disappointment and love for young Theodore."

Chapter Three - Wednesday

Groping for the phone on the bedside table she peered at the clock. *Oh no, it's 1:30 in the morning. This can't be good news.* She cleared her throat of nighttime phlegm.

"Ruthalice here."

"Mary Scott," came the brisk reply.

Ali's brain snapped to attention.

"Pennington Place is on fire; I'm notifying all senior administration; the fire department's on the scene."

The staccato words delivered in enunciated drill sergeant form pierced her stomach making Ali wince. Now fully awake, Ali swung her legs over the edge of the bed. *Oh, God, this can't be happening!*

"Is anybody hurt?"

"A few students are complaining about the smoke of course, but since no one's in Penn Place at night..." Mary's voice faltered for an instant. "Richard wants staff on campus to help maintain order," she added quickly as though suddenly remembering why she'd called the campus minister in the middle of the night. "Most of the kids are in their rooms or at least still in the dormitories and we're hoping to keep them there." She took a deep breath. "But, it's pretty chaotic so it's all hands on deck."

"OK, Mary, I'll be at the meetinghouse as quickly as I can."

Cliff raised his head and stared groggily at his wife.

"Now what?" He reconsidered. "Off to campus?" That seemed obvious even in his diminished mental state. "Who was it?"

Ali fell back across the bed, took his face in both hands and kissed him firmly on the forehead. "Answered in the order asked: Pennington Place is on fire, yes and Mary Scott. OK?"

"Sounds like Richard's calling out the guard," Cliff mumbled into his pillow.

"Nope, not yet, just the administrative staff. So, my dear lowly tenured biology professor, you get to go back to sleep."

Ruthalice rolled back off the bed, straightened her navy blue skirt and grabbed a pair of wool socks from the dresser. "I'll just stay on campus and call you when I know what's up. "

She quickly braided her hair, realized it was now 1:45 and dashed across the living room frantically buttoning her maroon cardigan. "I love you," Ali called over her shoulder as she nuked a mug of last night's left-over coffee then slammed the mud room door behind her. Lemon Drop scattered gravel behind them as Ali raced down the driveway still wrestling with the seat belt.

As she drove through the pre-dawn darkness, all the inner voices began their annoying speculation: *those girls must have been planning arson after all – I simply refuse to believe that - Regina told me herself her 21st birthday party was awesome – but what's that got to do with letting Priscilla Brinkley off the hook? Rani only overheard bits and pieces don't forget.*

"All right already, cut the speculation, ok?" she scolded herself. "At this point you haven't the faintest idea what's happened."

Cliff tossed and turned until the down-filled quilt slid to the floor then got up and headed for the shower. *Something doesn't fit here* he thought as he shoved the faucet handle to "H". The water streamed out scalding hot. *Our committee met for months but we finally did decide to completely remodel Pennington including total rewiring, so how on earth did the old girl catch on fire?*

Cliff toweled off his thoughts still on the Building and Grounds Committee. It seemed that at every meeting Professor Charles Hopkins shared his little joke: he and Pennington Place had something in common. "Penn's the oldest building on campus by nine years, and I'm the oldest professor by nine years. But by Jove, I'm less expensive to maintain!"

The first couple of times the BGC members chuckled appreciatively, but then like Curly, the joke wore thin after awhile and now they tended to ignore him.

Sad, Cliff reflected, wondering which he meant, the man or the fire, a*ll those college historical records and one-of-a-kind Quaker books in the second floor reading room. My God, the old historian really will go ballistic!*

Cliff dug in the pocket of his corduroy jacket for his keys then followed his wife's trail down the drive. As he drove into town the undulating thick black finger of smoke rose relentlessly into the star-studded sky backlit by the nighttime lights of Oakes Quarry. He finally located a parking spot a block from campus and quickly made his way through the maze of emergency vehicles.

He paused at the edge of the Fine Arts parking lot now agonizingly certain that none of Emerick's old records could possibly survive unscathed.

A half-hour earlier, Ali had come to a similar conclusion. In the middle of the campus lawn Pennington Place burned drawing attention to itself. The other buildings were clustered around the edges like kids at a campfire. A few students, their silhouettes flickering in the shadows, were starting to gather and clump together under the trees. The sharp rotating lights of fire trucks and police vehicles pierced the outer darkness. Yellow hoses wound like enormous snakes through the grass. The occasional shouts of fire fighters rang through the air. In spite of all the activity, an eerie waiting dread encompassed the crowd. *Everyone and everything is holding its breath.*

Ruthalice headed toward the students huddled together under a large maple tree to see if she knew any of them. Dressed in a collection of floor-dragging sweat pants and oversized Emerick College tops, the kids wore the haphazard get-out-of-the-building-immediately clothing of those tossed outside by fire in the middle of the night. It seemed as though everyone was peering at miniature screens on purple, black or red cell phones. *Who in the world are these kids talking to at this ungodly hour?* Ruthalice wondered. She spotted a student from her Bible class typing furiously her thumbs flying over the tiny keyboard she held in both hands and she slipped in behind her. *One of these days*, she promised herself trying unsuccessfully to ignore the tension growing in her stomach, *I'm going to take the plunge and join the 21st century technology-wise!*

Her trusty Wal-Mart Trac-fone vibrated against her thigh. Not recognizing the number, she pressed talk, listened for a moment and hung up. One more cursory glance at the faces flickering in the shadows under the tree convinced her there was nothing nefarious in the excited chatter and texting generated by the fire so Ruthalice stepped back and turned around. The only ones to notice her were pressed against the dark brick wall of Fox Hall. Though Ruthalice was clearly out of ear shot, they stopped whispering and watched until she disappeared into Jones Student Center.

Ruthalice turned right inside the glass-fronted lobby and started up the concrete steps to the "pub-flavored ambience" of the student hangout affectionately known as The Rat. Stopping to catch her breath, she surveyed the collection of tables around the edge of the room. A shriek of dismay burst from the conversation pit.

"Oh, dean I'm so sorry! Oh my gosh, did you burn yourself?"

"I'm quite all right, thank you, just a little damp."

She's done it again, Ali realized watching Evelyn Feller administer control and comfort simultaneously. *I could take a leaf out of her play book!*

"Oh Ruthalice, join us won't you?" The dean indicated the space beside her with an imperceptible nod. "We've had a little accident," she commented gently as she accepted the wad of napkins the flustered coed thrust at her. "Do you know Jennifer Blake?"

Ruthalice smiled. "I don't believe we've met though your name is certainly familiar."

"Jennifer Blake, but uh, everyone calls me just plain Jen," she stuttered still mortified by the great coffee spill incident. "I'm umm, Prissy's Little Sis. I mean Priscilla

Brinkley." She looked around miserably. "We're umm both Delts."

Before Ruthalice could come up with a suitable reply the Big Ben look-alike in the corner bonged four times. Evelyn leaned wearily against the cushioned sofa back and flipped her cell phone open. After a weary "Ok", she struggled to her feet and clapped her hands. The handful of students slumped in a few of the chairs scattered about the room raised their heads. "The fire chief just indicated the water pressure is back up in the dormitories so if you need to use the bathroom you're now free to do so." Chair legs scraped as several took her up on the offer. Jen Blake took advantage of the situation to make herself scarce as well.

Watching her go Ali's nervousness returned. "Where's Priscilla I wonder," she muttered to herself.

"Hmmm?"

"Oh, I'm just curious why Jen's here by herself. This is the most exciting thing to happen on campus in a long time, and Priscilla Brinkley strikes me as somebody who'd be right in the thick of things."

The dean shrugged. "My only contact with Ms. Brinkley is over academic issues." She glanced out the second story window at the porch lights across Mulligan Street. "God, how I wish Babs were here." *My goodness Evelyn's suddenly feeling in over her head,* Ali realized struck by the pleading in her colleague's voice. *That's a side of you I'm not used to.* "You can throw the academic side of things at me, and I know exactly what I'm doing, but the emotional histrionics which always seem to accompany episodes like this one baffle me."

Someone shouted from the street below as a car door slammed.

"That's why I insisted you come to campus, Ruthalice." Picking up her jacket Evelyn gave the campus minister a pensive smile. "You can blame me for the wake-up call." Her gaze and voice returned to 'take charge" mode. "We could all use some pastoral care right now, Ruthalice. The fall out from this unfortunate fire is going to take its toll on every single one of us since we're all affected by this tragedy one way or another."

Lost in thought Ruthalice followed the Academic Dean down the cement steps and back out into the night. Under the trees knots of curious students had untangled themselves and were heading for the dorms leaving the rubber suited fire fighters to do the mopping up. The police chief surrounded by college staff and a handful of faculty, appeared to be holding court. As the two women slipped into the circle, Evelyn gently took her secretary's arm.

"Mary," she whispered, "I think you really must take the day off."

"And leave you to cope by yourself?" Mary Scott turned back to catch the rest of the instructions. "That's just plain ridiculous!"

"...so no one is allowed to cross the police lines under any circumstances. I don't care who you are!" The Chief aimed this last comment at Professor Hopkins who was sputtering about not being allowed access to the building.

Evelyn gazed across the little circle at Patrick Turner, Oakes Quarry's Chief of Police. Clifford Mowry moved over and placed his arm around his wife's shoulders as Ali stepped between him and Charles Hopkins. To their left Angus Bailey the facilities director stood at attention like a well-trained soldier on review. President Richard

"Skip" Willson, his slim body silhouetted against the rotating lights of the fire engines, stood beside the fire chief. Once again she felt the absence of Barbara Carroll, Dean of Students who was attending meetings in Chicago.

Curly Hopkins abruptly threw himself into the middle of the circle and glared at the police chief through blood-shot eyes. "This is unconscionable!" he shouted. The officer's right hand slipped down and unsnapped the cover of his gun.

Oh for heaven's sakes, Charles, Evelyn thought indignantly, *cut the hysterics. It's uncalled for, and you're only going to succeed in embarrassing yourself.*

Ali leaned into Cliff's side a look of shock and dismay on her face. *Dear God, what's going on here? Curly's having a break down right here in front of You and everybody! Tell me what to do!!*

Oblivious of the ruckus he'd stirred up, Charles, his clenched fists pounding against his thighs, paced the space afforded him by the surrounding circle: two steps forward then two steps back, spin around and do it again. Mesmerized by the spectacle before them every member of the horrified little group prayed that somebody else would do something and do it quickly. But as abruptly as the ranting had begun it stopped. Ali stared in disbelief as a look of defeated sadness softened the old professor's scowling face.

"I simply must be allowed into Pennington Place" he moaned, then added almost as an after thought, "to ascertain the damage to the archives."

"Be reasonable Charles old chap." Clifford ever the solid rock of reason stepped in front of Curly and placed both hands on his shoulders as a collective sigh of relief swept around the little gathering. "The fire's still smoldering, but surely you'll be one of those allowed access when the situation's under control." Clifford looked meaningfully at President Willson who nodded at Chief Turner indicating it was not entirely his decision to make. "And besides, my friend, the sad truth is the damage has already been done."

Shrugging off Cliff's words and his hands, Professor Hopkins crossed the sodden grass and placed himself squarely in front of President Willson.

"Charles," Richard said firmly raising both hands as if to forestall any further onslaught, "we'll move as quickly as we can. That's all I can promise you at the moment."

Still unsatisfied Professor Hopkins grunted and turned his back. As he hobbled away Ruthalice felt numb. "What on earth is wrong with him, Clifford," she whispered wincing as Charles stumbled across the grass. "I've never seen Charles so worked up about anything. His behavior strikes me as way out of proportion to damage done to a bunch of old books."

"Which proves you're not an historian," Cliff shot back. Ali flinched at the unexpected reprimand. "But I agree with you," he added quickly. "Charles is way out of bounds on this one." Aware of how tense he'd become, Cliff stuffed his shaking hands into his trouser pockets. "But it doesn't matter what you and I think, Ali. Curly's determined to get inside Pennington Place come hell or high water."

With the departure of the fire chief, the impromptu staff meeting had disintegrated into private conversations. Dean Feller and her secretary were the first to leave. Picking their way over limp fire hoses, the remainder wandered off in various directions. Wondering how any of them were going to get through the rest of the day, Ruthalice grabbed Cliff's hand.

"You know what? I'm simply starving!" She pulled up her sleeve and checked her watch. "Come on," she urged dragging her reluctant husband toward the parking lot, "we've got time to drive to the fallen arches for an Egg McMuffin."

Hopping into her little yellow car sporting its 'Follow a Friend to Emerick College' bumper sticker, the M&Ms joined the drive-thru line at McDonalds. "I always wondered who ate breakfast at a fast food joint this early in the morning," Ali said through a mouthful of biscuit as they sat watching a steady stream of folk place their orders. "Now I know."

Cliff tossed the grease-stained wrappers in the trash bin then lightly touched his wife's shoulder. "We'd better head back. I've got to prepare for Invertebrate class this afternoon."

"Ah ha! Must be mollusk time again!"

"Yup, we're finally at that point in the syllabus where I really get to shine! So, what's your plan?" He fastened his seat belt. "Are you staying on campus?"

"Absolutely." She backed out of the parking space where they'd consumed their breakfast and headed toward campus.

"Ok, then I'll leave the sorting out and hand holding to you."

Ali grinned happily and planting a powerful smooch on his cheek, sent him on his way to Dalton Science Hall munching the remains of his second sausage and egg biscuit his mind already turned to things malacological.

Clifford relished this chance to teach his specialty: bivalves and gastropods. Snatching the textbook from the shelf, he plopped onto the wooden desk chair, swiveled a quarter turn and tilted back just enough to grab the set of slides from the shelf behind him. Carefully setting the carousel on his lap, he noticed the blinking red light on his phone. Half listening to the litany of 'please get back to me' messages, his eyes wandered to the still smoldering building. Sagging yellow do-not-cross police tape hung between the trees and metal posts hastily pounded into the wet ground to secure the site. A police officer was keeping watch from the curb of the cul-de-sac drive in front of Pennington Place. Clifford spotted a lone figure approaching the black and white squad car.

"How like her," Cliff whispered proudly. "Our trusty campus minister is making a pastoral call."

The brass ID bar pinned to her navy blue uniform read ROSEMARIE HARRIS. The young black woman rolled the window down as Ruthalice approached. Recognizing the Leaky Cup's signature Santa Claus Red cardboard sleeve with the tilted mug logo, she accepted Ali's offering. Expertly popping off the plastic lid, she took a tentative sip, sighed and grinned at her benefactor.

"I'm never one to pass up a cup of good coffee. Thanks!"

"You're quite welcome." Ali nodded at the badge. "My name's Ruthalice, all one word, Michels. My family calls me Ali, but around here I pretty much insist people use my full name."

Rosemarie nodded. "My folks call me Rosi with an 'i" but everyone else calls me Lieutenant Harris or just plain Harris. I prefer Rosemarie myself."

"Mine's with an "i" too. I'm the campus minister here at Emerick."

With the introductory chit-chat out of the way, the two women fell into easy conversation before getting to what really occupied their minds this smoke-scented Wednesday morning.

Coming straight to the point often elicited a frank response, so Ruthalice dove in. "What's your take on this fire, Lieutenant Harris?"

"All's I can say with certainty is the fire began in the basement. The State Fire Marshall's Office will have to determine the cause." She surveyed the black streaks reaching up the outside brick wall to the second story. "I expect there is a lot of smoke and water damage upstairs."

Though she welcomed the opportunity to test the theory forming in her mind, Rosemarie paused wondering how much surmising was within bounds. *I know all the regs against hypothesizing with the public* she reminded herself, *but this gal's a minister. If you can't trust the minister these days, then who can you trust?*

"Do you know what's in the basement?" she asked.

Ali closed her eyes trying to picture the lay out.

"As I recall there's not much down there. I've only been in the basement a couple of times over the years hunting some old folder in one of the metal file cabinets." She shivered. "The last time I got caught in the middle of a thunderstorm, and all the power went out. You can't believe how creepy that basement is! I'm telling you, Rosemarie it was like Tom Sawyer in that cave. Remember when their candles went out, and Tom couldn't see his hand in front of his face it was so pitch black?" Ruthalice shook her head. "I worked my way to the stairs each time the lights flickered back on. I had visions of being lost in the bowels of that darn basement for the rest of my life. Man oh man I was glad to get out of there!"

The lieutenant wasn't about to admit she'd never read Tom Sawyer and Huckleberry Finn though her mom had told her about him often enough!

"So, you're saying there's no windows?" Ruthalice nodded. "So the only way into or out of the cellar is down a flight of stairs."

"There's an outside door off the back kitchen." She squinted as she imagined herself going down the cellar stairs. "There is something interesting about that wall though. Like maybe a third of the way down there's an indentation in the wall like a little cave. You can't really tell how deep it is by looking, and I've never been tempted to reach inside."

Rosemarie looked up sharply.

"Big enough for a person to fit in?"

"I kinda doubt it. I'm trying to picture it exactly, but it's more like somebody cut a rectangular cubicle in the wall. I've heard Ernestine Perkins, she's our Alumni Relations Director who works on the second floor, tell visitors it was a place to store canned goods in the pre-refrigeration days."

"So who's in the basement now?"

"Nobody. It's only used these days to store ancient alumni records and discarded parlor furniture. The Quaker archives are housed on the second floor, but since the college doesn't have an archivist per se, there's usually a student worker staffing the desk up there."

"So what's the history of this house anyway?" Rosemarie straightened up and stretched against the vinyl seat back.

"Oh goody, I was hoping you would ask," Ruthalice responded eagerly. "Hannah Elizabeth Emerick was our first head of school during the Civil War Days, and she lived in the house during her six-year term. It was known then as the Dean's House. After Hannah died the name was changed to Pennington Place, and it was home to all the presidents until five years ago when the trustees remodeled it into a place for receptions and alumni gatherings, stuff like that." Aware that her companion was losing interest, Ali concluded pensively, "it *was* a wonderfully elegant spot for a tea party."

"Fire in a structure as old as this often traces back to faulty wiring or a mouse chewing on something it outtn't to." Lieutenant Harris was back to business.

Ruthalice frowned. "Maybe, but I don't think wiring's a factor in this particular instance, Rosemarie because it's all been redone recently." Placing a hand on each knee for balance, she leaned forward and spoke through the open driver's window. "Rosi, could this be arson?"

The policewoman shrugged but refused to speculate. "That's up to the Arson Squad to determine." Lieutenant Harris ran both hands around the steering wheel. "To change the subject if I may?" She glanced up at Ruthalice. "My son Russell's a senior this year at Oakes High, and he has his heart set on playing ball for the mighty Quakers next fall. Coach Adams says he's got an excellent chance of starting as fullback."

"Hey, that's great! Have Russell look me up when he gets here. I'm partial to football players."

Harris pulled her police cap over her black curls as Ruthalice stood up, opened the door and got out of the squad car. She leaned her slender body against the car.

"Listen, I'm gonna be here the rest of the afternoon but please don't be bringing me any more coffee 'cause if you do I'll just have to find a place to pee!"

Ruthalice laughed, took the empty cups and leaving Rosi to her solitary vigil, ambled back to her office. Unable to concentrate, Ali straightened the jumble of pamphlets haphazardly littering the shelf above her desk, watered the drooping hibiscus in front of the window and was about to resort to dusting when she was saved from further puttering by a tentative knock. The sight of Rani in the doorway nearly took her breath away.

She was spectacular, all 5 feet 10 inches of her. Dressed in iridescent blue Rani's body glistened like royalty as she stepped into the room. Upon closer inspection, Ali realized that what looked like purple and yellow blobs running along the dress hem and down the length of each sleeve were intricately embroidered flowers.

"Where on earth did you get that fantastic dress?" Ruthalice blurted out. "Those flowers look hand-embroidered. I can't even begin to fathom the amount of time and patience required to do the work. How many flowers are there?" Breathless, Ali stopped jabbering.

Rani smiled her dark eyes beaming. "There are exactly 93 flowers. Each one took me 15 minutes to embroider. The plant is the lignum-vitae, our Jamaican national flower. It was my project for Senior Sewing Class." Her clear voice uncharacteristically confident dropped to a hush as if she were suddenly afraid of succumbing to hubris. "I received a Highest Mark and was awarded a scholarship to continue my homemaker course for the rest of the year."

Standing perfectly still Ali managed to resist the overwhelming urge to throw her arms around her young visitor certain the gesture would embarrass her needlessly. For a brief moment the two women relaxed into the simple pleasure of each other's company then Rani seemed to crumble as she sank into the gaudy orange chair. As her left hand began gently tracing the flowers on her right sleeve, Ruthalice softly closed the door and sat down. Rani's restless fingers ceased their movement as she bent forward and pulled a tissue from the Kleenex box.

"She said it would be spectacular. You could see it for miles around." Rani hugged her elbows. "Did those girls set that fire, Ms. Ruthalice? I'm so afraid that's what Priscilla and the others were talking about in the bathroom." Gasping for breath, she began sobbing, "Oh sweet Jesus, forgive me!"

Ali leaned forward, touched Rani's sleeve then firmly squeezed her arm. "You do not need to ask God's forgiveness. This fire is not your fault, Rani Sequoia Brown!"

At the sound of her full name, Rani lifted her head.

"My father calls me by my full name when I'm in trouble," she replied, a far-away look in her eyes. "My mother calls me Rani Sequoia Brown when she wants to say how much she loves me." Wiping her cheeks with the back of her hand, Rani reached for the green book bag on the floor beside her feet, wrapped both arms around it clutching it to her chest. "I am frightened. I saw one of those fire starting persons – what do you call them?"

"An arsonist. You call someone who starts fires on purpose an arsonist."

"Yes, an arsonist."

"Rani, are you saying you saw an arsonist, and you think it was Priscilla?"

Rani dropped her head. "I could not see the face – it was too dark and the head was hidden inside a hood."

"Too dark? Where exactly did you see this person?"

"From our room. When I can't sleep I stand at the window. The campus looks so different in the dark." Tears welled up and spilled onto her bag. "Anyway, I saw a figure darting between the bushes. It was one person, it could have been Priscilla."

"Rani, it's up to the fire marshal to determine what caused this fire. It's no good jumping to any conclusions."

"What will happen now?"

"Let me think some more about what you've just told me, and then I'll decide what to do next. The police must be informed, but it's not up to you and me to solve this case by ourselves."

Rani got to her feet, slipped her right arm through the strap and hoisted her book bag across her shoulder. "I will try not to worry about this. And," she added lightly, "I promise not to play detective."

"Good," Ali replied somewhat mollified knowing full well she was not about to make the same promise to her young confident. "I'm positive this episode will soon be behind us and life on campus will get back to what passes for normal around here."

Reassured by Ruthalice's words, Rani slipped the key into the lock and opened the dorm room door being careful not to bump her roommate's bed. Their freshman year Sally Pratt's father built a sleeping loft on her side of the room and brought a desk, chair and her mom's best reading lamp from home. Content with the institutional furniture which came with the room, Rani settled for the single, iron-framed bed, the wooden desk with a crack in the bottom drawer and a straight-backed chair with a distinct wobble. The vase her grandmother gave her as a 16th birthday present stood proudly on the dresser flanked by two photographs of her parents. A large handmade basket served as laundry hamper. Rani had completed her interior decorating by placing a mat beside her bed so that every morning when her bare feet touched the rough hemp, memories of home washed over her. But best of all was the large poster Sally had given her last year for Christmas. *I know you can't smell the sea from our window, Rani,* the poinsettia-covered gift tag read, *but now you can see it from your desk. Love, Sally*

The poster, hanging at the foot of her bed, was a photograph of Kingston taken from one of the surrounding hills – sea water an incredible shade of blue, soft-green mountains caressed by light puffy clouds, the majestic city spread out below - Rani loved the poster because her hometown appeared as inviting as any other city on earth, its congestion, poverty and decaying neighborhoods invisible from that distance. When homesickness tugged at her heart, Rani starred at Kingston-by-the-sea until she felt better.

There'd been other gifts that first fall. One afternoon when the weather turned cool, the girl who lived at the end of the hall dropped by. "My mother doesn't give a rip what I do with my stuff," she stated bluntly thrusting two gorgeous Pendleton wool blankets into Rani's arms. "She's just relieved I'm out of the house so I don't interfere with her social life."

"But, I can't take these," Rani protested.

"Sure you can! Besides, I have more than I need." Priscilla Brinkley, with the dorm reputation of 'way wealthy and full of herself' had added softly, "Rani listen, it's going to get cold and you're going to need these. Besides I want you to have them."

Smiling at the memory Rani dropped her book bag on the desk. The acrid smell of smoke drifted across the college commons and through the open window. She could see the yellow police tape fluttering in the gentle breeze. Rani placed both hands on her stomach as the butterflies returned in an attempt to quiet the growing apprehension. As her breathing slowed she noticed the blinking light on her wall phone, walked over and punched the call-waiting light.

"Hi, Rani, this is Luther." His rich Arabic-accented English sounded excited. "Are you coming to the International Students' Club meeting tomorrow night? Call me, okay? Thanks, bye."

Luther Mouana enrolled in Emerick College the year before Rani. As two of only a handful of non-white students, they quickly became friends. His stick-thin African body and deep-set eyes shining from a gaunt black face, reminded Rani of the slave child running behind its mother she'd seen in a statute at the Cincinnati Freedom Center.

Rani lifted the receiver and punched the little squares – 475 – informed Luther's answering machine she planned to attend the club meeting and would be pleased to stay afterwards. That task completed she rummaged through her back pack, opened the Western Europe history text and was soon lost in the gory battlefields of World War I.

Lieutenant Rosemarie Harris yawned and stretched until her hands pressed against the ceiling of her squad car relieved to see it was almost four o'clock. As the police radio crackled, she dropped her arms and reached for the handset.

"Harris, here." She listened intently then opened the door and hopped out of the car relishing the crunch of dry leaves under her sturdy black shoes. "Ah, fall," she opined ducking under the yellow tape "and we've even got the smoke to go with it."

She crossed the porch gingerly testing each board before trusting it with her weight and peered through the opening where the battered front door had kept the rain and snow out of Pennington Place for over 125 years. Rosemarie braced herself with both hands and leaned inside. She could just make out two charred lumps hunched in the back corner all that remained of a splendid pair of wing-back chairs. As her eyes adjusted to the hazy interior, Lt. Harris spotted the outline of a stove and refrigerator through gapping holes in the wall between the kitchen and the front parlor.

As she surveyed the damage it suddenly struck her that she and Russell would never get to attend the traditional Tea with the President in Pennington House on Parents Weekend. The fact that Rosemarie had gone directly from high school to the Police Academy and never set foot on Emerick's campus until today didn't alter her mood. *Funny how the thought of missing something I've never even experienced makes me feel so sad!*

Shaking herself Rosi retraced her steps keeping an eye out for anything that felt out of place and began a quick tour of the outside. She lightly ran her fingers over the rough surface of the foundation as she walked. The silver-flecked beige sandstone blocks which held the first floor of Pennington Place at hip level were warm to the touch. Just as she rounded the corner Patrick Turner climbed out of his Chief of Police cruiser and marched across the lawn.

"Harris" he barked.

"Chief."

"You're relieved. See you in the morning."

And with that Chief Turner disappeared around the corner of the building.

"So much for, 'did you find anything suspicious, Lieutenant Harris?'" she grumbled under her breath. Glad to call it a day, she ducked under the tape. Just as she started to pull away from the curb, a man careened toward her frantically waving his arms. Lieutenant Harris stopped immediately and began a quick professional assessment as she ran the window down on the passenger side: *he's in his late 70s, probably used to getting his own way, probably lives alone...*

"Officer," he gasped placing both hands on top of the car to catch his breath. "Officer, a word please."

Add to that 'out of shape'. "Yes, sir?"

"It's terribly urgent that I assess the damage to the Quaker Archival Collection." Bending down he popped his head inside. "Can I gain entrance to Pennington Place yet?"

"Chief Turner's in charge of the investigation. You'll have to check with him."

With a sputter the head withdrew like a turtle into its shell.

"Chief Turner's still inside the building," she called to his backside as the old professor headed across the lawn. Lieutenant Harris shrugged her shoulders. Grateful her work day was finally over she drove down Division Street toward the police station wondering what that was all about.

Also intending to go home, Ruthalice was half way to her car when she witnessed the encounter between Charles and Rosemarie. Her curiosity peaked she did an about face and headed across the commons. She ducked under the tape before gingerly climbing the front steps then paused to allow her eyes to adjust before stepping across the threshold. The late October sun barely penetrated the soot covered windows. Ali groped instinctively for the light switch and flipped it up. Nothing. *Duh, what'd you expect you dummy!*

Stepping inside she yelled, "Charles, it's Ruthalice! Are you still here?"

Hearing footsteps above her Ali moved cautiously toward the bottom of the stairs avoiding the enormous jagged holes in the charred wooden floor. Biting her lower lip she cautiously worked her way up the steps.

"What are you doing here?" Chief Harris loomed menacingly at the top of the stairs.

Startled, Ali paused. "I don't think we've officially met, Chief. I'm Ruthalice Michels, the campus minister. I thought I saw Professor Hopkins come in here." Taking courage in hand Ali climbed the remaining four steps. "I share his concern for the condition of the archives, and…"

"He came and went! You'll have to leave when I do so make it quick." And with that he brushed past her and disappeared down the steps.

Moving into the middle of the large upstairs room Ali did a quick scan. The three overstuffed chairs which formed a semi circle around a large marble-covered table looked unscathed and except for the strong acrid smell of smoke the room appeared ready for its next researcher. She hurried over to the small desk under the window and read the green plastic plaque: *Priscilla Brinkley, student worker.*

"That's what I thought. No wonder her name sounded so darned familiar when Rani said it."

"You coming?"

Clearly 'no' was not an acceptable answer, so Ali joined Chief Turner at the bottom of the stairs. The pair of them moved cautiously across the porch and went their separate ways.

Using the eight mile drive home to 'decompose' as she humorously referred to this uninterrupted chance to mull things over out loud if she wanted to, Ali allowed the day's accumulated stuff to assume its proper place in the larger scheme of her life. Today as she drove east on Symmons Road and got stuck behind a load of soybeans, Ali was content to chug along at a steady 25mph until the tractor finally pulled into a driveway allowing the six car lineup to pass. Making the hard right onto Fair Ridge, she stopped a quarter mile down the road, collected the mail and newspaper from their respective plastic boxes and headed up the hill into the garage. She gathered her belongings strewn across the passenger seat, exhaustion threatened to take over. As she dragged herself into the kitchen it slowly dawned on her that even though she'd been up since 1:30 this morning she hadn't given dinner a thought until right this minute.

"I'm too pooped to be creative so unless there're some buns in the freezer I can nuke, it's beanie weenie time again." There weren't, but she did uncover a box of Stouffer's Apple-filled Tarts in the freezer door and half a bag of broccoli. "Good thing my sweetie's not a picky eater," she mused carrying her find to the microwave. By the time Cliff arrived 15 minutes later the smell of baked apples filled the house.

"Hmmmm, that smells good. I figured we'd be making do with cereal tonight." He planted a kiss on her cheek. "Shall we finish the merlot?" Without waiting for a response Cliff poured wine into two glasses and set them on the table. "Ahhh, merlot and beanie weenies!" he exclaimed as Ali set a plate in front of him. "Who says we M and Ms ain't suave and debonair?"

Ali dug hungrily into her supper quietly rejoicing that this wonderful man came home to her every single night, and for the next ten minutes they ate in companionable and exhausted silence. It wasn't until after the apple-filled tarts that either of them had the energy required to start a conversation. Cliff went first.

"So, what did you learn from that police woman?" he asked laying his fork across his empty plate with a contented sigh. "I spotted you heading for the patrol car and figured you were about to ply her for information with a cup of the Leaky Cup's finest brew."

"Me? Plying for information? Geez, Cliff, I was simply offering good Emerick College hospitality." Ali failed in her attempt to look aggrieved, and Cliff ploughed on undeterred.

"Ok, so, what did you learn with your good Emerick College hospitality, then?"

"She spells her name with an "i" also." Ali favored him with her biggest grin.

"And?"

"And she's at least relatively certain the fire began in the basement and that it'll take a couple days to get the fire marshal's final report." Ali licked the back of her fork. "She was pretty curious about that cubbyhole part way down the basement steps, the one Ernestine claims our Hannah Emerick used to store jars of canned food in the summertime."

"What else did your police woman say?" Cliff asked as he began sticking plates, silverware and glasses haphazardly into the dish washer.

"She's not 'my police woman' – her name is Lieutenant Rosemarie Harris. She has a son by the way named Russell who's planning to attend EC next fall and play football." Ali yawned. "And that's about it."

Cliff turned off the light over the sink before heading for the living room and sank into his 'man's recliner' and reached for the remote. "Ready for Game One of the National League Playoffs? I'm counting on not needing to expend any intellectual energy watching the Cubs and the Dodgers."

Ali settled into her matching forest-green recliner and wrapped up in the Ohio Bicentennial coverlet a grateful mother had given her after she'd convinced their distraught son that suicide was not his only option. Sufficiently shaken by their child's determination to leave school one way or the other, his father informed him he could do whatever he wanted, and at last count son Rudy was happily tossing Caesar salads and stuffing chicken pot pies at the local Bob Evans.

"If you insist on lying down in that recliner," she opined, "you're not going to make it past the pre-game hype let alone the 9th inning!"

"You know me only too well!" he replied tucking the pumpkin covered afghan under his heels and pulling the remainder up to his chin. "Oh, by the way," Cliff rolled his head sideways and glanced at his wife. "Did you see you have a message on the answering machine?" Ali shook her head.

"Well, you do. It's Skylar."

Ruthalice clambered back out of the recliner and vanished into the kitchen. Fifteen minutes later she re-emerged. "No wonder he's been on my mind lately," she said resuming her seat. She arranged the afghan over her knees. "He just wanted us to know that he and Alyse are finally settled in their new apartment on Amberly Drive, and can't wait for us to come up and visit." She smiled contentedly. "He really just wanted to chat."

Their attention back on the tv, their eyes began to glaze over and by the middle of the 2nd inning with two outs and a man on third, the M&Ms were sound asleep so neither saw the third baseman clobber a home run into straight away center field, putting the Cubbies ahead two to one.

As evening slipped into night, Professor Hopkins ducked under the yellow tape and scurried across the lawn.

"Calm down, old boy, just calm down," Curly counseled himself, grateful for the heavy clouds obscuring the moon. He paused under the ginkgo tree by the back porch and surveyed the campus for movement. Seeing none, he mounted the four steps and using his shoulder, shoved the splintered back door open. Suddenly hesitant about barging into the kitchen uninvited, Curly paused. The old house seemed forlorn and abandoned, her once elegant interior ravaged by fire.

Charles moved toward the basement door carefully avoiding the broken window glass under foot. The linoleum floor felt sticky. Digging the pencil-sized laser flashlight out of his tweed jacket pocket, he shone its skinny beam down the basement stairs.

"Got to do this alone, old boy" he whispered pressing down on the top step with his left foot. The heavy smell of smoke and dampness nearly choked him. His face buried in his left arm his body convulsed in a spasm of muffled coughs. His eyes bleary, tears running down his cheeks, he worked his way step by tested step until he felt the welcome cement of the basement floor. Digging a handkerchief out of his breast pocket Charles tied it across his nose and mouth (*like a damn Yankee cowboy,* he mused wryly), and pointed his inadequate light at the stubborn darkness.

Following the narrow illuminated path he passed three file cabinets standing along the north wall. As he shuffled his way forward the old professor waved his left hand in front of his face feeling the darkness with his fingers the way he had as a kid in the dimly lit tunnels of the London Underground. His right shoulder brushed the new furnace in the middle of the room. Finally reaching the wooden wall which separated the front two-thirds of the basement from the rear, Curly switched off the flashlight and felt his way along the divider until his fingers found the door he was seeking. Lifting the metal latch, he stepped into the old boiler room. Sidestepping the original furnace he bumped into the waist-high half wall between the furnace and the coal bin a few yards later, turned the flashlight back on, and quickly played the beam across the stone floor.

"Gideon's right," he rasped with relief. "Everything's out except his blanket pack."

Squatting down he ran his fingers over the rough woolen bundle. Inside he found a leather-bound Bible wrapped in a flannel shirt, a packet of loose-leaf lined paper and three ball point pens. Underneath were a pair of trousers, one flip flop and some underwear. Suddenly uneasy pawing through another man's belongings, Charles retied the blanket and gathered it into his arms. A quick glance around the coal bin satisfied him that no trace of occupancy remained. Tucking the blanket roll under his right arm Curly retraced his steps and climbed up to the kitchen. Peering through the shattered kitchen window he stood motionless for several minutes before stepping out onto the narrow porch.

In front of Harvey Library the streetlamp lit the sidewalk in both directions, but the light did not reach the back yard of Pennington Place. Grateful for the safety the dark spots afforded him, Charles ducked under the police line tape and reached his car just as campus security turned into the parking lot. Curly unlocked the door and slipped inside, quickly placing the bundle on the floor between his feet.

"Hey Professor Hopkins," the blond uniformed guard called as he drove past. "Have a nice evening."

With a curt nod and his best nonchalant British wave he turned the key and the old Beetle sprang to life without its usual grinding and sputtering. Passing the police station at a law-abiding 35mph, Charles drove the few blocks to Sheppard Place and turned into his one-car garage. He made sure the garage door closed all the way then walked the short distance to the kitchen door.

"It's me, Gideon," he called softly moving into the unlit living room. "I've retrieved your parcel." Silence filled the room. Charles turned on the table lamp beside his favorite chair creating a softly lit circle on the beige carpet. "There is no one else here, Gideon. You are safe now."

Sensing movement behind him Curly sat down, laid the bundle on the carpet and waited. A slender black man materialized in front of him. Lifting the soft packet with both hands, he smiled broadly then bowed.

"Thank you, Professor Curly. You are my friend."

Gideon Boseka squatted and began unpacking the frayed plaid blanket. Tucked under the clothes was a small square package wrapped in a red bandana. The young Somali removed a wooden picture frame, a beaded necklace with a gold cross hanging from the middle and a small roll of US bills. He raised the cross to his lips then slipped the necklace over his head. He gently kissed the photograph before standing it on the little square table beside Charles' arm chair. Next he counted the bills, nodded and twisted the brown rubber band around them before re-wrapping the roll in the bandana.

"My mother and my father and my little sister, Corinne." Gideon cradled the framed photo with both hands. "They are all dead now, Professor Curly," he added staring blankly at the wall over Curly's right shoulder.

"I know Gideon." Charles pondered how much of his own childhood story to share. "You and I have much in common," he began deciding empathy would help his young friend feel more at ease. "I survived the London bombings of World War Two by hiding in the Underground, but after the Germans bombed our London flat killing both my parents, I was parceled out to my granny in the countryside." Charles pointed a finger at the harpsichord in the corner of the living room. "Do you see that picture, Gideon? That is my ma and my poppy standing on the beach at Dover celebrating their 10th wedding anniversary. They died two weeks later." Charles cleared his throat. "That photograph is the only one I have of them."

In one fluid motion Gideon rose and moved to the far wall. Bending over he squinted at the reddish-brown photo. "She is very pretty your mama, and your poppy he is very handsome." Then a smile lit up his entire face. "We share…we are both orphans…we are like brothers now… No, that is not right." A frown creased his forehead. "You are my uncle!" he amended quickly. "Yes, my Uncle Professor Curly!"

Gideon resumed his seat on the carpet, his dark eyes darting anxiously from object to object as if expecting one of them to jump up and come at him. He ducked his head as the cuckoo clock began to chime. When the little wooden bird finally reached twelve, the professor staggered wearily to his feet.

"Gideon, my good man, I'm done in and simply must retire. Put your photo and other belongings in your room."

Gideon sprung obligingly to his feet, collected his belongings and headed to the basement door. "Tonight I am safe in my new home," he whispered softly. "Thank you, Uncle Professor Curly."

Professor Hopkins stumbled into the bedroom at the end of the hall, kicked off his shoes, wrestled out of his jacket and collapsed on the bed. He located the coverlet with his left hand, tugged it up over his shoulders and instantly began to snore. Alarmed at the unfamiliar noise, Gideon crept down the hall and listened outside the room. Finally reassured that all was well, he tiptoed down the wooden steps to his metal-framed cot in the unfinished basement.

Before climbing into bed, Gideon dropped to his knees and closed his eyes. Having learned from experience that it was foolish to expect his life to ever be truly safe, he refused to let down his guard. When suddenly forced to evacuate in the middle of the night he became once more the terrified young refugee escaping with his life. With the temporary safety of the coal bin sanctuary literally going up in smoke, Gideon fled to the only person he knew would shelter and protect him.

Praying softly Gideon pleaded, "Gracious Father, cast me not away from Thy presence and take not Thy holy spirit from me." Rising to his feet, he touched his new bed and ran his hand over the soft blanket. "Two bed pillows, a warm duvet and four clean towels! Thank you sweet Jesus, thank you for my Uncle Professor Curly!"

Grateful for its warmth Gideon pulled the black hooded sweatshirt over his head, climbed into bed and entered the light sleep of one accustomed to terror in the night.

"Finally!" Jennifer Blake whimpered close to tears. Sitting up in bed she fumbled for the bedside lamp. "Where have you been?" She scowled at her roommate who seemed completely unperturbed by the outburst. "I've been worried sick about you."

Priscilla glared scornfully in the general direction of the voice. "Who asked you to be my keeper?" She dropped onto her bed and bent to untie her Nikes. "If you must know, Bobby and I had a date, remember."

"But it's after midnight. You've been gone since *last night*!" Jen hated the way Priscilla always made her feel like an idiot for bothering to care. "That's more than twenty-four hours, Prissy!"

"Geez, my roomy's a mathematical genius!"

The air felt electric. Jennifer stared gloomily across the room waiting for the explanation she knew from past experience would come eventually.

"We got a little high." Priscilla rubbed her forehead with the heel of her right hand. "And then Bobby had to have his joint in order to relax," Prissy made quotation marks in the air with her left fore and middle fingers around 'in order to relax', "and by then the damn campus was crawling with cops 'cause of the fire…" She collapsed backwards onto the bed arms splayed wide on either side and yawned loudly. "Bobby will be thrown out of school if we get caught again, so the only smart thing to do was wait for the smell of booze and dope to just drift away." She fluttered her fingers in the air. "Satisfied?"

Jennifer felt sick to her stomach. Knowing better than to reprimand her wayward friend, she simply turned off the light and slipped back down under the covers. "So you were at Bobby's?" she asked already knowing the answer.

"Where else?" Priscilla propped herself up on one elbow and stared across the room. "Listen, Jen, are you thinking what I'm thinking about this fire?" Her query was met with silence. "Don't worry, kiddo, Bobby and I kept constant watch from outside Fox Hall, and nobody was going inside to investigate last night. It was still way too hot."

I guess I'm supposed to feel better with that piece of information, Jennifer thought miserably still unwilling to voice her apprehension. It didn't matter anyway. Priscilla had tipped over and was snoring like a passed out sailor. Jen pulled the pillow over her head and willed herself to think about anything besides what had set off the fire.

Chapter Four - Thursday

The next morning brought the first frost. Determined not to light the furnace until the end of the month, Ali set plates on the table her plaid flannel bathrobe wrapped tightly around her.

"Our fire made the front page of the Out-County News," Cliff announced folding the Dayton Daily News so he could read and eat at the same time.

"Let's see what we've got here. Headline: ***Historic building burns at local college.*** 'A fire broke out early Wednesday morning at Emerick College, a small liberal arts school (founded by The Religious Society of Friends) 50 miles southwest of town. Pennington Place built in 1863 and designated a Historic Site in 1993 by the Ohio Historical Society, suffered extensive smoke and water damage.' Then there's the usual stuff about our heritage as an institution of higher learning dedicated to Quaker principles and testimonies, etc. etc. and – oh, 'President Richard "Skip" Willson is relieved to inform parents that no one was hurt. Quote, Emerick's students were never in danger unquote. There's a picture of Penn before the fire and another post-conflagration."

Cliff leaned into the newspaper. "Whoa, wait a minute! Hand me that magnifying glass would you, Ali?" He waved his right hand in the direction of the stack of papers on her side of the table. “It’s on the crossword puzzle.”

Cliff peered at the photo. “Well, I’ll be dad burned. What do you make of THAT?” He slid the paper and glass across the table.

“Exactly what am I looking at?”

“Just look at the street.”

Ruthalice brought the magnifying glass to rest above the police car parked at the curb and squinted. She made out a woman leaning against the side who appeared to be in earnest conversation with the officer inside.

“Apparently I’m married to a celebrity.” He leaned back a self-satisfied smile on his face. “How many malacologists do *you* know whose wife’s picture is featured in a major metropolitan newspaper? Man oh man, our phone’s going to be ringing off the hook!”

“Oh, for pity’s sake, Clifford, get a grip. Nobody can tell it’s me but you.” Ali’s grin undermined her attempt at annoyance. “Besides, I was just fulfilling my pastoral care responsibilities, remember. And,” she lowered her voice, “hoping for some inside information.”

“Is there any mention of arson?” Cliff asked dribbling honey on his English muffin. “That’s what concerns you and Rani the most, right?”

Ali raised her chin enough to see through the lower portion of her trifocals and began to read: “‘The fire marshal continues investigation of the predawn fire at Emerick College. The captain at the scene indicates that the blaze, which began in the basement, was caused by an explosion. According to college security personnel their guard checked the outside doors at 12:30am and found them both locked.’”

Ali put the newspaper down and stared at Cliff.

"What do you make of that interesting tidbit of information?"

"Has an ominous ring to it. I suspect the campus rumor mill's in over drive." He bent over and kissed the top of her head. "Speaking of high gear, I've got to run." Zipping his EC wool jacket, Cliff called over his departing shoulder, "Have a good day, sweetheart. I'm sure it will all get sorted out before long."

Ali dressed in a daze, trying unsuccessfully to rein in her sense of complicity. She re-emerged from the closet buttoning a blouse lavishly strewn with raspberry and sky-blue orchids. Her trusty all-purpose black skirt lay in a heap on the chair.

"Maybe I can make up somehow for not taking this whole fire talk more seriously," she muttered braiding her hair. *By doing what? What exactly is it you should have done?* Ali sighed. "There you go again, arguing with yourself like some kind of multiple personality!"

Pausing in front of the full length mirror long enough to reassure herself that she 'passed muster', she grabbed her canvas bag on the way through the kitchen and headed for campus.

"This morning's wide open," she reminded herself as she turned the engine off. "I've got time to do some poking around if I go right now. I've got to *do* something or I will go nuts."

Having made up her mind Ali headed straight for Pennington Place. The lone policeman slipped out of his black-and-white and intercepted her at the front porch. Stepping artfully between Ruthalice and the bottom step, he placed a hand on each hip and assumed the stance Ruthalice always thought of as official police posture:

legs three feet apart, weight solidly on the balls of both feet.

"This site's still under investigation, ma'am. You can't go in there."

Smiling brightly Ali snuck a surreptitious peek at his badge. *It looks like Doff but in this glare that last 'f' might very well be a 't' for all I know.*

"I'm Ruthalice Michels, campus minister here at Emerick," she said brightly extending her hand. The young officer shook it with little enthusiasm. "I spoke at length with Lieutenant Harris yesterday." She paused dramatically hoping the age-old tactic of name dropping might improve her chances of being given some slack.

"All's I know, ma'am is I'm not to let no one in the house until the chief gives the thumbs up." Anticipating her next question he added, "And I don't know when that will be ma'am."

Darn, Plan A didn't work so it's on to Plan B.

"Can I bring you a cup of coffee, Officer Doff?"

"No thanks. I don't drink coffee." A hint of a smile softened his face. "That's Dorft actually." Relaxing for an instant, he added "They left the 'r' out of my name. The bursar claims she couldn't read my handwriting, and the next order for badges goes in at the end of the month, so in the meantime I'm stuck with Doft I reckon."

"Ok, Officer Dorft. I guess sometimes we've just got to live with the mistakes of others."

"That's right, ma'am, and some of them are real doozies!"

Ruthalice waited to see if Dorft was going to elaborate but he remained motionless, staring across the damp lawn at Dalton Science Hall.

"Well then I guess I'll move along. Have a nice day."

Her curiosity still unsatisfied, Ruthalice set a leisurely pace along the west side of the house, marveling at how well the bushes had survived the onslaught of heat and water. Glancing back she watched as the police chief's car pulled to the curb. Unwilling to push her luck any further she strode along the red brick walkway back to Frame Meetinghouse.

Normally on campus by 8am, Professor Hopkins grew increasingly antsy as he lingered over a second cup of tea. By 8:30 he'd read the entire *New York Times* and concluded that Gideon was going to sleep until noon, when he heard the basement toilet flush. Sliding out of the vinyl-covered dinette chair, Curly hollered down the stairs.

"Gideon, are you finally up?"

"Yes Professor Curly," came the sleepy reply. "You want me to come up?"

"Yes. I'm dreadfully late - should have been on campus an hour ago - but first you and I must talk."

Gideon climbed the stairs massaging his temples with both palms and followed Charles into the kitchen. Curly thrust a mug of tea into his guest's hands.

"Sit down, Gideon. You're making me nervous hovering around like that." *God, you're a grumpy old man this morning*, he chastised himself. "Listen, Gideon the reality of our situation dictates that we be very circumspect now. You have to lay low for a few days until this damnable fire investigation is over."

Gideon frowned. "What is this 'lay low', Professor Curly?"

"It means you are not to go outside, answer the phone or the door under any circumstances," Curly stated flatly beginning to feel like a boys school principal.

A look of alarm skittered across Gideon's face. "What about my job? I do not want to lose my job, Professor Curly."

"Bloody hell! You didn't say anything about a job!" Lowering his voice he growled, "Where are you working, for pete's sake?"

Gideon's head dropped. "At the warehouse out there," he muttered pointing vaguely with his left index finger.

"Speak up, Gideon. I can't hear a word you're saying. Remember I'm an old man."

Without raising his head, Gideon tried again to explain. "At the home improvement store. I sweep the floor and stock shelves. I work three nights a week."

Charles shook his head in disbelief. "And no one's ever questioned you?"

"Never. I fill out form and get job two months ago." His confidence restored, Gideon raised his head and pronounced proudly, "I save money and go to Twin City!"

"Twin City? Oh, you mean Minneapolis-St. Paul." Now it was the professor's turn to look puzzled. "But why the Twin Cities?"

Hugging the mug of tea against his chest with both hands, Gideon fell silent his half closed eyes hiding whatever he was thinking.

"Oh, never mind. What matters now is that you stay put! Lay low, whatever."

Gideon opened his mouth to respond but Charles cut him off.

"Do you understand, young man? Your presence in this house must not be discovered or we're both in a heap of trouble."

Still shaking Charles rose to his feet and began rinsing his cup and plate. He took a deep breath. "By the way," he asked casually, "who is your supervisor out at the warehouse?"

"Miss Green. She's the boss lady. She come in at four o'clock every morning."

"So this Miss Green, she's at the store now?"

"I think so." Gideon stared earnestly at Curly. "She want me to have stocked shelves on Saturday. What I do, Professor?"

Charles slipped his arms into a gray London fog and settled it over his worsted blazer. "It's only Thursday, Gideon," he replied opening the kitchen door, "which gives me a couple of days to figure a way out of our muddle."

Suddenly feeling old and befuddled, he smiled tenderly at the young man sitting at the table, his elbows propping up a boney chin. Dressed in baggy pajama bottoms and a bright orange XL Bengals sweatshirt hanging loosely from his thin shoulders, Gideon could easily pass for a graduate student in his early twenties.

"I'll be home for supper, Gideon. Remember, you are quite safe here as long as you remain in the house." Embarrassed by the strength of unaccustomed emotions, Charles looked at his feet and blinked.

"I trust my friend Uncle Professor Curly," Gideon replied breaking into his million dollar smile. "OK I will, what you call it? stay put!"

Hugging himself with crossed arms, Gideon waited until his benefactor had closed the kitchen door and backed out of the garage before slipping down the narrow hallway into the living room. Lifting a corner of the poplin drape, he followed Curly's progress down the street until he disappeared out of sight. The sun glared off the picture window rendering all movement invisible from the outside. Gideon watched the neighborhood children gather on the corner and board the yellow school bus. He remained motionless as they too disappeared around the corner. Twenty minutes later the curtain dropped silently back into place.

Resisting the impulse to head straight for the warehouse, Charles stuck to the original plan he'd concocted this morning whilst waiting for his unexpected house guest to emerge. *Damnably tricky turn of events, this.* Braking he turned into the Fine Arts parking lot and shut off the engine. *Haven't shared a flat with another human being since my Swarthmore College undergraduate days, and I don't fancy starting to now! We're chalk and cheese.*

"Steady old bean, you've been in deeper scrapes before," he reassured himself. "Poppy always said there's a way out of every bag." He set his jaw and stepped onto the sidewalk. "Just don't get careless," he counseled himself still rattled by the swing and depth of emotion he experienced that morning.

On the ground floor of the Fox Hall Administration Building, President Willson nodded at Mary Scott's cheerful greeting then stuck his head in Dean Feller's office.

"Evelyn, can you spare a minute?"

"Of course, Richard."

"Let's go up to my office."

Walking beside him Evelyn Feller felt the weight of responsibility on the president's narrow shoulders. During administrative meetings he was the man-in-charge; the bon-vivant when dealing with the public; the firm but lovable parental presence with students. However, around his closet colleagues, Richard Willson often seemed aloof as he retreated into some personal private space. This morning his hands trembled as he poured their coffee.

"Not much sleep last night," Richard admitted aware of his colleague's concern, "and an overabundance of coffee." He nodded toward the door to his office. "I need a frank 'where do we go from here?' conversation with you, Evelyn."

Four chairs were arranged in a circle around an elegant glass-topped mahogany table. The president sank into the nearest chair, shut his eyes and slipped away. Evelyn quietly assumed the chair next to his and sipped her coffee, content to wait as long as necessary. On the wall clock, the minute hand passed silently over bright white numerals pasted on top of a photograph of Fox Hall. Richard abruptly opened his eyes and sat up, swallowed a mouthful of coffee and uttered a disgusted 'yuck'. Reaching behind him he tapped the intercom.

"Could you bring me another cup of coffee, Lynn? This one's stone cold."

The president waited while his secretary closed the door, then slide a photo out of the manila folder on his lap and handed it to Evelyn.

"Turn it around, you've got it upside down," he indicated kindly, waiting while the dean rotated the picture and studied it through narrow silver-rimmed reading glasses. "It is a bit difficult to decipher. What you're seeing there are the back steps from the kitchen to the basement. Chief Turner informed me that most of the fire damage to the parlor floor was caused by flames from the over-stuffed furniture the college was storing under the stairs.

Evelyn laid the photo on the table. "Is there any decision about what started the fire? That upholstery would need a pretty good blaze to ignite it I should think."

Skip handed her the next photograph. "That's a closer view."

Evelyn tilted her head and frowned. "What's that?" she asked pointing to a darker spot in the foundation wall.

"It's a recess for storing canning jars. Apparently our dear Hannah Elizabeth, frugal Quaker that she was, placed jars of food in that recess in the wall to keep them cool." Richard fiddled with the flap on the manila envelope. "For some reason that western foundation wall is two rows thick instead of the usual one. It's the only building on campus built that way." President Willson favored her with an amused smile. "You'd have to check with Hopkins to get the full story."

The dean returned his smile. "Ok, now I can make out the cubbyhole." She set the photos on the table. "I've only been in that basement once or twice and just never noticed it before." She raised both hands and removed her glasses, folded them and began tapping the frames against the open palm of her left hand. "Are we assuming the fire started in that cubbyhole?"

"Seems unlikely, doesn't it because as far as I know there's nothing in that space."

He paused at the light knock on the door. "Yes?"

"You're 10:30 appointment's here. Shall I postpone her to this afternoon?"

"What do I have after lunch today, Lynn? I can't seem to keep on top of my schedule these days."

"That's totally understandable," Lynn replied sympathetically. "You've got an awful lot on your plate." Remembering his question she added quickly, "Mr. Cope is coming in at 2:30. He's the father of that soccer player Coach Stevens was telling you about yesterday, the one who broke his foot."

Richard gave an impatient nod. "Yes, I know exactly who he is! And he's Ted's uncle not his father."

Momentarily taken aback by his curtness, Lynn paused before delivering the rest of her message. "Chief Turner called a few minutes ago and wants to see you at four."

"OK, put my 10:30 off until three. That will give me a good excuse to terminate the visit with Sidney Cope," he added as an after thought.

Lynn nodded and closed the office door.

"Well, well, so Sid Cope is Theodore's uncle. I didn't realize the connection. A visit from him ought to take your mind off Pennington Place for awhile. I doubt he gives a hoot for the demise of dear old Penn. If it isn't sports forget it, right?"

"It's not quite that bad. However, if athletics wants new locker rooms and a basketball court, it behooves me to see what's got him all riled up this time." He sighed. "Cope's got very little use for Bob Stevens."

Evelyn rose to her feet. "Is there anything else I can do, Richard?"

"Join me at four if you can."

Feeling every one of his 72 years, President Willson met Evelyn's concerned look with a weak smile. "Don't worry. I'll be fine with a good night's sleep."

Keeping her thoughts to herself Evelyn walked down the hallway and stopped at her secretary's desk.

"I'll join Richard at 4 o'clock and hear what Chief Turner's got to report."

Mary Scott ran her finger expertly down the date book in front of her and made the entry. Watching as the inter office door closed behind her boss, Mary pondered the latest scuttlebutt texting its way across campus and picked up the phone.

Ruthalice spent the rest of the morning in her office reassuring parents about a variety of concerns. "Of course I can talk with Robbie about anger management, Mrs. Flanders. I understand your distress. Judicial Hearings for dorm misconduct are meant to be taken seriously." Ali, thankful she was on the phone, rolled her eyes as Mrs. Flanders continued fretting over her son's behavior and possible sanctions.

She had just completed a quick review of her teaching notes on the prophet Isaiah for Friday's Bible class, when the telephone rang again. "Yes, of course it's appropriate to reflect on being thankful for the bounty all around us at Thanksgiving time," she assured the volleyball coach who had agreed to speak at All College Worship November 18th. "Do you want to sing '*We Gather Together*' as the hymn?"

Everyone needs affirmation today, she reflected staring at the reprint of her favorite Monet hanging above her desk. There was something so incredibly soothing about the way the clear water played with the reflection of the small brown boat floating on its surface. Ali could not remember how many times she's longed to trade places with the calm figure sitting in the dingy and trail *her* fingers in the pond and listen to the call of French birds hiding in the trees.

The bright red sticky note stuck to the picture frame caught her attention. *Jeesh, that's right, I promised Skip I'd deliver a short tribute to Pennington Place tomorrow at noon for his little commemoration. You'd better pull your thoughts together and get something down on paper-unless you're planning to wing it again* her annoying inner voice chimed in.

"I'll get right on it after I eat lunch," she promised herself as she crossed the green and joined a group of students in the cafeteria line. "A little sustenance always gets my brain in gear."

Since the walk back to her office took her past Pennington Place, Ali decided to take another look at the rear wall. Finally satisfied there was nothing her untrained eyes could learn by gawking at the smoke-streaked walls, she was about to give up when a large marmalade cat emerged from behind the corner bushes. Twitching its tail the cat paused for a moment then slunk behind the next bush. Following its route Ali caught a glimpse of black metal in the sandstone blocks. Curious, she stepped between the bushes then dropping to her knees realized she was looking at a small door. Ruthalice reached out and gingerly touched the cast iron handle wrapped in silver metal coil.

"That's got to be the door into a coal bin. Dollars to donuts there's a room down there like the one we had in our house."

Ali pictured the huge furnace with its octopus arms. After her parents bought the enormous stucco house on Lincoln Avenue, her father had converted it from coal to gas. Whenever it was Ruthalice's turn to fold laundry her best friend always refused to do it in the cellar. Spooked by the ominous noises the boiler emitted, Annie always insisted they bring the clothes up to the kitchen "where it's totally safe. There's no way I'm staying down there. It totally weirds me out!"

Chuckling at the memory Ruthalice placed both hands against the sun-warmed stones, pushed and got to her feet. By the time she drifted back to her office it was nearly two o'clock. *Time to tackle the testimonial to Pennington Place* she reminded herself. She grabbed a yellow pad, sat in the orange comfy chair and gathered her thoughts: *A member of our community was badly burned Wednesday morning* she began and spent the next hour scribbling and crossing out. By 3:30 she had a decent speech.

"Whew, I gotta pee," she stated matter-of-factly. She stretched then wandered across the hall into the bathroom, washed her hands and stared gloomily in the mirror above the sink.

"The bags under my eyes are definitely getting bigger!" she moaned. Then switching to self-lecture mode she scolded, "if you don't start getting more sleep, you're going to have to resort to make-up." Splashing cold water on her face she grumbled, "with my luck, TV 7 will be at this commemoration around Angell Pool tomorrow with their cameras rolling, and Cliff's celebrity wife will look like she's been through the wringer!"

Hearing Sid Cope's arrival well in advance of the knock on his office door, President Willson straightened his tie and tugged his shirt sleeves making sure they covered his wrists. Resolved to soldier through this interview with as little damage to himself and the college as possible, Richard got to his feet.

"Come in, Sidney."

Sid Cope extended a well manicured hand then dropped into the chair occupied by Dean Feller a few hours earlier. "Damn shame about old Penn burning, Skip. I remember interviewing the head of PR in the parlor when I was a student in the 80s."

"I'd forgotten that public relations used to be in Pennington," Richard replied content to let Sid set the pace for their conversation. "You graduated cum laude in, what, '85 if I remember correctly."

"Yes, siree, the class of 1985, all 115 of us. I prided myself on knowing everyone's name!" His face lit up. "We played one heck of a game of football back then." As the best quarterback Emerick College had ever seen, Sidney R. Cope claimed the right to boast.

Hoping to avoid a lengthy recitation on the glory days of Quaker football, Richard remained mute. His visitor guzzled his coffee then tossed the Styrofoam cup into the wastepaper basket beside the president's desk.

"Still got it!" he crowed.

Richard shifted in his seat, pulled up his left sleeve and pointedly consulted his watch.

"But, that's for another time." Sidney adjusted his jacket. "It's about this business with my nephew and Coach Stevens. First Coach kicks Ted off the team for a god-damn accident, so the kid threatens to withdraw from school and run home to mommy." His angry recitation turned into scorn. "I thought this was a Quaker institution – all lovely-dovey and forgiving and crap like that! Whatever happened to supporting our athletes, forgive and forget?"

Momentarily taken aback by the indignation spewing across the table, Richard fought the urge to wipe his hands on his pant leg. As the verbal barrage ceased he regained his composure.

"Bob Stevens has a good reason for everything he does, Sidney, and furthermore, I trust his judgment when it comes to team discipline." The president paused braced for another outburst. When none was forthcoming, he continued.

"Theodore's a good kid and an outstanding goal keeper. I suspect he's feeling pretty miserable about the whole thing. Some kids deal with their disappointment by, as you put it, 'running home to mommy'. I don't know any of the family dynamics other than the fact that Theodore is one of our first generation college students. For some of those kids being the first in your family to go to school can become a daunting burden to try and carry."

Sid Cope gazed impatiently out the window.

"Yeah, yeah, I know all that, Richard!" he retorted. He turned and fixed his steel blue eyes on Richard's face. "My brother RJ thinks this college stuff is a total waste of money. He seems almost eager for his boy to fail, come to his senses and get his butt back to the farm where it belongs."

The words slowed to a trickle, the bravado suddenly gone. The big man leaned forward over clasped hands, his elbows resting on the arms of the chair.

"I talked with Stevens yesterday, and he told me about the fight." The anger spent Cope chose his words carefully. "The true story. Apparently Ted's version of how he broke his foot is a bit creative." Sid snorted and shook his head. "Kids!"

Richard waited, curious to see where his visitor was going now that he'd gotten the worst of his indignation off his chest. The transformation from in your face rage to well-hidden sorrow reminded the president of an inner tube as it gradually softened and shrank from a slow leak.

"My sister-in-law's pretty upset. She's always been the one keen on having their oldest child in college, 'to set a good example for the rest of the kids' as she puts it." He shook his head in amazement. "Somehow Emma persuaded Roger to let Ted give college a try but with this turn of events my narrow-minded brother has gotten the excuse he needs to jerk Theodore out of college handed to him on a silver platter. When he heard about the incident he started in again reminding the entire family that quote he's not paying for no fancy education if'n his boy can't play soccer unquote. Apparently the only acceptable reason for going to college as far as his father's concerned is that his son's the star player for the Hustlin' Quakers."

Sid re-crossed his legs shifting his weight to his left hip.

"But my little brother doesn't know the entire story. Seems Ted called his mom sometime Monday, and Emma immediately contacted me begging me to please do something." His eyes softened. "My sister-in-law's one of those solid down-home gals you can bet the farm on. I'd never heard her so upset. So," he continued vigorously rubbing the tip of his nose with his right index finger, "that's why I came by today – to try and do something about it."

"So your nephew's withdrawn?"

"His mother and I came up this morning, treated Ted to a Bob Evans' breakfast, and as of eleven o'clock this morning we've got him persuaded to tough it out at least until the end of the semester. I've extracted Steven's promise that if Ted stays in shape, he'll put him back in goal next fall." Sidney straightened himself up to his full height. "I assured Coach I'd take personal responsibility for his conditioning. He'll be ready." Cope remained motionless, the veins on the back of his hands threatening to pop from the death grip he held on the chair. "Since I'm now the one paying for this kid's education, he damn well better knuckle down and work out until he drops!"

"So, Theodore remains here at his uncle's expense. That's mighty generous of you, Sidney." Richard relaxed for the first time that afternoon. Here was a side of Sidney Cope he'd never seen before. "Am I to assume the true story of how Ted broke his foot remains between his mother, his coach and his uncle?" *Well not quite*, Skip realized as soon as the words were out of his mouth. *There's Mary Scott, who seems to know everything, Evelyn and now me.*

Sidney Cope snorted. "The whole team sure as hell knows, rumors have made the rounds all over campus, but yeah, other than that, only his mother and I know!" Cope looked at the floor and shrugged. "But, that's life on a small campus, isn't it? Times may have changed since my day but you can dad-burn count on the old rumor mill to churn out the good stuff." He sighed and raised his head. "Some things never change."

Inhaling heavily Sid got to his feet. "Ted says the campus minister pried the truth out of him," he added wryly. "I reminded him confession's good for the soul even if she's only a Quaker and not a Catholic priest. No offense, Richard," he added hastily.

"None taken, Sid." Willson stood up. "Ruthalice Michels is a good listener. I hope he'll talk with her again." He reached for the knob as Lynn's gentle knock officially ended the interview. "I'm pleased you found a workable solution, Sidney. Let's have that golf date the next time I'm up your way, shall we?"

"Oh, that reminds me." Cope reached into his breast pocket and extracted a fistful of Ohio State basketball tickets. "Distribute these however you wish, Richard. Opening game of the season. A present from Cope Sporting Goods compliments of the management."

And with his habitual we're-in-this-together wink, Sidney Cope walked out the door. Richard and Lynn stood side by side watching him wend his way down the hallway and disappear into the elevator. The president looked around for his next appointment.

"Here she comes." Lynn nodded toward the coed trotting down the corridor. "Her name's Roxanne Dubois, by the way."

"Ok. What's on her mind?"

"Roxy, as she prefers to be called, addressed the faculty meeting last April about our moral obligation to speak out against the Iraq War."

"Ah, yes, now I remember." He grinned. "Not shy about offering her opinions is she?"

"No comment," his secretary replied softly retuning his smile. "But today she wants an interview for the student paper."

"Ah, Roxanne please come in. I understand you want to talk about the unfortunate fire in Pennington Place." Richard's voice trailed off as he shut the door.

The president's secretary glanced up from her notepad and caught a glimpse of a harried coed as she dashed into Room 306. A minute later the phone rang.

"President's office." She listened for a moment, nodded silently then replied smartly, "Yes, sir, I'll be sure to tell him. Thank you for calling."

Content with the tone of Roxanne's interview, President Willson leaned heavily against the back of his desk chair, dropped his chin into both hands and stared wearily across the room grateful for a few moments alone. The blinking intercom and a very full bladder vied for his attention. *I can ignore the former but had better attend to the latter,* he murmured hoisting himself to his feet.

In spite of an unspecified sense of urgency, Professor Hopkins presented a decent lecture on *The Rise and Fall of Mayan Civilization* to his two o'clock senior seminar. After class he wandered down the hall pondering his options. He felt like a shuttlecock being bandied about, back and forth over the badminton net. One minute he was confident of the way forward and the next minute he felt overwhelmed by the nagging fear he was committing a sin of omission.

Now as he gazed around his cluttered office, his brother's words intruded and momentarily occupied his mind. *You're getting a bit absent-minded old bean. You know Molly and I would be delighted to have you live with us, Charlie. Do retire and come back to England.* His words to the contrary, Curly remained convinced that if he ever did take up his younger brother's invitation he would be mortified. But more to the point the notion of sharing a flat with his flighty sister-in-law made Charles shudder. So every year Charles' reply was the same. *That's terribly decent of you and Molly, but I'm quite content here. After all I've lived in the States for nearly 50 years, and as they say, 'you can't go home.'*

Determined to dismiss for one more year his brother's concern that he rejoin what was left of the Hopkins family, Curly reached for the telephone, dialed and waited.

"Yo!" said a strong male voice at the other end.

"Is Luther in?"

"Just a minute – hey, man it's for you."

The phone changed hands. After a quick introduction, Curly delivered his invitation. "I have someone staying with me I'm quite eager for you to meet. Please come by my home early this evening.

"I have the International Club Meeting at 7pm, sir," came the startled reply.

"Luther, my request is pertinent to your work as an international student, specifically as an African student. It is my humble opinion you will quickly discover that honoring my invitation is much more important than a club meeting. And," he added quickly almost as an after thought, "I can feed you dinner."

Charles heard soft breathing at the other end of the line as his invitation was reconsidered.

"I will be at your home this evening as you have requested, Dr. Hopkins. I will take my supper in the cafeteria and come at 7pm."

"Oh that's jolly good!"

Greatly relieved that his persistence had paid off and he'd taken a first step, Charles picked up the open volume on his desk chair. Planning to distract himself by preparing a book review for the Ohio Historical Society magazine the loud knock made him jump. The president and academic dean stood grinning at him through the doorway.

"Didn't mean to startle you, Charles," Richard said apologetically.

"That's quite all right." He leaned back. "To what do I owe this auspicious interruption?"

"Evelyn and I are on our way to meet Chief Turner, and knowing you're deep concerned about the state of the Quaker Archives, we thought you might like to join us. Can't promise we'll be able to go upstairs yet, but you're welcome to come along."

"Jolly thoughtful of you, Richard." Placing the open volume spine up on the chair, Curly stepped around his desk and accompanied them down the steps onto the sidewalk. "Is cause determined yet?" he asked as nonchalantly as possible.

Richard spotted Chief Turner standing stiffly on the front porch of Pennington Place, a female officer by his side. "Maybe that's what the chief wants to talk with us about."

Pat Turner removed his hat and dark glasses as they joined him on the porch. "Ok folks, we'll take a quick tour of the building so you can see the extent of the damage. Then we'll need a place to sit and go over the department's final report."

Curly felt his stomach knot with tension. Praying no one noticed his nervousness he rubbed his sweaty palms together before shoving his hands into his pockets.

"We'll start upstairs," the chief announced leading the way.

They followed behind in single file keeping a respectful distance from the wobbly banister, Lieutenant Harris bringing up the rear. Evelyn paused half way up and gazed forlornly at the scene below.

"A sad sight, isn't it Evelyn?" Richard stopped behind her. "The trustees will have to determine whether to restore the old girl or tear her down."

Evelyn dug a handkerchief out of her pocket, quickly wiped her eyes then climbed the rest of the stairs. The subdued little company moved into the center of the archival room.

"As you can see this area suffered extensive smoke and water damage." Turning to Charles Chief Turner added, "You may begin assessing the condition of the files and books up here. You are the one in charge right, Professor Hopkins?"

Curly shuffled his feet uncomfortably. Richard quickly jumped in. "Dr. Hopkins is the college's senior faculty member, and because his field is history, he's nominally in charge of this collection."

"Whatever," the chief replied with a shrug recognizing departmental wrangling over turf when he heard it.

Looking into the Alumni Office, Evelyn blinked. "Do the Alumni folks have permission to go through their files?" she asked stifling a sneeze.

"Your physical plant needs to lay plywood over the holes in the parlor floor and repair this railing so no one falls, and then, yes, they may begin to clean up."

The president unclipped the cell phone attached to his belt. "I'll check with Angus and get boards down yet this afternoon."

"He'll need to cover the doorways too," the chief said heading back down stairs. "The building must be completely secured before we will release police presence."

Turner led the little group around the outside and into the kitchen through the back door. "The on-site investigation is complete," he announced as the little group gathered forlornly around him.

Richard looked at Charles. "As long as Ernestine Perkins can get upstairs I think she'll be satisfied. We have a student worker who can assist with the clean up. That should be sufficient don't you think, Charles?"

"Ah, surely," Curly replied. "Apologies, Richard," he added hastily seeing the puzzled look on the president's face. "I was still thinking about the cellar." Turning to Police Chief Harris, Charles blurted out, "Has anything been found in the basement that explains the cause of this unfortunate fire?"

Turner replaced his police hat then tugged on the brim settling it firmly on his head. "We've got probable cause." He looked directly at Willson. "I'll explain further when we have privacy."

"Yes, of course." Richard glanced quickly at his watch. "Let's head up to my office. I'll call my secretary and order beverages and sandwiches sent up. Will you be joining us, Lieutenant?"

"Officer Harris will be with us," Chief Turner replied nodding at Rosi who leaned against the door jam. "She has an observation that's pertinent to this investigation."

"Shall we adjourn to my office, then, gentlemen, ladies?"

They shuffled through the leaves as students sauntered to the Rufous Jones Student Center and the cafeteria line. Keenly aware of how hungry she'd become Rosi was delighted that the president ordered food along with their drinks. Looking over her shoulder she spotted the campus minister having an animated conversation with herself as she struggled through the door of Frame Meetinghouse.

"Hi, Ali with an 'i'," Rosi whispered. "It sure feels mighty fine knowing at least one person on campus."

When they reached Fox Hall President Willson lightly touched Professor Hopkins on the shoulder. "Charles, I'll be giving a full report to the faculty as soon as I have something specific to share, but for right now, this conversation needs to stay at the President's Council level." Without waiting for a response Richard followed the lieutenant into the hall allowing the door to shut behind them.

Suddenly flooded with rage and disappointment, Curly pounded the brick wall in frustration. "Damn and double damn" he snarled kicking the door for good measure. "Tossed aside like a leaky, old bucket!"

Still furious at his abrupt dismissal from the meeting with the police, Curly stopped at the hardware store, selected the brightest flashlight on the shelf, added two packs of D batteries and headed to the check out counter. Ignoring the 'have a nice day, sir' from the twenty-something clerk, he stuffed himself into the battered VW and drove home.

Inside the little house though quiet as usual, nonetheless felt occupied. Laying his purchases on the kitchen table, Charles wandered into the living room announcing his presence by whistling softly. The curtains were drawn back allowing the last rays of sunlight to fall on Gideon's back as he sat on the love seat, the Bible open in his lap.

"Good evening, Professor Uncle Curly." He placed a thin black index finger on the well-worn page. "Was it a good day today?"

"Hello, Gideon. It will be a better day after I have some sherry." Uncorking a bottle of Dry Sack, he poured half a glass, raised it and nodded at Gideon. "Cheers!" Taking a swallow, a long satisfied 'ahhhhhhh' slipped out. "I take it you do not partake?"

"Partake? What is 'partake'?"

"You will not be joining me in a drink this evening." Curly held the glass gently between his fingers and thumb. "I assume you do not drink liquor."

"That is right. I do not drink liquor."

The silence lengthened. Gideon ran his finger up and down the page before shutting the Bible and placing it on the cushion beside him. Caught unprepared by the strength of his emotions, Curly swallowed the lump growing in his throat. *It's like waiting for a statue to move,* he thought suddenly aware that Gideon hadn't moved a muscle since closing the book. Coughing lightly, Charles began to pace.

"Gideon, I have what I hope will be a pleasant evening in store for us tonight." Except for a quick brightening in his eyes, Curly might have been talking to a deaf man. "Are you aware there is a student at Emerick from Chisimaio? He's a junior and a biology major."

Gideon's thin body shifted on the cushion as he leaned forward a fraction of an inch. "No, I did not know this. What is his name, Professor Curly?"

"Luther Mouana. Do you know him by any chance?

"No, I do not, but Somalia is a big country." A ghost of a smile touched his mouth. "I have some family on my mother's side called Mouana, but because of civil war in our country I do not see any of them since I am a child."

Curly uncorked the decanter and refilled his sherry glass. "I have invited Luther to join us at 7pm this evening. I thought you might enjoy having a fellow countryman around to converse with. I expect you've been dreadfully lonely these past five months, all alone in that dank coal bin with no one to chat up."

Feeling slightly chilled, Charles took his favorite chair and set the sherry glass on the table. From across the room Gideon sat ramrod straight, his bony hands resting lightly in his lap watching his benefactor closely. "I have not talked with a Somali since Serita died." He closed his eyes for a moment, a shadow of grief resting on his face. "Then I come back to Oakes Quarry for assistance from my friend."

"Yes, I remember Serita quite clearly. Such an enchanting woman and so charming at your wedding." Curly stopped unsure how much more reminiscing was appropriate.

"It was a short marriage, only three years." Gideon briskly rubbed his fingers as if he too were chilled. "Now I cannot be American citizen because my American wife is dead." A note of bitterness crept into his sorrow. "I must hide so INS not send me back to my death in Somalia!"

"Damnably rotten this new US policy, isn't it old chap? You had already filled out the paperwork and had your first interview." Curly nearly choked on the sour taste in his throat. "I've said it before and I'll say it again, it's a rotten way to run the country where Lady Liberty proclaims bring me your tired and your poor!"

Gideon shrank against the back of the couch. "I huddle and hide and run again. All I want is to breathe free air of America!"

The cuckoo sang seven times into the gloomy silence. Professor Hopkins jumped to his feet as the door bell rang.

"Ah, this is our guest, my young friend." Curious, Gideon rose to his feet. "Come, we shall welcome Luther to our humble abode."

Their meeting over, Richard accompanied the police officers to the bottom of the stairs. The campus security lights came on as they were shaking hands.

"You've put in a long day, chief. I'm grateful to you and the lieutenant for your time."

"Not at all, President Willson. That's what the good folks of Oakes Quarry pay us to do." Stepping onto the pavement Turner added, "I'll get that written report to you first thing Monday morning. Be sure Pennington Place is completely secured."

Skip leaned back against the sun-warmed brick wall content to survey his beleaguered domain. A boisterous group of male students swaggered down the walk headed for the brightly-lit soccer field. As they disappeared Richard pushed himself off the wall and went inside.

"Still here?" he asked sticking his head through the doorway of the Academic Dean's office.

Evelyn looked up from the files on her secretary's desk. "Just checking on Mary's progress with those student academic difficulty alert forms, Richard." She straightened up. "Are you headed home, now? You look exhausted."

"I am – going home, that is, and exhausted."

His smile struck her as incredibly sad. "What do you make of the broken Coleman lantern by the old furnace?"

"I'm not sure. Does seem an unlikely place for a campout, doesn't it?"

Moving toward him she inquired gently, "When are you issuing a formal statement to the college community?"

"I'll call the President's Council together first thing in the afternoon."

Watching him wander back to his office, Evelyn was relieved that Richard had showed no inclination to discuss the situation further. His tendency to think things through before sharing with her often drove her nuts, but tonight Evelyn was grateful to be alone. She trudged down Wood Avenue to her condo, unlocked the unit's front door and stepped into the foyer. The smell of freshly baked bread filled the house. *My programmable bread machine comes through again!* she sighed slipping out of her shoes. *Black bean soup, French bread and a glass of wine. Not a bad way to spend an evening.*

"Who is Alexander the Great?" she informed the Jeopardy contestants. "No, not who is Socrates for heaven's sake!" Setting her meal on the TV table, Evelyn raised her wine glass. "May I have an uninterrupted evening, Mr. Treback."

The dean got her wish and by 8:30 was sound asleep in her chair.

Chapter Five - Friday

The terrified little girl dove under the empty cardboard boxes at the back of the alley and held her breath as black figures loomed above her hiding place, kicking boxes, shouting and swearing, "Come out, come out wherever you are! You little bitch!"

Rani sat bolt upright in bed shaking uncontrollably. Pulling the blanket to her chin, she gasped for breath grateful for the street light leaking around the heavy draperies.

"You ok, girl?" Her roommate raised her head.

"I was having an awful dream, that's all."

"Oh dear, not again, Rani. I'm so sorry." Sally rolled over. "What time is it, anyway?"

"It's only 5:30. I'm all right, really I am. You can go back to sleep."

Rani sank back into her pillow relieved that she did not have to put the reoccurring nightmare into words. For the moment the terror had retreated. Determined to keep it at bay Rani concentrated on Luther Mouana.

Why didn't he show up for our Club meeting last night? It's not like him to forget. Something unexpected must have come up. She pulled up her knees and in the process untucked the blankets from the end of the bed.

"I wish I'd taken Sally's advice and asked for a tall mattress," she sighed annoyed by her own hesitation to assert herself. "This bed's too short!"

Rani closed her eyes. Remembering Sally's well intentioned advice their freshman year made her smile. "You've got to take care of Numero Uno 'cause that's the American Way. The sooner you figure that out the sooner you'll be like the rest of us and fit right in." Taking a step back Sally had quickly run her pale blue eyes up and down her new roomy's 6'1" frame sizing her up. "You ought to try out for basketball. The Lady Quakers are desperate for women over five-and-a-half feet who are coordinated and can run and shoot!"

Rani threw off the blanket and stepped onto the mat which always reminded her of home. Embarassment at her curt response still made her blush. *I came to USA to learn my lessons and complete my teacher training not to play ball games! After I graduate I will return to Kingston and open the Friendly Little Red School for all the street ragamuffins who wander the alleys of my neighborhood.*

It had taken six months of sharing a dorm room for Rani to realize how much she liked and admired Sally Pratt. This morning as she listened to her friend's gentle snoring, Rani could envision the rest of her day dream plan. *I will invite Sally to come for a visit and teach the little children how to solve their disagreements without hitting each other.*

Grabbing her towel and cosmetics case, she headed for the bathroom. In the relaxing heat of the shower, her thoughts returned to last night. Afraid she had misunderstood him, Rani went to the Leaky Cup thinking Luther might be waiting for her over there. But except for five women sharing a text book at the oval table in the middle of the room, the coffee house had been empty.

As she walked back to her room, Rani knew what to do next. "I feel bolder already" she whispered. "Sally will be so proud of me."

Taking a deep breath, Rani dialed Luther's room.

"Yeh?" said a sleepy male voice after six rings.

"Luther?"

"Yes."

"This is Rani. Do you want to have breakfast with me this morning?"

"I can't, Rani. I've got class."

"This is Friday, Luther. You don't have an eight o'clock class on Fridays. Besides, you were supposed to meet me at the Leaky Cup last night, remember?" For the first time in a long, long time Rani responded in annoyance. "Did you forget?"

Her angry query was answered by labored breathing, then a painful swallow.

"Luther, are you sick?" she asked suddenly alarmed. "You sound like you don't feel well."

"I don't feel well, Rani. I was up until five this morning and barely got to sleep before you rang me." Luther cleared his throat. "Listen, Rani, I'm going back to sleep. I'll call you later," and with that he hung up.

"What was that all about?" Sally sat up in bed her mousy brown hair sticking out in tiny spikes.

"Oh, nothing."

Rani hung up turned her back and pulled her panties on under her loose-fitting terry cloth bathrobe.

"Nothing?" From across the room Sally regarded her skeptically. "If I had to guess I'd say you got stood up last night."

"Luther asked me for a coffee last night but he never came." Rani watched her roommate's face in the mirror.

"I suggested we go for breakfast, but now he sounds ill. I'm a bit worried about him that's all."

Sally pulled back the floor length curtains. The morning sun light streamed across the tile floor.

"Well, maybe he changed his mind. Men do that sometimes, you know."

"It's not like Luther."

"Just go over to Gurney, knock on his door and ask him then." Sally reached for her robe and towel. "That's what I'd do."

"I know that's what you'd do," Rani replied unhappily. Calling had stretched her sense of proper boy-girl relations far enough for one day. The idea of walking into the men's dorm made her blush. "But, I can't."

"Whatever," her roomy tossed back. "I'm headed for the loo."

Dressed in ankle-length denim skirt and long-sleeved polka dot blouse, Rani felt properly covered. She braided her black hair into a thick braid, secured it with a band of plastic flowers and headed for the dining room. On her way past Gurney Dorm she glanced furtively at Luther's first floor window. The Venetian blinds were drawn tight.

I have to do this my own way and wait for you to call me back.

Luther Mouana curled into a ball feeling wretched. He lay motionless under the heavy wool blanket until his roommate finally left at 8:15. Exhausted and a bit queasy, he slowly sat up and reached for the cord dangling from the blinds. After vigorously rubbing his short black hair he squinted quickly out the window. Stumbling to the dresser he rummaged through the top drawer feeling for his beaded necklace and after kissing the gold cross, he pulled it over his head.

Exchanging pjs for Boxer shorts and jeans, Luther patted his pocket to be sure the room key was still there, grabbed a hooded navy sweatshirt and hurried down the hallway. He hit the fire bar with both hands, shoved the metal door open and made a bee line for Jones Student Center. In the bookstore he bought a Coke and peanut butter crackers then drifted toward Pennington Place as casually as his racing heart would allow. Rounding the corner he stopped at the edge of the back porch. He longed to bore a peephole through the foundation rock into the cellar below.

His eyes began tracing the foundation stones and suddenly there it was: Gideon's secret entrance. The black cast iron door half way up the second row of stones was barely visible behind the shrubbery. Luther slipped between two bushes and crouched down, the thick green foliage closing behind him sheltering him from anyone passing by. With trembling hands he grasped the silver coiled metal handle, pushed down and felt the inside bar slide up and out of its latch. Jerking the door open Luther squinted into the inky black space where his countryman had lived the past five months. Torn between curiosity and dread, he placed both hands on the sill and forced himself to lean forward. Praying for a glimpse of the floor below, his eyes followed the shaft of sunlight but the blackness refused to surrender the size or shape of the space below. Luther dropped back on his haunches and began to weep.

Sweet mother of Jesus, how could Gideon bear living in a hole blacker than our Somali nights without a star to comfort or guide him? Luther's thoughts tumbled over one another. *A lantern – Terrell Martin gave him a gas lantern – did Gideon get careless and leave it burning Tuesday night when he was at the warehouse? Oh, please God, no!*

Luther slammed the door, made sure it was securely latched then crawled between the bushes. Now that he'd seen the actual hideout for himself, Luther felt the warmth of a kinship bond begin to grow in his heart and soul. In spite of a nagging uneasiness, he crossed the campus green with a sense of renewed purpose. Back in his room, Luther kissed his grandmother's cross and laid the necklace gently on the handkerchief in the drawer.

"Gideon is safe with Professor Hopkins," he whispered gratefully. "That's all that matters for now."

"Ali, get a load of this!" Cliff's fork clinked against the plate as he set it down and began paraphrasing from the morning paper. "Two artists built a secret apartment in a Rhode Island shopping mall and lived in it for up to three weeks at a time without being detected. Quote, the artists built a cinderblock wall and nondescript utility door to keep the loft hidden from the outside world, unquote."

"No way!" Ali rested her hands on his back and read over his shoulder. "'The apartment was fully furnished including a Sony Playstation 2 and since there was no water, they used the mall bathrooms!' What a hoot! A bunch of incredibly unperceptive people must be running that mall for them to get away with something that outlandish!"

"I suspect some poor lowly Pinkerton man is going to loose his job over this." Cliff folded the newspaper. "Listen, honey I've got Vet Club at five this afternoon.

Let's car pool today and meet at the Leaky Cup around six."

"Great! We'll decide then what to do for supper."

President Willson was wide awake at 6:30am. Unable to go back to sleep, he walked the six short blocks to Fox Hall where with the exception of the housekeeping staff scrubbing and flushing toilets, he had the place to himself. Unable to concentrate, he lay the *Chronicle of Higher Education* aside and turned to watch a red-bellied woodpecker work its noisy way up the maple tree outside his office window.

"Makes my head hurt just watching you pound away." He stretched then got to his feet. "This is a Starbucks morning," he thought pulling on his overcoat.

As he approached the Leaky Cup his eyes drifted to the green sign dangling from the porch soffit. **"For those who know; There's no such thing as too much Joe!"** The glass front door was securely latched. Skip checked his watch then leaned against the porch rail. Five minutes later Missy Springer, her hair still in pin curls, opened the door and waved her broom at the day's first customer.

"Good morning, Richard. You here for a cuppa java?"

He nodded then bent over and stroked the marmalade cat rubbing against his gray slacks. "How's old Biscuit this morning?"

The neon lights crackled and a bright red scripted OPEN lit up as Richard followed the proprietor inside.

"The usual?" she asked turning to the espresso machine.

"I think a tall French vanilla will do the trick this time."

He wrapped both hands around the cup grateful for the warmth and worked his way back across campus. Maple leaves too weary to hang on any longer, decorated the grass still drippy with dew. Slowing his pace, Skip watched the tall dark-skinned woman pull her black sweater tightly around her body then disappear inside the student center.

"You're bright and early this morning," Bev observed cheerfully.

"See if you can catch Rani Brown. It's been awhile since we've chatted, and I'd like to hear how her semester is going."

Bev watched him fondly. "I see you've had your coffee already."

The president nodded and hung up his coat.

"I'm calling a Council meeting for three this afternoon. Please notify everyone." Skip tossed his empty cup into the wastebasket. "Be sure to include Ruthalice this time," he added walking to his desk. Skip opened the manila folder which lay on top. "Keep that 10:30 slot free, Bev. I need to work some more on my remarks for the campus gathering circle this noon."

At one o'clock, the remembrance ceremony behind him, President Willson walked briskly over to Pennington Place intending to check on physical plant's progress in securing the building. "Do Not Enter" was spray-painted across the middle of the plywood sheet covering the kitchen doorway. "For access, call ext 600" was printed underneath in Angus Bailey's careful script. Richard extracted his cell phone.

"Could you send someone over to let me into Penn?"

Within minutes the little blue Campus Security cart scooted up the drive. The guard unlocked the padlock, wrestled the plywood door open and the president walked carefully into the abandoned kitchen. The entrance to the basement gaped open and through it Skip could see two-by-fours standing upright on the basement floor with planks nailed between them. Keeping his left palm against the stone wall, he slowly descended the make-shift stairs. Reaching the bottom he slipped his cell phone out of his pants pocket.

"Physical Plant, this is Judy," the voice bubbled from the other end.

"Judy, Richard Willson here. Ask Angus to remove this burned furniture. That's where much of the smoke smell is coming from."

"Yes, sir," she replied. "I'll put the order in right away."

"This weekend, Judy," he added forcefully, "and get a crew down here to clear the debris and clean this place up. Ashes and soot and who knows what are everywhere."

Skip winced as a rat darted under the charred remains of lounge chairs heaped haphazardly under the steps. Back upstairs Skip leaned into the plywood door with his shoulder, relocked the padlock and strode back to his office. Relieved that no one was waiting for him, he collected his thoughts.

The basic facts were straight forward enough. An anonymous 911 call came in at 1:13am Wednesday morning alerting the police to a fire underway at the college. Richard reviewed his transcription copy of the interview with the dispatcher.

"He had kind of a foreign accent."

"The voice was male?"

"Yes."

"What kind of an accent?"

"Maybe kinda African? The voice was soft spoken and polite." Pause. "The man spoke slowly almost like he had to think before pronouncing each word."

Richard studied his notes from last night's conversation with the police. Chief Turner was clear the fire started in the cubbyhole then rapidly spread to the discarded furniture stored under the steps. When the fire department arrived shortly after 1:40am the fire was burning its way up the wooden stairs into the kitchen.

Ten minutes later Richard joined his colleagues around the dark oak conference table after having made a pact with himself that he would not nor would he allow anyone else to engage in speculation.

"Evelyn and I met with Chief Turner and Officer Harris in my office yesterday afternoon," he began without fanfare. "Here are the facts as we currently have them."

Ruthalice, tucked between Barbara Carroll, Dean of Students, and Angus Bailey, Director of Facilities, wondered why she'd been included. Four years ago when she was summoned to the second floor conference room, the need for her pastoral care and counseling had been obvious. The sophomore class president was found dead in his garage from a self-inflicted gun shot, and the entire campus community was in shocked disbelief and grief. Somehow a fire in the basement where no one was hurt didn't seem like campus ministry material, unless, she suddenly realized, there was more to this whole incident than meets the eye.

Fresh off her new insight Ali sensed a shift in the president's mood. Richard coughed lightly and fiddled with his pen before placing it on the table. Evelyn took a sip of water, replaced the cap and set the bottle squarely in the middle of her paper napkin. A collective hush filled the room as everyone's attention focused on the head of the table.

"Friends, this was the easy part." Skip's troubled smile drew them all into the circle. "We have a real mystery on our collective hands." His gaze settled on the Director of Facilities who stirred uncomfortably in his seat. "Angus, I authorized storage of the old parlor furniture four years ago."

Hoping to defuse the self-defensive stare from across the table Richard continued.

"In light of the events of the past few days this may not have been one of my better decisions, but that's all water under the bridge at this point I'm afraid."

Evelyn took up the narrative.

"There were fire crackers in Hannah Emerick's storage compartment hidden behind wads of crumpled up newspapers and cardboard boxes."

Ruthalice felt her stomach tighten. "*I don't* like the direction this is going one little bit," she thought unhappily. Next to her Babs Carroll fidgeted.

"How did that happen?" Angus swiveled his chair back and forth, its arms repeatedly bumping the table. "That building is locked up tight as a drum the minute Ernestine goes home."

"Why would anyone stash explosives in Penn in the first place?"

"To blow it up"

"Oh surely you don't believe that, Angus! Don't tell me you're thinking this is a student protest gone awry."

Evelyn Feller and the facilities director seldom saw eye to eye on anything from the color to paint the women's restrooms to the fundamental nature of humankind.

"Who says it's students?" Angus shot back.

"Well, for one thing why would any of us store fireworks on campus when we can take them home?" *Dear God, I don't like where this is going* the Dean of Students whispered uncomfortably to herself. "But our students can't do that."

"Ok, that's enough speculation." Richard was out of patience with himself and his colleagues. The bickering immediately ceased. "Permit me to read from my notes of last night's conversation with Turner and Harris." He peered at his colleagues over the top of his glasses. "Quote, all evidence indicates that the newspaper in the recess ignited first, subsequently fire spread to the box of fireworks which then exploded spewing burning material out of the cubbyhole igniting the furniture below unquote."

You call someone who starts fires on purpose an arsonist. Ali's own words raced in her head. *Rani's mysterious figure; a spectacular fire.* Her forehead began to pound. *My God, what is happening on our campus?*

"Ok, that's all very well and good but so far we have no explanation for how the newspapers caught fire." Angus crossed his arms and surveyed his colleagues. "Am I right?"

Richard decided to ignore Angus' taunting.

"I've been promised the complete report will be on my desk first thing Monday morning. If this turns out to be an in-house issue, we will deal with it through the college judicial system, unless it has wider implications. In the meantime if you must speculate, keep it amongst yourselves. Everyone clear on that?"

Richard's no-nonsense stare surveyed the table. Ruthalice spoke into the awkward silence.

"I'd like to summarize things a bit if I could. Someone disguised the fact they'd placed fireworks in the cubbyhole by stuffing newspapers and old boxes in front of them. So," she paused as a new question posed itself inside her head. "Does anybody even go into the basement of Penn anymore?"

"Someone certainly did, unless we have a case of spontaneous combustion!" Angus retorted.

"Ruthalice's question is a good one though." Babs Carroll straightened her gold necklace. "Ernestine Perkins runs a tight ship over there. It seems to me she's the logical person to ask about access."

Heads nodded in unison around the table. The president rose and disappeared into the hallway. As the little group occupied itself drinking from water bottles and gazing out the window, something tugged at the back of Ali's mind. *Firecrackers are gorgeous and loud; they call attention to themselves and can be seen all over town! Maybe Rani's girls are involved in this after all.*

"What are you pondering over there, Ruthalice?" Babs Carroll asked, gently nudging her elbow. "Your eyebrows are bobbing up and down like corks."

Ali blushed.

"Oh, I'm trying to figure out what someone wanted fireworks on campus for, that's all."

"Ernestine Perkins assures me no one from her office has been in the basement since June 2," Richard announced settling back into his chair. "She needed records for an article she was writing about the class of 1876." He paused, a pensive look crossing his face. "Emerick's first graduating class with its seven students."

"But those records are in the Quaker Archives," Ali protested remembering her promise to write a short history for the new brochure being prepared for Parents Weekend. "I know because I asked for them myself just last week,"

"Well Ernestine must have forgotten that because she sent her student worker to the basement."

"So what does this intriguing piece of information tell us?" Angus grumbled.

"That as far as our alumni director is concerned no one's been in the basement in three months, but she's clearly wrong." Evelyn scratched above her left ear with her index finger. "Whoever it was either has a key or was in the basement during office hours unbeknownst to Ernestine."

"The later is more likely I should think," the Dean of Students offered. "Penn's accessible every weekday during the day. It'd be pretty easy to slip in undetected."

Richard cleared his throat.

"There's more." The room fell silent. "I got my coffee at the Leaky Cup this morning. Missy Springer told me she saw two college-aged men hanging around between Pennington and the meetinghouse at approximately 12:30 Wednesday morning. I urged her to inform Chief Turner which she has now done."

Richard finished the bottle of warm water in front of him.

"Bev told me that while I was on the phone just now with Ernestine, Turner called to inform us he's issued a request for anyone with information about two young men seen loitering around the southwest end of campus Wednesday morning to contact the witness hot line at the Oakes Quarry Police Department or the Boone County

Sheriff's office. Quote, a reward is offered for information which leads to the arrest and conviction of the party or parties involved in Wednesday's fire at Emerick College, unquote."

Richard rose wearily to his feet.

"Ok folks, now you know as much as I do, so let's all go home and sleep on it. Give me a buzz if the bright bulb of insight lights up in the middle of the night, ok?" His steady smile belied his uneasiness. "And remember, your conjectures are welcome in my office and nowhere else."

As the council members filed out the president lightly touched Ali's arm.

"Ruthalice, may I have a word and with you also, Barbara?"

He quietly closed the door.

"Ali, I need you to keep your ear to the ground, to coin a rather corny phrase. The students trust you, and you're often told things in confidence. " He paused looking slightly uncomfortable. "I'm well aware of the confidentiality of the confessional so to speak, but I'm requesting that you report anything you hear immediately and directly to me whether it seems pertinent or not."

Turning to the Dean of Students he added, "Babs, I'm asking the same of you."

"I'll call my RAs together this evening," she replied without hesitation, "and see what the rumors are in the resident halls. Our students often hear things they don't want to pass along to me."

"Well someone on this campus knows who, why and probably how. The president of our Board of Trustees is worried that if this does turn out to be arson, the insurance adjustor may try to finagle out of as much coverage as possible."

Ali suddenly felt miserable. "I dread the thought of where we're going to end up with that line of investigation."

The president sighed. "I just hope someone figures this out in a timely manner so we can get on with the business of higher education."

"Let's go down to your office," Ruthalice said watching Evelyn disappear down the hallway. "One of our international students shared a conversation she overheard in the bathroom. I think you should know about it."

Twenty minutes later, Richard opened the office door and reached for his coat. "Try and have a good weekend you and Clifford," he said attempting to sound chipper.

"Isn't this the weekend your sister visits?" she replied waiting while he turned out the lights.

"Yup," Skip replied. "It will be mighty good to see her in spite of all the furor."

Cliff returned to his office at 3:15, nudged the partially closed door with his elbow and nearly collided with Charles Hopkins pacing impatiently between door and window.

"What brings you to my humble abode in the middle of the afternoon?"

"Are you and Ruthalice free tonight?" Before Cliff could answer he hurried on. "I'd be dreadfully appreciative if the two of you could join me at the house for dinner. I'm in a bit of situation and want your collective advice."

"Sounds positively intriguing."

"Then that settles it. I'll see you both tonight."

Wondering what on earth this was all about, Cliff dutifully left a message for the campus minister on her answering machine then sat down determined to grade at least five student lab books before he had to meet with the *Vets of Tomorrow Club.*

It was one of those cloudless-blue-skies-gorgeous-crisp afternoons only a Mid-west fall can produce, so Curly decided to mull over his upcoming evening with the M&Ms whilst taking a walk. He headed briskly across the city park and sat on a warped wooden bench beside the deserted picnic shelter. Closing his eyes the turmoil of the past 24 hours marched across his mind.

It was 2am before he finally bid his Somali drop-ins goodnight and tumbled into bed fully clothed for the second night in a row. Shuffling into the kitchen at eight this morning and finding no trace of either one of them, Charles had begun to fret. When he reminded himself he was not Gideon's babysitter he'd felt a tad better, yet halfway through his dry toast and tea the fretting returned. It became abundantly clear to the old professor that this entire business was just too complicated to handle alone. Too many secrets were pilling up, there was too much coming and going to watch over and manage. And worst of all he could not escape the terrifying image of his nosey next-door neighbor popping round uninvited for a look-see if she got even the slightest whiff of a rumor that Professor Hopkins might be harboring an undocumented alien. Charles could see it all unfolding with appalling predictability. The very idea of an illegal African male (*and no doubt a Muslim!)* living on her lily-white Sheppard Place with its law-abiding citizens would send

Laverna Stroodle into a tizzy, and it would be out of a flurry of patriotic fervor that she'd rise to the occasion and turn her disloyal neighbor over to the proper authorities.

Curly got to his feet clear that his top priority was to head this particular scenario off at the pass. He walked vigorously back to the Fine Arts parking lot, started the engine and was filled with relief as his ornery VW Beetle carried him home one more time.

Entering his familiar kitchen the soft strains of Beethoven's *Pastoral Symphony* greeted him and for an instant the elderly eccentric resented the fact that his domicile had been invaded! *There's never been someone to come home to before,* he grumbled suddenly uncertain whether or not he liked the idea, *still.* His head bobbed slightly with the notes of the orchestra. Reluctant to interrupt the music Charles Hopkins, professor emeritus bent over the kitchen sink and began peeling potatoes and cutting up broccoli and cauliflower before tossing the vegetables into the pot roast.

"Oh, hello Gideon. I didn't hear you come in." Curly flipped off the garbage disposal. "I have a little surprise for you," he added wiping his hands on a faded dish towel. "Our campus minister and her biology professor husband are joining us for dinner this evening." Seeing the panic dart across his friend's smooth black face, Curly quickly added. "Ruthalice and Clifford are colleagues of mine. We've been friends for years and years." He leaned his back against the sink. "Gideon your situation with me is precarious. We must confide in someone we can trust. Ali and Clifford will most assuredly assist us in determining how to keep you safe."

"You are in trouble Professor Curly because of me," Gideon said dejectedly. "I should not be here." His eyes darted toward the basement door. "I go now."

"Whoa, whoa!" Charles grabbed the young man by both shoulders. "You're not going anywhere me laddie," he exclaimed loosening his grip. "You are perfectly safe in this house as long as no one realizes you are here." Taking a step back he surveyed the young man from head to toe. "Listen Gideon, I want you to stay here with me, but I can't do this alone. My friends are kind, generous and sensible people who will be delighted to meet you. They will want to help."

Gideon raised his head. "Can my cousin join us also?"

Charles reached for the white plastic wall phone and waited for the answering machine to pick up. "Luther, this is Professor Hopkins. Gideon and I would like to talk with you again, so please come to my house as soon as you get this message."

"Thank you, Uncle Professor Curly." Gideon's mercurial emotions were back on delight. "Now I get clean shirt and help you to set the table for our guests."

"Excellent! I'm headed for a quick shower. Oh, and be a sport would you and turn on that outside light? The switch is on the wall by the front door," he added disappearing down the hall.

Ali got Cliff's message when she darted into the office at 5:57.

"Hi, sweetie, it's me," she said struggling into her jacket as she braced the phone against her left ear with her shoulder. "I'm heading for the Leaky Cup right now. Meet you there."

She pushed open the outside door and inhaled the evening air grown nippy with the setting of the sun. Ali felt like skipping across Division Street.

"Thank you, God for this most glorious time of year! Nights like this are one of your better ideas and I am truly grateful."

"Hey, good lookin', you goin' my way?" Cliff slipped his arm through hers.

Standing on her toes, she kissed his cheek.

"Did you get my message?" he asked pulling her to a stop.

"About dinner with Professor Charles Eugene Hopkins? That one?"

"Yep, that very one."

"Sounds mighty dang good to me right now. I'm pooped, and it means neither one of us has to cook tonight." Ali dug the car keys out of her bag. "You wanna drive?"

Cliff held the remote at arm's length and pressed the unlock button. As he turned on the ignition, a newscaster's voice blared from the radio.

"Yikes," Ali squeaked and with a fierce punch of the on/off button cut Michelle Norris off in mid sentence. "*All Things Considered* requires way too much brain power for me tonight."

She rolled her head back and forth against the head rest then turned to gaze out the window as the colorful autumn foliage and brick walkways of Emerick College were replaced by the dull black asphalt pavement of the local strip mall.

"So, my dear, do you have any idea what this is all about?"

"Not really," Cliff replied easing into traffic. "Charles was unusually tight-lipped and a bit anxious. Says he's gotten himself into a bit of a muddle that quote wants our collective advice unquote." Cliff frowned. "Didn't sound like take charge Charlie at all actually."

"Interesting." Ali stared fondly at the side of her husband's face. "It's not like Charles to alter his customary solitary Friday night fish and chips in front of *Washington Week in Review*. It must be pretty serious."

Ali recalled the last time Curly sought their opinion. He'd been worried about an uncle, a low level diplomat in the British Embassy, who lay dying in a hospital in Istanbul. Would his father's youngest brother appreciate a visit from a nephew he hadn't seen in over 35 years or consider it an intrusion? Ali listened carefully, asked a few gentle questions then urged him to follow his own inner nudges and do what felt right. After studying her for what had felt like hours, Charles pronounced, "Right then, I'm off to Istanbul." Uncle Doyle Hopkins died peacefully in his sleep two days after his nephew arrived at his bedside.

"You're awfully quiet."

"I'm just remembering Uncle Doyle."

"Hopkins was terribly grateful as he put it, that he sought your council on that one." Cliff slowed down to make the turn into Sheppard Place. "You're a very good listener, you know." Affectionately patting her knee he added, "That's partly why I keep you around."

"What's the other reason you keep me around?" she asked coyly, squeezing his hand.

"Oh, let me count the ways."

"Oh, let's not. It'll take way too long and cold kidney pie will be our lot!"

Cliff chuckled. "Have it your way."

Ali joined him on the sidewalk and hand in hand they strolled up the front walk. "Perhaps you can fill me in tonight," she teased tugging on his hand.

"Now you're talking. You're a woman after my own heart!"

In the distance a loud speaker crackled. "Second and three, the ball's on the 8 yard line".

"Ah Friday night high school football, the Oakes Quarry Founders versus the Miller's Run Cougars." A roar filled the air as the M&Ms waited on the little cement porch. "I do believe the mighty Founders have just scored a touchdown."

"A reasonable deduction, my dear Watson," Ali replied stepping back so their host could open the screen door.

Amid the 'so glad you could come on such short notice,' and the 'wouldn't miss it for the world', Ali caught a glimpse of movement out the corner of her eye. *Good heavens*, she thought stepping onto the worn beige carpet. *Has Curly gotten a cat?*

While the professor took a shower, Gideon had gone straight to his basement room and changed his shirt. After slipping on the only vest he owned, he headed back upstairs eager to show Professor Curly he knew how to set the table for dinner. At the top he paused to pray.

"Jesus, you lay right upon my heart. Please to give me courage and peace. I am very nervous." Gideon lifted the crucifix to his lips. "I trust Professor Curly." He hesitated, "And his friends."

Gideon opened drawers until he located the silverware, took four of everything and began placing knives, forks and spoons around the kitchen table.

"I put knife on right and fork on left," he reminded himself at each placemat. Humming happily Gideon added plates and glasses then stood back to admire his handiwork.

"Jolly good, old boy!" the professor's voice thundered behind him. "Not bad for a bloke who's been camping out in a basement for five months." Curly thumped the young man on the back. "But the spoon goes over here."

"It's too soon to start the veggie water," Curly noted glancing up at the wall clock. "Let's go through to the front room. I could use a drink."

Gideon assumed his place on the love seat whose rustic English hunting scene upholstery had seen better days and laid his right arm on the herringbone throw pillow. Curly sank into his favorite arm chair and uncorked the port.

"Gracious we're becoming damnably predictable in our habits, Gideon! Like a couple old duffers assuming their self- designated seats in a gentleman's club." He raised his glass. "Well, cheers! Don't you want something to drink whilst we wait? A coke or lemonade?"

"I get a coke."

Gideon disappeared into the kitchen then resumed his position on the sofa. Setting the can on the carpet, he placed a palm on each leg and starred at the picture on the opposite wall. Charles watched the young man study his hands then slide them back and forth on each pant leg. Gideon shivered then vigorously rubbed the bottom of his nose with the heal of his hand. Finally unable to sit still he began to fidget.

"You are worried about my colleagues, and wonder if you can trust them. Am I correct?" Curly asked sipping his port.

"What do I tell them, Professor Curly?"

"The truth. You and I will tell them the whole truth, my friend. That is what we both are required to do." As the door bell rang, Curly set his drink on the side table then got to his feet. "I will get us started. Do not fret, my young friend. Together we shall hatch a cracker of a plan."

Gideon took a deep breath and pressed his back deep into the cushion. At the sound of strange voices, the familiar cramps seized his intestines.

"Sweet Mary, mother of Jesus, help me," he implored rising quickly to his feet and slipping into the shadows cast by the floor lamp beside the professor's chair. Squeezing his eyes until tears formed, he begged silently, *Do not let them send me back, please, no! I rather hide away in America than die in Somalia.*

"Gideon, I want you to meet my dear friends Ruthalice Michaels and Clifford Mowry." Sweeping his arm toward the young man Charles added in his booming voice, "Ali, Cliff meet my young friend Gideon Boseka."

At the sound of his name Gideon slowly opened his eyes. Ruthalice smiled warmly. "How nice to meet you, Gideon," and stepped forward extending her hand. Seeing his hesitancy she stopped moving.

"I taught at the Friends Theological College in Kaimosi, Kenya for six months." She paused lowering her arm. "We had one student, Salome Kutosi whose mother lives in Mogadishu."

Fascinated, the two men held their collective breath as Gideon, his left hand in the crook of his right arm, tentatively offered his hand. As their hands clasped, the heavy cloak of tension seemed to slip off the young man's shoulders and tumble to the floor.

"I am Somali from Doolow on the Jubba River. I am a Christian," he added hastily, "not a Muslim."

"I know, Gideon," Ali replied softly. "That is a lovely beaded necklace."

His hand flew instinctively to his throat.

"Oh, yes. I wear the necklace my grandmother makes for me." His face relaxed into a charming smile. "It is grandmother who names me Gideon."

"The faithful judge of the Israelites whom the Lord chose to lead his people out of oppression by the hand of Midian." Ali turned to Cliff. "My husband teaches biology here at Emerick College. His office is in Dalton Hall across campus from mine." Determined to keep the conversation going she added, "And I am the college's campus minister."

Clifford shook Gideon's hand then stepped back. Completely at ease, he crossed his arms, a reassuring twinkle lighting his green eyes and cocked his head.

"If I remember my geography correctly, Doolow is located on the northern border of Somalia near Ethiopia and Kenya where the three borders come together."

"Yes, yes! My people raise many cattle. Cattle are wealth and status so many herders get hurt or killed in the too much fighting over grazing and water." He sighed. "But the land is too dry."

Cliff scratched his chin.

"I am curious, Gideon, have we met somewhere before? You look vaguely familiar."

"Dear me look at us standing like stumps in the doorway." Hastily closing the front door, Curly shoved Cliff into the room. "I'm not being much of a host. Do sit down and I'll get us a drink. Sherry or port?"

About to object, Cliff reconsidered and sat down as Ruthalice settled on the love seat. Gideon shyly joined her. After handing glasses to his guests, Curly assumed his chair on Cliff's left.

"My goodness, Charles, something smells simply delicious!" Ali inhaled deeply. "Can I be of assistance?"

"Not quite yet, my dear. All that remains is to put veggies in boiling water and warm the muffins."

Content for the moment with their pre-dinner small talk, Cliff sipped his sherry and agreed that the Cincinnati Bengals were off to another lousy start. Having concluded that Cliff was safely diverted from his trip down memory lane, Curly accepted Ali's offer of help, and the two of them disappeared into the kitchen chatting happily about the upcoming Oakes Quarry Nature Club color tour on Sunday.

Left unattended, Clifford tried again.

"I pride myself on never forgetting a face. It's one of my little quirks, I guess. My version of hubris."

Gideon looked confused and was about to speak when Curly reappeared.

"Dinner is ready now, my friends. Please come through."

They followed and dutifully took their places around the kitchen table. A confirmed bachelor Charles felt absolutely no need for a big house. Content with his two bedroom bungalow he entertained the occasional dinner guest at the oak table in his modest kitchen whose color scheme was the result of a serendipitous visit from his next door neighbor. Dropping in unannounced as was her wont, and finding him totally flummoxed by the little squares of paint from the Sherman Williams store, she offered her unsolicited opinion: wheat and daffodil yellow compliment the cabinets and will bring out the luster in the table!

Curly let out a heavy sigh. As a look of concern flitted across Ali's face, he added quickly, "Just thinking about Mrs. Stroodle and her poodle next door."

Ali burst out laughing. "Mrs. Stroodle and her poodle! Surely you can't be serious."

"Quite so I'm afraid," he said shaking his head. "Frankly I no longer find her amusing but the old gal is spot on once in awhile – the wheat walls with daffodil trim being my primary example."

"I thought something was different in here." Ali exclaimed as all eyes turned and dutifully surveyed the room. "It's quite lovely, Curly, very warm and welcoming, just what you want in a kitchen."

"I've got it!" Cliff slapped his palm on the table, a look of triumph on his face. "I told you I never forgot a face." He beamed at Gideon across the table. "You were in my human biology course six or seven years ago. Yes, I'm sure of it."

Petrified, Gideon froze. Curly's fork stopped halfway to his mouth, a piece of lettuce descending to his lap. Ali's internal monitor screamed 'say something!" but no words came to her. Nodding vigorously, Cliff plowed ahead.

"You turned in the most professional looking lab reports I've ever received from a student. And, your drawings!" Cliff's voice trailed off as he became aware of the awkward silence engulfing the room.

Ali gently took her husband's hand, her warm smile radiating compassion as she encompassed first Gideon then her husband's old friend at the end of the table. Curly finished raising the fork to his mouth and began to chew. Without warning the roar of delirious hometown fans poured into the kitchen through the half-opened window, providing Ruthalice with words.

"Do you like American football, Gideon?"

His eyes downcast, Gideon remained motionless. Momentarily stymied, Ali reached for the muffins.

"Anyone else want one?" she asked tucking the napkin around them and raising the basket.

The deep bong, bong of the grandfather clock began its laborious announcement that it was now eight o'clock. Into the silence which followed, Gideon began to speak.

"You are right, Professor Clifford. I was in your class." He stopped abruptly and starred self-consciously across the table with his coal black eyes. "I was a student at Emerick College. I graduate almost five years ago." Gideon's smile, always just beneath the surface, burst across his face. "Thank you for the compliment, Professor Clifford. I work very, very hard on my laboratory report notebook. I like to draw."

"Well, it showed, Gideon. You were an 'A' student." Cliff leaned back in his chair. "So, I was right after all."

"You never forget a face," Gideon repeated. "You never forget my face." A pensive look replaced the grin. "I like Emerick College very much. It was good time for me. I learn many new things."

Curly got to his feet relieved the excruciating tension had eased. He turned on the coffee pot and began scooping prodigious amounts of Neapolitan ice cream into four mismatched earthenware bowls. Cliff pushed back, rose and cleared the table. As the rich smell of freshly brewed coffee filled the kitchen, Gideon produced a box of Chips Ahoy chocolate chip cookies from the shelf above the toaster. A series of short taps on the window interrupted the comfortable domestic scene. Ruthalice glimpsed a face peeking through the kitchen door window, fore finger raised to tap again. Gideon sprung to his feet in terror, but before he could bolt, Curly's arm shot out and grabbed his wrist.

"Steady there mate, it's Luther, remember; Luther is joining us."

As the young man stepped into the room, Gideon went limp with relief and joy. As Charles let loose of his wrist Gideon fell into the other man's arms as they embraced.

"Come in, come in, you're just in time for dessert." Curly waved his hand in the air indicating the rest of the table. "You probably already know these folks, Luther. This is Ruthalice Michels, our campus minister and her husband Clifford Mowry, professor of biology."

Luther acknowledged them with a low bow from the waist.

"I am taking the invertebrate zoology class this semester from Clifford," he replied enthusiastically. "I'm studying to be a large animal veterinarian and teach our Somali herdsmen how to provide good care to our cattle."

He stuffed his hands into the pockets of his nylon wind breaker.

"And I have seen you on campus, Pastor Ruthalice."

"Everyone go through to the front room, and I'll bring the dessert tray. Gideon, put those biscuits on a plate," he added as Gideon opened the cookie bag. "We have much to discuss this evening."

The four guests obliged, Clifford heading for the second arm chair, Ruthalice chose the love seat and Gideon hovered. Luther perched on the edge of the harpsichord bench.

"Oh, no, that seat is dreadfully uncomfortable." Curly set the battered silver tray on the table between the two arm chairs. "Clifford, be a good sport and fetch that chair with the padded seat for Luther, would you? It's in my study."

Cliff rose to comply.

"Who wants high test and who needs cream and sugar? I've also brewed tea for us English sorts who can't abide coffee more than once a day."

"I like black coffee at night," Luther replied. "It keeps me awake so I can pull the all-nighters."

Returning with the chair for Luther, Cliff placed it beside the small sofa then picked up the remaining ice cream bowl and sat down.

"So, Luther what brings you here this evening other than the fact that Professor Hopkins summoned you?" His mischievous smile invited Luther to join their little private joke.

Exchanging a nearly imperceptible glance, Luther and Gideon quickly checked in with each other.

"I invited Luther to join us tonight." Curly paused then added lamely, "I thought they might have something in common since both boys are from Somalia."

That was an awfully intimate greeting for two men who've just met, Ali reflected. *But, I'll play along.*

"So, Gideon, do you and Luther have something in common?" When neither answered, she turned to Gideon who had settled in beside her on the love seat. "Gideon, I have known Charles Hopkins for more than nine years.

He and Clifford and I have shared many secrets with each other."

Ruthalice smiled affectionately at the two professors across the room. Charles' thoughts were indecipherable. Her dear Clifford thoughtfully licked his ice cream spoon as he waited patiently. Out of the corner of her eye Ali saw Luther softly touch Gideon's knee with his left hand. She continued gently, "Whatever you share with us tonight stays in this room."

"Gideon," Professor Hopkins said with gentle resolve, "it is time to tell the truth." Frozen in place, Gideon began to pray under his breath, his lips moving silently. "Luther Mouana and Gideon Boseka are cousins."

"That is correct," Luther stated plainly. "My mother is Gideon's mother's youngest sister." He paused then turned to address Ruthalice. *He has already accepted me as a confident. What a trusting soul this young man is.* "My mother has ten older sisters, and finally two younger brothers." Grinning broadly he added, "Our grandfather was very pleased to finally get his sons."

Ali glanced at Cliff who sat with legs crossed, a pensive look in his eyes. As his gaze moved from Gideon to Luther and back again she realized he'd put something together.

"I'm still a bit puzzled here, guys." Cliff's tone was casual. "You graduated in, what was it, Gideon, 2000?" Without waiting for a reply Cliff went on, "and you Luther came to Emerick in 2004. You must be a junior because you're taking Invertebrate Biology." He added quickly reassuring himself his math was accurate. "And you're from the coast of Somalia, what's the name of that town?"

"Chisimaio," Luther replied quickly, "on the southern coast of Somalia. Chisimaio is one of Somalia's most important commercial centers. The port there is very deep. My father works at the docks and unloads enormous ocean liners which steam in and out of the Indian Ocean."

The pirates, Ruthalice thought shifting in her seat, *what about the pirates*? She was about to ask when Luther silently passed the conversation baton to his cousin.

"Professor Clifford is right again," Gideon unfolded and sat up straight on the sofa. "I graduate in 2000. Then I get a job in Cleveland and work in hospital laboratory. It is there I meet my wife Serita."

He stopped abruptly. Dropping his head, he squeezed the corners of his eyes with thumb and forefinger.

Charles took up the story. "Serita and Gideon were married for three years. Serita was an American citizen of Ethiopian descent." He cleared his throat. "Both she and their baby girl died in child birth."

The only sound in the room was the steady tick-tock of the grandfather clock.

"I already start my application for citizenship, but when my wife die, the US government agent come and tell me I am going to be deported." Gideon seemed to wilt. "They do not trust a young, single Somali man in America anymore."

"Nine-eleven," Charles declared. His angry gaze landed briefly on each one of them. "Our young friend here is one of the numerous nameless and unaccounted for victims of this government's knee jerk response to the terrorist attacks. "

"Yes, nine-one-one," Gideon spoke haltingly choosing each word carefully. "I am not a Muslim man, but Immigration not care. I am alone and black and from Somalia – an Islam country with much poverty, violence and killings -an enemy of America."

Fingering the crucifix around his neck Gideon raised his eyes.

"I tell them I cannot go back. There is no home for me. My house is destroyed in the fighting. My mother and my father and my little sister are all killed. I am refugee in my country too but they never accept me in USA." Gideon's gulp punctuated his story. "I beg to finish my citizenship process so I can keep my job at the hospital. Then I can go to graduate school in Ohio, but INS tell me, how you say? 'no go', and refuse me to stay."

Gideon's hands rested heavily in his lap. As he thrust himself into the back cushion of the love seat, a look of utter despair settled on his face. The little audience remained motionless, mesmerized by the telling of his plight.

"Immigration send a man to put me in detention so they can deport me. So, I must disappear from Cleveland and hospital job. I escape to my mentor." Gideon shrugged as if to say, what else could I do? "Dr. Martin find me a safe place to hide– he call it my sanctuary."

"His sanctuary as dear old TM dubbed it, is right here on campus." Dr. Hopkins had their undivided attention. "Gideon has been living in the coal bin in the basement of Pennington Place." Curly poured himself a third glass of port. "Refill anyone?"

Cliff held out his glass. Luther frowned and shook his head, a look of utter disbelief on his face. Ruthalice blinked. *Charles, what did you just say?* But one look at Gideon told her it was the truth.

"So, who's this Dr. Martin?" she managed to ask waving off a refill. "What's his connection to Emerick?"

"Dr. Terrell Martin was the Romance Languages professor from the 50s." Cliff looked at Charles for confirmation. "But how on earth do you know him, Gideon? Terrell had been retired for years by the time you came here as a student, and as far as I know seldom came to campus anymore."

"I meet Professor Martin in US Embassy in Mogadishu. When I fly to Cincinnati, he meets me and brings me to campus. He buys clothes and books and blankets for me." Remembering his delight at the sheer bounty of his benefactor's generosity, Gideon beamed. "Dr. Martin is very kind man."

"Now wait, wait!" Ali pleaded raising both hands as if to ward off any further information. She looked sternly at Charles Hopkins sitting cross-legged on the other side of the room. "Charles Hopkins, are you telling me that this young man has been sequestered and all alone right here under our noses and you never said one word to anybody?"

Ali sputtered to a stop. The notion of being summarily dumped and abandoned like that appalled her. Taking a deep breath she collected herself. "Gideon, you've actually been hiding in the basement of Penn Place?" Ruthalice struggled to keep the horror she felt out of her voice. "For how long?"

"Five months," Curly stated flatly answering for him. "Gideon came to Oakes Quarry in April."

Gideon nodded and took up the dispassionate recital of his story apparently unperturbed by the interruptions.

"When I get in trouble with Immigration, I call Dr. Martin. He tells me to come and he take care of me. I stay with him until one night Immigration is coming so Dr. Martin takes me to hid in the basement. He tells me I will be safe in the basement of Pennington House. He says no one goes down there anymore." Gideon jumped as a car door slammed somewhere down the block and glanced nervously over his shoulder at the curtained window behind them. "He is almost correct. No one comes down into basement very much. When the girl comes I hear her steps and stay quiet. She never knows I am there." His voice trailed off as a memory slipped across his mind. "In Somalia I stay quiet and I survive the soldier raids on my village."

Once again the little cadre slipped into silence. Ali marveled at the sense of communion that enveloped them. *We've known each other for less than a day and yet...*

"This is utterly amazing!" Cliff leaned forward. "How on earth did you manage to get in and out of the basement undetected?"

"Dr. Martin show me metal door behind the bushes."

"Of course," Ali exclaimed, "the coal bin door on the south side!" She shook her head amused by her private joke. "Biscuit led me to it."

Seeing the quizzical looks all around her Ali quickly explained. "I was poking around Penn Place Wednesday afternoon looking for I'm not sure what exactly. Biscuit, Missy Springer's cat, was in the bushes, and I caught a glimpse of a metal door handle. Since we had a coal bin in the house where I grew up it didn't strike me as anything significant."

She paused as an involuntary shiver slide up her spine. "How on earth did you manage, Gideon? It's gotta be pitch black down there and damp and oh, I don't know," she shuddered, "creepy!"

Gideon smiled proudly. "Dr. Martin give me oil lantern. He brings me blankets. I have my clothes and some books." Seeing the look of horror on her face, Gideon added reassuringly. "It's okay to live in Pennington Place, Miss Ruthalice. I go out at night sometimes and sleep in day."

Charles picked up the narrative. "Our friend timed his nightly comings and goings with the routine of the Alumni Office workers and the security man who I might note, patrols in a frightfully predictable pattern every week night. So, Gideon remained totally undetected."

"They built a non-descript utility door to keep their loft hidden from the mall shoppers," Ali murmured under her breath.

"Say what?" Curly looked lost

Cliff grinned. "Ali's just recalling an AP story from the *Dayton Daily News* she found unbelievable at the time. I believe 'no way!' was her analytical response to the purported episode."

"Ah, quite." Charles set his sherry glass on the table. "I thought the same thing when I read that story." He and Ali exchanged an amused wink.

Unable to follow their banter, Gideon studied his cousin's face. He was certain Luther's mind was filling with unanswered questions despite his placid face and unfurrowed brow. Only his cousin could truly understand his need to remain hidden. They were first and foremost countrymen and family after all, witnesses to unspeakable times of torture, rape and murder as Somalia deteriorated and sank into a violence which no one seemed able or willing to control. *If they catch you, my son, they will kill you.*

Gideon forced himself back to the present and the temporary safety of Professor Curly's dimly lit living room. "I eat what Professor Martin bring me sometimes and sometimes I go to dumpster behind Jones Center. That way I always eat. I finally work courage up and apply for job." Once again Gideon checked the curtains behind him. "I sweep back store room. Then stock boy quit so now I restock shelves," he added pleased with his accomplishment. "If warehouse is clean and shelves full when boss lady come at 4am, I keep good job."

Encouraged by his cousin's courage, Luther joined the story telling.

"We Somalis have learned how to live on very little. We live what you Quakers call the simple life." He grinned. "And now, my cousin you are saving money to join our aunts and uncles in Minneapolis-St. Paul someday."

The two men chuckled at some shared family memory. Then Gideon's face clouded.

"I was safe for five months, Professor Clifford, until Tuesday night when fire drive me out. Now I am fugitive and must run and hide again." Gideon's smile filled with sadness. *This time, Papa, I never look back.*

Ali bit her lip afraid of bursting into tears if she so much as glanced at the young man seated next to her on the love seat. Cliff studied the bottom of his empty glass, pondering the unfairness of it all. Charles, recalling his own childhood terror every time the air raid sirens sent him into the unlit tunnels under the streets of London, wondered how his young Somali friend kept his sanity. Luther observed his cousin thinking of him now as 'born-again Gideon'; and wondering what life might be like if he were to stay in town. There would finally be someone he could share the terrible night mares with and the fear that often came with the night.

Sometimes when I walk across campus in the middle of the night I hear the screams of terror from the villagers, screams that would pierce the walls of our tiny tin-roofed shack.

It was Gideon's calm voice which broke into the heavy silence. "The coal bin is my home. It is okay." He smiled his gentle smile. "It is very quiet. I like quiet." The cousins exchanged another private glance.

Clifford leaned forward. Resting his elbows on his knees, he intertwined his fingers and gazed intently at Gideon.

"I'm curious, Gideon. Didn't anyone ever stop and question you?" Always the practical one, Clifford unwittingly moved the conversation into a place less fraught with emotion.

"One time on way back from my job a police woman stop me in parking lot."

Ali froze certain that her heart had just leapt into her throat and she'd stopped breathing!

"She ask me where I am going and I say 'to the college', and she ask me where I live and I say 'at the college', and she happy with that and say 'goodnight'. So," he grinned contentedly, "I not lie, I tell truth."

"And that was that?" Ali managed to ask.

"Then I go home and she walk away." Gideon laughed and clapped his hands. "That was that!"

A sense of relief rippled around the room. Curly rose to his feet and without a word disappeared into the kitchen returning with another round of coffee and hot tea. Cliff stretched his legs in front of him, stuffed both hands into his jacket pockets and gave an enormous yawn. Rolling her shoulders to relieve the tension, Ali raised her arms above her head, swallowed – *my heart back into my chest-* she thought with amusement, and turned to Luther who sat in the ladder-back chair silently watching the movement around him.

"So tell me, Luther. Did you know your cousin was living on campus?"

His eyes immediately filled with delight. "We knew nothing of each other's whereabouts until last night when Charles forced me to come to his house." Luther burst out laughing and he pointed his index finger at the old professor. Reminded of their phone conversation, Curly chuckled appreciatively.

"Our family is very large," Gideon said. "My cousin and I are separated by civil war when we are young children. We never see each other until last night in this house!"

Ali took Gideon's right hand then reached across the space between them and gently clasped Luther's left one in hers.

"Loving and ever-present God," she prayed in a firm voice. "We are filled with thanksgiving for your mercy and we thank you from the depths of our being for reuniting these two precious people. I ask a special blessing for our dear Charles who made it possible."

She released their hands and fumbled in her skirt pocket for a tissue. She blew her nose then dropped the damp kleenix in the wastebasket beside the sofa. "I've noticed that you are each wearing the beaded necklace made by your grandmother." The two men nodded. "It is your talisman?"

"Our birth mark," Luther stated smiling shyly. "That is how we recognized each other."

As the cookies made the rounds, the mood lightened. Voices rose and fell as parents walked by outside returning home from the football game. A high pitched yipping suddenly began in the yard next door.

"Ah," said Professor Hopkins. "The insufferable poodle of Mrs. Stroodle, out for his nightly doggy constitutional."

Ali nearly choked on her cookie. The barking grew louder then suddenly ceased.

"I had a dog once," Gideon began, a look of resignation on his face, "But one day he disappear. We find out a man eat him. The man say he is very hungry. We believe him."

Luther nodded sympathetically. "People are starving all over Somalia."

"But everything okay-dokay here in Ohio. I do not have to eat dog because I have job and nice bossy lady who come in at 4 am and never ask me questions!"

After the goodbyes and promises to get together again soon, Cliff turned on the car headlights and headed for Horsefeathers Farm. Curly's cul-de-sac was deserted by now lit only by tall streetlamps and an occasional front porch light. The curved slice of moon had begun its accent across the star strewn sky above Oakes Quarry.

"I'm still a bit stunned by Charles' complete involvement in this whole saga," Cliff said braking for a white cat that suddenly shot out between two parked cars, "though now that I think about it I guess I really shouldn't be. After all he was just a kid himself during the air raids on London and was forced to hide for hours in the Googe

Street Underground Station. He doesn't talk about it much, but the terror of those endless agonizing nights must be just below the surface. I suspect he has immense empathy for a homeless orphan and refugee to boot."

As they reached the edge of town Cliff clicked on the high beams and settled into a comfortable 50 mph. Reaching for Ali's hand he interlaced their fingers and squeezed gently.

"Tell me what thee is making of all this. What doth my dear campus minister have to say?"

Ali sighed. "Oh, I don't know what to think, Cliff. I guess I'm still marveling at Gideon's ability to remain undetected on our little campus for over five months when everyone seems to know what everyone else has said and done within minutes! And it does remind me of those mall rats we read about, hidden in plain sight!"

Ali gazed out the side window. Up in the coal black sky Orion the Hunter, his belt of three starts shining at his waist, stood poised to shoot his arrow. An enormous inflated Halloween pumpkin its insides aglow with artificial light wobbled in the front yard of Sky View Farms.

"Consumerism run amok," she observed cryptically.

"Hmmm?"

"Oh, nothing really, I'm just cranky." She continued gazing out the side window. "It's just that after listening to Gideon talk about subsisting on hand-outs and left-overs and Luther reminiscing about hundreds of thousands of people starving in Somali, I'm not in the mood for over-blown Halloween decorations, that's all."

Ali slipped her hand out of his and laid her palm against the back of his neck. Gently fingering his curly hair, she starred straight ahead alert for any movement at the edge of the road that might mean deer.

"Gideon indicated that his boss lady at the warehouse is sympathetic to his plight because her brother's an illegal alien."

"Undocumented is the correct term, Cliff, undocumented worker." Sensing his annoyance she added quickly, "I prefer that language actually because it's scriptural. According to the Bible we are all aliens living on land that belongs to the Lord." Ali ran her thumb along Clifford's hard jaw. "I don't think God worries a whole lot about national boundaries. And besides it's another reminder to the pastor side of me that we human beings are a family and have an awful lot in common."

"Her brother is undocumented." Cliff landed heavily on the last word. "At any rate, the fact that she assured him no one would ever ask any questions if he lay low and did his job, turned out to be correct. She and Charles were the only ones aware that Gideon was in town." Cliff slowed down and pulled off on the right hand shoulder as an ambulance came into sight in the rear view mirror.

"Terrell Martin knew."

"True, but after his stroke Dorothy insisted he come live with her, so Martin moved up to Toledo. He's effectively out of the picture all together by now I should think. And remember Gideon's only heard from him that one time when Martin sent a letter via Hopkins informing Gideon that he'd been 'kidnapped' as he put it by his youngest child."

"Ok, so five months ago only Terrell Martin knows Gideon Boseka is back on campus. When Martin moves up to Toledo he passes Gideon on to Charles to look after." Ruthalice pulled her cape around her shoulders. "I guess Immigration has lost track of his whereabouts."

Cliff stopped at the mailbox and retrieved a rubber-banded bundle of Christmas catalogs.

"I suspect that at the time Gideon disappeared from Cleveland, Charles didn't know anymore than anyone else did about his whereabouts and for some reason Martin wasn't ready to spill the beans." He laid the mail in Ali's lap. "So with a place to hide, a job, a boss lady to cover for him and a friend on campus providing occasional comfort, Gideon moved into the cellar of Pennington Place."

"It's incredible to me what people will endure when it's too darn dangerous at home to even contemplate returning there."

Ali retrieved her purse from the back seat, gathered up the mail Cliff had tossed in her lap and opened the door.

"I'm finding that it's impossible for me at this point to walk even a block in Gideon's moccasins, Cliff, let alone a mile! Even thinking about living in a dark, dank coal bin all by myself with no one to come home to feels totally unbearable!" She felt tears welling up inside. "Poor dear Gideon hasn't even had sufficient time to mourn the death of his wife and baby girl."

She climbed out of the car and started for the kitchen door.

"He's clinging to a tenuous present, escaping an unbearable past, and facing a future of what: endless hiding and running? What good does his hard earned Emerick College degree do him when he's been relegated to a furtive, secret existence underground, popping in and out like a gopher spooked by his own shadow! Dear God, all I want to do is take Gideon in my arms and weep!"

Cliff slammed the car door, slipped between Lemon Drop and the truck and gathered his wife into his strong, loving arms. When they'd both stopped shaking, he opened the kitchen door. Still clinging to each other, they stood in the dark mud room lost in their own private thoughts. Finally, Ali moved into the kitchen, set the catalogs and purse on the kitchen counter and filled the tea kettle with water.

"I can't possibly get to sleep yet, Cliff. I'm too wound up." Slipping out of her coat, she took two mugs off their hooks under the kitchen cabinet. "Will you join me for Chocolate Raspberry Delight cocoa?"

"Sure. If we're going to be up for awhile what do you say to a little fire?"

Without waiting for a reply Cliff headed for the living room. By the time Ali slipped off her shoes and shook out the "*horses on parade*" afghan, the fire had popped into life.

"You know what I want to do, Cliff?" she asked gingerly cradling her hot mug. "I want to move Gideon out here in the country and say to heck with it to the authorities."

She lowered herself onto their old leather couch. Cliff removed his glasses, rubbed his eyes and squinted at his wife.

"That's your intuitive side speaking, right?" he asked fondly, "the side which says let consequences be damned, I'm acting on faith and Christian principals and all that radical stuff?"

"I guess so." Ali stared at the fire and asked herself as she had so many times before, why basic human justice was so hard to come by. "It's just that Gideon doesn't deserve to be sent back home. He was a small boy when he got caught up in the Somali civil war, managed to hang on by the skin of his teeth and finish school."

She stopped speaking as tears slid silently down her cheeks.

"I don't want him deported just because the fire forced him out. I can't stand the idea!"

Setting her mug on the floor, she blew her nose. Cliff replaced his glasses and carefully sipped his cocoa. As the logs settled, a pop like a gun shot exploding made them both jump.

"Well my dear, if it's any consolation I can't imagine Hopkins sitting idly by and allowing Immigration to get its hands on Gideon. For one thing it would signal betrayal of old Doc Martin's trust in Curly's ability and commitment to keep the young man safe."

"I suppose you're right. Betrayal of trust and an inability to keep his promises and follow through are at the top of Curly's no-no list!"

"You can add loyalty to that list because in my humble opinion Curly's grown quite fond of young Gideon Boseka." Cliff sighed. "But, you know what troubles me about this whole sorry affair?" He turned to face his wife. "Only Doc Martin knew Gideon was in the basement until that fire and now there are four of us who have been added to that exclusive list of one."

Clifford got up and jabbed the fire with the black poker lying on the hearth. "It's just a hunch, sweetheart but from where I sit I see no good way out of this refugee mess." A shower of sparks flew out of the logs as Cliff continued to stab them. "I don't like anything about this right now!" Ali gave him a startled look. "Look," he began coming back to sit beside her. "Why does a fire breaks out in the Old Dean's House in the first place? It makes no sense to me at all. And in fact the more I think about it the more I'm convinced that this fire is going to upset more than one apple cart."

As they sat watching the fire dance and hiss, exhaustion finally got the upper hand.

Let's sleep on it, shall we, honey?" Cliff kissed Ali gently on the forehead. "Can you do that, let it rest 'til morning?"

Taking his head in both hands, she pulled his face down and returned his kiss.

"I think so, sweetheart. I'm sure willing to give it the old college try." *And place my worries about Gideon's future into your hands, dear Lord.*

Chapter Six – The Weekend

Ali's left arm swept lightly over the empty space now grown cold beside her and leapt out of bed. Reluctantly she stepped on the bathroom scale for her weight control program's required weekly weigh-in. Bending forward she peered at the illuminated red numbers.

"Well at least I'm headed in the right direction," she sighed making a mental note of one hundred and eighty-two pounds. "But I'm still too much the traditionally built lady!"

Pulling on pink sweatpants and matching sweatshirt with SLEEP HERE WHEN IT HAPPENS! plastered across her ample bosom, she followed the delicious smell of coffee through the living room into the kitchen and back again.

Looking up Cliff watched his wife draw back the floor length drapes then turn and head his way. "I see you're sporting your good old Packfield's town motto this morning – the earthquake epicenter of the USA!"

Ali grinned. "When you said let's honeymoon in Monterey, California, I pictured sea and sand otters not the sand of a sleepy, dusty mountain town, population 18!"

Cliff held his mug over the braided rug hoping to avoid spilling hot liquid as Ali plunked down beside him and tousled his hair.

"But what a find, eh? Dozens of small earthquakes every single week, seismic instruments on every hillside and valley. Remember that cafe? I ordered The Big One well done and you had Magnitude Six medium rare." Cliff chuckled. "With Aftershocks for dessert!"

"I still can't get over that highway bridge over Cholame Creek, the rails and supports all bent and crooked by over five feet since it was built." Ali placed her right hand on the lettering on her chest and recited from memory. 'The edge of the North American tectonic plate where the next-door Pacific tectonic plate butts up against it!' That was one of your better ideas, my dear Clifford. Who woulda thunk it'd turn out to be such a funky honeymoon location!"

Ali placed her slippered feet on the coffee table and starred at the field stone fire place.

"So, how long have you been up?"

"Oh, not very long." Cliff dropped this week's *Around Boone County* on the floor. "You up for the Saturday morning special?"

"Sure." Ali got to her feet. "I'll go see if the hens laid yesterday and feed the cows while I'm at it." She pulled her plaid wool barn coat over her sweatshirt, tugged on a pair of rubber boots and headed out the door. She soon disappeared behind the cedars between the house and barn leaving Cliff happily banging around the kitchen collecting the ingredients for his fabulous pancake and sausage breakfast.

"So, what's on your plate today, sweetheart, anything in particular?"

They stood on either side of the king-size bed tugging the polka dot sheets and vermillion down coverlet over the mattress.

"Have you seen my work boots, by the way?"

"Egads Clifford you're a big boy now, keep track of your own stuff!" Ali scowled at him across the top of the bed. "In answer to your question, nothing other than raking leaves."

Ali slipped around the end of the bed as Cliff bent over to check for his wandering boots, wrapped her arms around his backside and squeezed tightly. Grasping his left boot firmly in his hand, he wiggled out of her grasp.

"There's the other one," he cried triumphantly as he spotted the toe of the second leather boot poking out from under the Carharts draped over the rocking chair in the corner. "Hey, good looking now that I've got my boots, want to take a hike? We haven't been along the creek in a long time."

"Sure beats raking leaves!"

Five minutes later Ali tossed a water bottle and OSU ball cap at Cliff, tugged her knit Emerick hat on and stepped onto the wooden porch. They hiked across the pasture strewn with iron weed and dried milk weed pods then started upstream following the stream bank. Ali grasped the occasional skinny hawthorn to keep from slipping into the water.

"Let's go to the point and sit on that oak log," she suggested cheerfully.

Cliff stepped around her and pointed. "We can get through here," he announced just before losing his footing and slipping ingloriously into the creek.

"Rats!" Cold water seeped through the boot soaking his wool sock. "Don't step on that rock! It's tippy."

"I can see that," Ali observed dryly as Cliff hopped around madly shaking his sopping wet left foot. "You're gonna end up back in the water if you don't watch it," she said grabbing his arm.

They clambered up to the wide oak log, lichens clinging to its sides like empty dirty shelves. Ali spread her wool shirt on the deeply scarred surface of the old tree and sat down. A crow called raucously from the buckeye tree as a red-tailed hawk whistled overhead. Lulled by the steady gurgle of creek water, Ali felt warm and content. Leaning back she watched the raptor circle and soar correcting its flight with a powerful flap of its wings. Breaking a stalk of tall grass in half, she stuck the sweet tasting end in her mouth. The seed head bobbed up and down as she nibbled. Cliff rested his back against the rough bark and sighed as Ali's fingers gently twisted his red curls.

"By the way, you haven't filled me in on the big conference with all the president's men - and ladies," he added quickly, hoping to head off his wife's corrective stare!

Ali leaned back on her hands enjoying the soft prickle of warm wood on her palms. Closing her eyes she tilted her face back and began a blow by blow recital of yesterday's meeting.

"Hold on a minute, what's this about fireworks?"

"Somebody's been storing fire crackers in the basement. It now seems virtually certain the fire started in the cubbyhole that's partway down the stairs. Apparently by the time the 911 call came in, the steps and furniture below were burning like crazy."

Cliff struggled out of his wet boot and wiggled his toes.

"It's a good thing Gideon came back from work when he did," he said hopping clumsily on one foot, "and had the good sense to call the fire department, otherwise historic old Penn might be a total goner. There're no windows in that basement, so it might very well have been quite awhile before anyone noticed smoke or flames."

"The college owes Gideon a huge thank you, but I doubt he'll ever get it." Ali rubbed the wood chips from her palms then flicked the mashed grass blade into the creek. "Our secret unsung hero took a big risk by calling the cops." She raised her legs and crossed them on the broad back of the log. "For some reason Angus kept insisting in adnauseam that no one ever goes into the basement anymore."

"How can he be so sure about that?"

"I don't know, but he's partially correct because Ernestine did tell Richard that no one from the alumni office has been in the basement since last June."

"Be that as it may, they're obviously both mistaken."

Cliff placed his wet sock on top of the dry boot, and joined Ali on the log. "We know of at least two people who've been in that cellar, Gideon and our elusive arsonist."

"But no one knows about Gideon, Cliff."

"I'm simply stating the obvious. If Gideon didn't stash fire works in that nook, then some heretofore unnamed individual most assuredly did. And what's more whoever put fire works in that hole went to great lengths to hide the fact which leads me to suspect that he or she knows full well that it's illegal to even have fireworks in your possession in this state." Cliff shifted his weight. "That fire did not start itself."

"Could a wire or fuse box socket or whatever those things are called have shorted out? It's an old building after all."

"In the cubbyhole?" Cliff vehemently shook his head. "That makes no sense whatsoever. Besides the college upgraded all the wiring when we did the renovations."

Ali swatted at a black fly buzzing persistently around her face.

"I just hate the idea that someone in our college community is to blame for the damage to Penn Place. And it's even more horrible to realize we probably know the person who set that fire."

"And forced Gideon out of his hiding place."

"That too."

"Well just remember, sweetheart, neither of us knows yet if this fire was set on purpose or was an accident." Cliff paused to watch a brown wooly worm work its way up the leg of his jeans. "I for one remain convinced that it is a human being who started a fire in Pennington Place Tuesday night."

"But why?" Ruthalice squinted and pulled her forehead into a masterful crease.

"Why what?"

"Why hide contraband explosives on campus in the first place? What on earth were this mysterious 'they' planning to do with them?"

"The more pertinent question is who?"

"Who, what?"

"Well, for starters WHO has access to the basement?"

"Somebody's whose presence there wouldn't raise suspicion."

"You're probably right, though the way this campus operates just about any normal looking individual could come and go as they please especially since the building is unlocked much of the time." Cliff pulled his cap back on. "Does anyone sit at the reception desk in the parlor anymore?"

"Nope, that position was eliminated when Quaker Archives was moved upstairs."

"That's what I thought, so really anyone could mosey into the kitchen, descend the basement stairs with a bag full of fire crackers tucked under their arm and sequester their loot completely undetected." Cliff managed to swat the fly which had finally landed on Ruthalice's head. "It keeps circling back to who was in the basement Tuesday night doesn't it?" Cliff poked at an ant hustling across the top of the log. "Whoever our culprit turns out to be, he or she must have arrived after Gideon went to work at 9:30 and was gone when he returned at 1am."

"I've been thinking about what starts a fire," Ali said vigorously rubbing her lower back. "Man I'm getting stiff, Cliff I've gotta walk."

"What starts a fire?" Cliff pulled his boot back on. "A match, a blow torch, lightening, a spark."

"An electrical short, but you pooh-poohed that one already. Gideon's lantern, but dear God I hope that's not true!"

Ali scratched her cheek and stepped carefully down the slippery bank. "A cigarette," she said bending over to pick up a painted turtle with its eyes closed sunning itself on a shiny flat rock lying at the edge of the small pool created by a submerged log.

Cliff stopped lacing his boot and starred at her.

"You're a veritable genius," he cried leaping to his feet. "A cigarette – that's perfect. So, who smokes on campus?"

"Good heavens, Cliff, lots of people but now that Emerick's a non-smoking campus they don't do it openly that's all."

"So, if somebody was smoking in Penn they did it on the QT."

"Like in the basement."

"Like in the basement, yes, or after everyone'd gone home for the day.

"In my limited experience," she said smiling, "it's darn difficult to disguise the smell of cigarette smoke. I at least always got caught!"

"Which is why, my dear, I think our dastardly deed was done after hours and in the dark of night!"

Ali watched the little turtle pull its head and legs and tail tightly into its shell. "We all do that, don't we?" she said looking pensively at the pointed little face. It returned her stare with unblinking eyes.

"We all do what?" asked Cliff.

"We all hide when we're feeling threatened. If we feel under attack, whenever we feel ashamed or are too embarrassed to admit something we keep it a secret. We hide. I guess that's the human thing to do."

Cliff smiled down at the top of her head. "It's an instinct, Ali. All the snails, all the little creatures I study, when threatened go into hiding. Pull themselves inside their shell or lay low and hope they're going to be safe."

"That's what I mean. And yet, we never are completely safe," Ali replied gently placing the painted turtle back on its rock where it immediately scrambled back into the water and disappeared into the muddy bottom. "God, you have been my hiding place, my shelter in the time of storm."

"God my fortress." Cliff helped her up the bank.

As dark gray clouds loomed on the Western horizon, the M&Ms hiked back across the field hand in hand, silently pondering where this investigation was taking them.

It started raining shortly after midnight; by 4:30 the ceaseless drumming on the tin roof drove sleep away. Fumbling for his slippers in the dimly lit room, he wrapped himself in a well-worn flannel bathrobe then stood beside the water-streaked window watching the drops pound the pavement. Crossing to the ladder back chair beside the bedroom door, he perched on its wicker seat. Unable to silence the chatter in his mind, he lumbered back to his feet to peer once again into the deserted street.

"Ira, honey, what on earth is the matter? You've been pacing the floor for hours."

Ira Ish turned from the window and gazed apologetically at his wife.

"I didn't mean to disturb you, Nora." He gently held her frail deformed hand between his sturdy rough ones. "I've got a lot on my mind this morning. You know me I can't think sitting down!"

Nora favored him with what remained of the smile that won his heart nearly 40 years ago. He kept his eyes on her face as she fumbled with the white afghan coverlet strewn with embroidered red roses. Remembering a long-ago reprimand, Ira resisted the persistent urge to straighten the bedding for her.

I can still manage to cover myself up, Ira. I'm dependant on you for nearly everything else, please don't take that away from me too. For now at least, he was willing to share the burden her rheumatoid arthritis had laid upon both of them by honoring her request.

Finally the afghan was where she wanted it. Nora looked up then nodded toward the bedroom's only chair.

"Husband, you're frightening me. Turn on a light, sit down and talk to me."

Ira placed the chair at the foot of her bed, straightened the yellow-stripped cushion and sat down. His eyes roamed the room where his wife now lived out her days, and was pleased yet again by its clean coziness and welcoming warmth. Nora's niece Polly cleaned once a week and since she insisted on flinging the window open to exchange the air, the room seldom had that "old folk smell" he associated with nursing homes. On Sundays after the second mass, one of the guild ladies from Holy Mother Church made certain the altar flowers found their way to Sister Nora's bedside stand accompanied by a tape of the service and the morning's church bulletin. Nora slipped every cover into its own plastic sleeve and saved them in a three-ring album.

"Look at those mountains, Ira," she'd say pointing at a favorite bulletin cover. "Isn't it pretty how they reflect so perfectly in the water?" She placed a trembling hand on the shiny surface. "From whence cometh my strength," she sighed softly. "No mountains and no strength anymore."

As happened more and more these days, the enormity of his wife's deteriorating condition and his own fear of the future rose up and overwhelmed him. Ira closed his eyes and began to weep. Watching the tears slither down her husband's wrinkled, pudgy cheeks and drop on the faded fabric, Nora stifled the scream welling up from within and managed to remain silent, waiting for the sobs to subside.

Finally Ira pulled a red bandana from his robe pocket, drew a deep breath and blew his nose. He scrunched it up then began picking at the edges of the material slowly unraveling the hem.

"Nora, I have done a terrible thing."

A shared sense of foreboding hung heavily between them.

"I fell behind in my work again." He lifted his head and stared into her liquid filled eyes. "My assignment was to service furnaces Tuesday night, but that old Bryant in Fox Hall required all new parts so it ended up taking much longer than I expected it to."

"I don't understand."

"I didn't finish in Fox Hall until after nine and since I was hungry, I went to Subway for supper. I knew I had to finish cleaning both furnaces before Wednesday morning or Mr. Bailey would've been all over me, so I went back to campus around ten o'clock to take care of Pennington Place."

Rubbing his eyes, Ira slumped in the chair and sighed heavily. He placed a hand on each thigh in an attempt to quiet the twitches which made his legs jump. In a voice heavy with exhaustion he continued his story. "I finally finished up around midnight and then came straight home."

Nora impulsively tugged the edges of her afghan until the fabric lay smooth across her narrow body. The task completed, her hands slid down and came to rest quietly at her side.

“Ira Ish, how can I help when you hold back and don’t tell me the entire story?”

Ira got up nearly upsetting the chair and walked to the closet. Replacing his pajama top with a clean white shirt, he began buttoning from the neck down. Nora’s pale blue eyes quivered nervously.

“Tell me where you are going,” she commanded watching him slip on a pair of black trousers. The long suppressed scream of despair lay coiled just below the surface of her controlled emotions. Nora knew with the certainty of the dying that she could not contain the anguish much longer.

Ira ran a black plastic comb through his thin brown hair then clipped a paisley bowtie to his collar. “I’m going to confession.” Pulling himself up straight, he stared into the mirror and addressed the ashen face reflecting back at him from the bed. “I’m going to talk with Father Paul, Nora. I have a sin to confess.”

“We have never kept secrets from each other, Ira. You must tell me also.”

“I am smoking again,” he admitted dejectedly.

“Oh, thank you, Jesus! I was afraid you shop lifted again!” Nora’s voice cracked as relief swept over her leaving her limp. “Father Paul will forgive you, my dear husband. Smoking is only a human weakness and failing.”

He tucked a clean handkerchief into his shirt pocket. “I’ll take the car; it’s still coming down in buckets. If I get to church before 7:30, Father will hear my confession right away.” His billfold felt exceptionally light this morning as he tucked it into his pocket. “I’ll plan to stay for morning mass.”

Sensing his confidence return Nora relaxed as he kissed her gently on the check.

"Say, how 'bouts I stop at Crater's and get us some of those custard filled long johns for breakfast?"

"How delightful, something to look forward to!"

Listening to his footsteps retreating down the hallway she was overpowered by a keen sense of disquiet. She waited until the front door slammed then began to pray softly:

"Lord Jesus Christ

Son and Word of the Living God

By the prayer of your most pure Mother and all the Saints

Have mercy on us and save us."

The steady rain hammered the shingles at Horsefeathers Farm as water gushed out the gutters onto the soggy grass. Ali leapt out of bed and dashed to the window. She grabbed the cold metal handle and began frantically cranking the window shut as an icy mist sprayed her face. Shivering she headed straight for the bathroom, grabbed the nearest towel and energetically rubbed her face and arms.

"Are you staying up?" a groggy voice questioned from Cliff's side of the bed.

"I'll never get back to sleep now, it's nearly seven." She kissed his warm forehead. "Do you want the radio on?"

A sleepy grunt answered her question. Accompanied by the twangy sounds of old tyme gospel, Ali lustily sang her way across the living room floor and into the kitchen.

"Shall we gather at the river, the be u tiful, be u tiful, river?"

Ali was busy scribbling and erasing when Cliff sauntered into the room a half hour later, his flannel sleeping shirt barely reaching his knees.

"Whatcha working on so diligently this First Day morning?" he asked pouring a cup of coffee. He crossed the room and noisily taking his first cautious slurp attempted to peer over her shoulder.

"Oh, I promised Mike Peters I'd have my part of the new publicity brochure ready by the end of this week, but since I didn't even get started on it, I'm attempting to make up for the error of my ways this morning!"

Cliff scooted in beside her on the cushion-covered bench.

"Let's see what you've got so far."

Oakes Quarry was settled in 1821 by two Quaker brothers Obadiah and Sterling Emerick who joined the large settlement of Friends (Quakers) migrating from North Carolina to Ohio escaping the institution of slavery. The brothers began farming and built a functional house of stone. In 1823 Sterling married Sarah Cluxton in a simple Quaker wedding. Hannah Elizabeth Emerick, the youngest of their seven children, founded Emerick College in 1872 as a school for women, the only institution of its kind for hundreds of miles around. Ms. Emerick taught English, French and Art History, and within four years of the date she courageously shared her vision with the town counsel, the Emerick School for Women graduated its first class.

"An excellent summation, Ali. I've only got two corrections."

Ali favored him with her best Cheshire cat grin. "I'm all ears."

"Ok, their wedding was in 1824 instead of '23, and technically Hannah was the youngest of *eight* children as the one born before her died at 2 months of age."

Ali marked the changes with her trusty red pen. "I'm going to add that Miss Hannah was the first woman to be recorded as a minister in our neck of the Quaker woods."

Cliff nodded his agreement. "Oh, by the way you'll be interested to know that it's now official. WKOA reported this morning that exploding firecrackers started our fire."

Ali looked up from her yellow pad. "Really!"

"The anchor man didn't elaborate, but that rules out Gideon's Coleman lantern as far as I'm concerned."

"Thank God for that." She wrinkled her forehead. "I think his exact words were, 'I always turn light out before I go'." Ali turned sideways on the breakfast nook bench and lightly laid her left hand on Cliff's arm. "Remember Gideon told us he smelled smoke the minute he opened the coal bin door..."

"and immediately jumped down into the bin, lit the lantern, grabbed as many belongings as he could get his hands on and scrambled back out..."

"calling the fire department from the campus emergency phone in front of Harvey Library."

Ali laid her pen diagonally on the pad of paper in front of her. "In order to use the phone Gideon had to stand under the security light in full view of anybody who happened to look out a window in that direction or wander by."

"It was the middle of the night."

Ali shrugged still convinced it was a gutsy thing to do.

"I no longer believe Ernestine has a clue about what goes on in that building in spite of her take-charge posturing because if she did there's no way she'd tolerate the storing of explosives in what she considers to be HER basement!"

Ali gave Cliff a bemused look. "So what ignited the newspapers, Clifford? All you and I've managed to do is eliminate a couple of possibilities." She briskly rubbed her upper arms. "We're just going in circles, and it's driving me nuts!"

"Ah, yes, well there in lies the rub." Cliff stood up and moved over to his side of the breakfast nook as if to say enough of this conjecturing. "I'm ready to eat." Ruthalice who was getting antsy and feeling a bit out of sorts herself, gladly took the hint. Desperately needing to do anything that would make her feel she'd actually accomplished something this morning, Ali sprang into action.

"Cold cereal or cinnamon oatmeal this morning?" she asked setting two hand-made stoneware bowls on the placemats with a thud.

"Oh, I don't care whichever's easier for you." Clifford reached for the sugar. "Is this the Sunday you preach for the Presbys?"

"That's next week," Ali replied setting an armload of cereal boxes on the table. She shoved the stack of magazines occupying the bench into the corner then slide in across from her professor. Pouring milk into her bowl she watched stray Grapenuts bobbing on the creamy white surface.

"Cliff, I've got an idea." Ruthalice raised her spoon and took a mouthful of cereal. "Since it's such a lousy day weather-wise," she began swallowing rapidly, "let's invite Charles and Gideon out for the afternoon. We can sit in front of a nice warm fire and watch football or NASCAR or whatever's on TV, and they can stay for dinner as well. What do you think?"

A warm smile slipped into Cliff's eyes.

"I love you, Ms. Ruthalice Michels," he said contentedly. "That's a wonderful idea."

"Do you think Charles will be ok bringing Gideon out of the house in broad daylight?"

"We won't know till we ask. I'll give him a call."

Ali buttered her raisin toast. "Tell them we'll be back from meeting for worship by noon so come anytime after that and plan to spend the rest of the day."

"Consider it done, my dear."

Licking the peach jam off his fingers, Cliff reached for the cell phone lying on top of the New York Times crossword puzzle book. Ali headed for the shower. A few minutes later Cliff flushed the toilet then knocked rambunctiously on the shower door.

"Come in!" she moved out of the way as her buck naked husband stepped through the opening, quickly closing the door behind him. She shoved the bar of soap into his hands.

"So, what did Curly say?"

"A jolly good idea! – says it'd do 'em good to get out." He chuckled as the water cascaded down his soapy chest. "Sounds like our old campus curmudgeon's having to make considerable adjustments to his solitary bachelor-weekend routine.

"Are you coming, Gideon?" Professor Hopkins growled impatiently. "It's nearly half-past. Ruthalice and Clifford were expecting us at one."

Getting no response he clumped down the basement steps. Reaching the bottom, he saw Gideon down on his knees running his hands along the bare floor.

"Lose something, old chap?" Charles inquired as Gideon peered under the cot.

"I cannot find my other flip flop, Professor Curly.

"You don't need flip flops, it's pouring outside."

"I do not have good shoes. Look."

He held up two ragged, dirty tennis shoes with holes in both toes.

"Forget the flip flops. We'll buy a new pair of shoes at the Wal-Mart on our way out of town." A look of uneasiness crossed his young friend's face. "Oh that's right I can't take you into Wally Mart, can I? Where is your head these days, Charles?" He waved both hands in exasperation. "Never mind. Just come on, Gideon. I'll just take one of your loafers in with me." Without waiting for a reply he plodded back up the stairs, Gideon following meekly on behind.

Forty-five minutes later with the shopping mission completed, the improbable duo chugged out of town in the little VW, wipers flapping at full speed. Gideon threaded the laces of his new red and white Nikes then slipped them on. Turning his feet from side to side, he inhaled the new-shoe smell and beamed.

"Thank you for socks too, Professor Curly." His soft lyrical voice made the words sing. "You are my friend." Gideon's stare eagerly flitted from the windshield to the side window. "This look different from town. There are hills and cattle out there." He pointed at a herd of Black

Angus grazing behind acres of field fence seemingly oblivious to the driving rain. "I like cattle."

"Do you miss Doolow?" The professor's voice was uncharacteristically gentle. "I jolly well miss the English countryside with 'The sun above the mountain's head, a freshening luster mellow; through all the long green fields has spread, his first sweet evening yellow.'" Charles chuckled appreciatively. "Ah, Wordsworth."

"Wordsworth? What is this Wordsworth?"

"Who my boy, who? William Wordsworth is England's Lakes District poet and in my humble opinion, is the best of our British poets."

Negotiating the turn Charles maneuvered the wheezing little Beetle up the winding gravel lane of Horse Feathers Farm and the Mowry Centennial Home.

"Well, Gideon, we've arrived; your first road trip since you skedaddled out of Cleveland by Greyhound!" Shoulders hunched Curly sprinted for the front porch hollering over his shoulder, "Come on, Gideon, it's bucketing down out here!"

Clutching his new shoes and sox against his chest, Gideon hopped over puddles in his bare feet and joined the professor on the wide wooden porch just as Clifford flung the door open.

"Come on in! If this keeps up old Noah's going to have to start building."

Cliff stepped aside as the two men crowded through the front door. "Here let me take your coats." Glancing at Gideon's feet he added, "and get a towel for you, my good man."

Charles headed straight for the handsome Victorian chair to the right of the fireplace and sat down. Gideon nervously edged his way into the middle of the room, his eyes darting to the large plate glass window dominating the west wall. Ali stepped into the room holding a piece of paper behind her back.

"We're all alone out here, Gideon. Please, come and sit by the fire. You must be cold."

"In Somalia we are very happy when it rain. It is always too dry. "

He moved to the leather couch and sat like a wary cat poised to slink away at the slightest sign of danger. His eyes surveyed the room. "Is that Africa?" he asked pointing to the large water color hanging above the claw-foot dining room table.

"You have a discerning eye, Gideon. That is Kenya, the Rift Valley to be exact. A Quaker friend of ours, Mateau Ketoyo painted it."

Cliff handed Gideon a soft yellow towel and joined him on the sofa.

"I led worship one Sunday morning at Nairobi Friends meeting. The pastor gave me the painting as a thank you gift. What I just love are those sprawling acacia trees and the intense blue of the African sky that seems to go on forever."

"Mr. Mateau is very good artist."

The opening chit chat, like lines forgotten in the middle of a play, slipped into an awkward silence. Curly, suddenly ill at ease re-crossed his legs. Cliff fiddled with the button on his shirt sleeve and wondered if he should poke the fire. Gideon, starring at the painted landscape, suddenly felt homesick for Africa. Ali determined to get the conversation going again, cleared a space in the middle of the coffee table.

"Gideon," she said calmly, "I'm woefully ignorant about your country so I went on the internet this morning." Ali placed a white piece of typing paper on the wooden surface. "I have printed out a map of Somalia. Would you show us where you used to live?"

In one fluid motion Gideon slipped off the sofa and sank to his knees. He turned the map a quarter turn then pointed to the upper left. "This is my town I grow up in, Doolow. See it is where Ethiopia, Kenya and Somalia borders come together."

"Ah, yes the Mandera Triangle." The others gave him a startled look. "The tri-border area is known as the Mandera Triangle," Charles explained, "where a man's wealth and status are dependent upon the number of cattle he owns. It is the most desperately poor area on the entire continent."

"Professor Curly is right." Gideon ran his finger down the map. "Here is Chisimaio where my cousin Luther come from down on Indian Ocean, about 100 kilometers south of Mogadishu."

He sat back on his haunches and stared at the map. "There is no peace in the triangle area of my country. There is too much fighting in our capital city. Many thousands of people get killed in Mogadishu and now come the terrorists," he added bitterly, "who kill anybody they don't like."

"Until 1941 Somalia was known as Italian Somaliland. The Italians occupied Chisimaio." Cliff tapped the middle of the map. "I remember reading about the 1995 siege of Baidoa. My nephew was serving in the Marines at the time, and when fighting broke out in September the family worried he'd be sent to Somalia. Hundreds of innocent civilians were killed in that particular siege."

Gideon moaned and grasped the edges of the coffee table with both hands. "My mother and my baby sister Corinne, they are slaughtered in Baidoa." He began rocking back and forth. "They go visit my auntie. My grandmother is not well, so mama and my sister go to help. The soldiers fire bomb the house…" His voice trailed off.

"May your dear ones rest in peace, Gideon." Ali gently covered his hand with hers. "Two more innocent victims of war. God help us all."

"A case of being in the wrong place at the wrong time. That's bloody awful." Charles rested his chin on his fist. "Gideon, did I ever tell you that both my mum and da were killed when a Nazi shell landed on the house and blew them and everything inside to smithereens?"

"No, Professor Curly, I not know that. It is very sad too." Gideon crumbled the tissue Ali held out to him then cleared his throat. "My father is part of resistance movement in Somalia. US soldiers shoot and kill him two years before my mama died." The logs shifted in the fire place filling the silence. "There is always civil war in my country," Gideon added, "and many fightings in the streets of Mogadishu."

"The Transitional Federal Government in Somali is totally incapable of governing the country." Charles' voice rose as he switched into lecture mode, the living room his classroom. "The United Nations reports that 1.8 million Somalis are currently in danger of dying from malnourishment. Four hundred thousand Somalis have been displaced from their homes. And now the government, such as it is, has Al Shabab to deal with which is waging a deadly insurgency in the south and center of the country. Even the African peacekeeping forces are attacked almost daily by roadside bombs and explosive vests. It's a desperate situation made worse because Al Shabab has begun preventing the UN from distributing food and other forms of humanitarian aid."

Unable to sit still any longer Cliff added more wood to the fire, rubbed his hands together and turned to warm his back side. "I heard recently on NPR that *Doctors without Borders* has withdrawn all their volunteers because of threats against their medical staff and the bombing of some of their clinics."

"And the waters off the Somali coast are rift with pirates," Curly added still in professorial voice, "so there isn't a ship willing to sail or dock without being afforded naval protection. The situation is deplorable."

Ruthalice closed her eyes and lifted the blood-soaked land up in prayer. Amidst pops and crackles the logs finally settled into a warm steady glow, and a comfortable silence mysteriously descended on the little circle of friends.

"Remind me again, Gideon." Ali opened her eyes and released his hand. "When did you come to Emerick College?"

"August, 1999. I flee to Mogadishu after my mother die. I live on the streets where I always try to not get killed. I eat and sleep in mission house. That is where Dr. Martin meets me."

Curly snapped out of some distant reverie and abruptly interrupted Gideon's story.

"Martin had retired from teaching and was engaged in humanitarian work for the United Nations in Somalia at that point in time. He and our friend here spent a good many hours together. Terrell took quite a shine to you, Gideon."

A dazzling smile swept across Gideon's entire face. "Professor Martin tell me to come to USA with him. 'How I do that?' I ask and he say 'get your papers'. So we go to Embassy and get a visa for my passport. 'You are good college material,' he say." The young man took a deep breath. "That is what he says." Gideon's face became somber as he mimicked his mentor. "Gideon will go to Emerick and make a future for himself in America!" He burst into laughter then held up his right arm, forefinger pointed toward the ceiling. "Gideon must go to Emerick, an excellent Quaker school.'"

"By Jove, old Martin was spot on that time, eh, Clifford?"

"I should say so!" Cliff grinned broadly. "Gideon Boseka learned to tell his clams from his mussels and snails in no time at all!" Delighted by the memory of young Gideon pouring over the department's meager collection of shells, Cliff began pacing in front of the fire place, his hands gesticulating with every step. "You were the one student I could always count on to be excited about wading knee-deep in Brush Creek! Neither rain nor snow nor dark of night keeps a true malagologist from his appointed rounds!"

"I love mollusks!" Gideon sat ramrod straight and lowered his chin as well as his voice. "Ohio has unusual number of species of fresh water clams. It is hot spot for clam biodiversity! That what my professor Clifford teach me."

Ali clapped her hands. "I'll bet dollars to donuts you can still reel off the definition of malacology." And like co-conspirators, their hands on their respective hearts, the campus minister and the undocumented alien recited in perfect unison: "'Malacology: the branch of zoology which deals with mollusks, the second largest phylum of animals in terms of described species…'"

"All right, all right, that's enough!" Cliff threw up his arms in mock distress. "Now you're making fun of me and my life's calling!" With a sweep of his arm he indicated the television at the opposite end of the room. "The Bengals game comes on in five minutes."

Gideon scrambled to his feet. "Oh, good, American football." He looked at Ali who remained seated with legs stretched out under the coffee table. "Thank you, Miss Ruthalice for getting map. You are very kind."

"You're quite welcome, Gideon."

Shifting to her knees, Ali, with considerable help from the coffee table, hauled herself up off the floor and placed the map on the mantle. "Popcorn anyone? I can have it ready by kick off."

Three hours later and thoroughly satisfied by the Cincinnati Bengals 24-17 win over the Chicago Bears, the friends lingered around the dining room table after supper listening intently as Gideon related his arduous journey to Oakes Quarry two years after the Civil War in Somalia had officially ended.

"My father die in September, 1993." Gideon wiped his mouth with the back of his hand, his voice assuming the tone of an impartial newscaster reading a script. "In my country are nearly 10,000 casualties from our resistance to UN and USA forces in Somalia. They all die between June and October, 1993."

His voice dropped so low the others strained to hear. "My mother and my sister Corinne are killed in September, 1995. The war lord Aideed was fighting for power." He paused. "How you say, Professor Curly? Aideed, is one bad ass man!" A look of defiance sparked in Gideon's eyes, then faded into resignation as he continued his sage. "Six hundred of Aideed militia men fight their way into Baidoa. It is these armed guerrillas who raid and bomb my auntie's house."

He stopped his black eyes filled with pain.

"There was nothing left of the house when the authorities finally got there," Charles added. "According to Martin, there was precious left to bury except a few bones."

Gideon ducked his head quickly squeezing his eyes with his fingers. "So, I stay in Doolow and finish my schooling but there is much hunger and no jobs so I go to Mogadishu to find how to leave Somalia." He paused then dispassionately announced "I am orphan living in Mogadishu streets. I eat a cat."

Ali winced in spite of herself.

"The old man strangles three cats, he see I am hungry and give me one to eat. It is only thing I eat in three days."

Curly nodded in sympathy his mind back on a scene which remained vivid in his memory of city streets and German bombs and the heartbreaking cries of lost children despite the fact it had all happened over 70 years ago. "We war refugees cannot afford to be picky can we, Gideon?" Their eyes met briefly before Charles looked away. "Terrell Martin was in Mogadishu and met Gideon one afternoon in the mission's charity soup line. They both spoke sufficient Arabic to communicate and by evening had become friends. Martin got it in his head that this kid needed to go to college and Emerick was the right place, so in typical take-charge fashion, he set about making it happen. And the rest, as they say, is history!" Charles shoved his chair back and stood up. "Come on,

Gideon, it's time for us to hit the road. This old lad's ready for bed."

Their thankyous and goodbyes completed the VW's headlights bounced down the hill and soon disappeared into the moonless, drippy night. As she watched them go Ali began to realize the depth of her attachment to this charming young Somali. Her inner ear heard once again the carefully selected and pronounced English words and her heart began to ache. N*ow that you have been a guest in our home and my soul has welcomed you in, I must do something to help you survive, dear gentle Gideon.*

Suddenly feeling chilly, Ali joined her husband in front of the dying fire. "They make quite a pair those two don't they, sweetheart. Two terrified little kids running from war yet somehow managing to survive. I can almost picture little Curly huddled on a pile of blankets deep under ground in the middle of London surrounded by a bunch of frightened neighbors and strangers, and a skinny little Gideon foraging through the dumps, running and hiding from the guns in the midst of all the killing and dying in Somalia. And all the while you're up here safe and sound on Horsefeathers Farm with an abundance of everything and I'm struggling to raise a son as a single mom! How can you and I possibly feel even a tiny little bit of their terror?" Ali's nose dripped. Fumbling with her Kleenex, she wiped her upper lip. "I simply can't imagine what it's like to always be on the run, not daring to look back and scared to death of getting caught by the wrong people! It's worse than being a renegade or fugitive because your only sin was to be born in a messy part of the world in the midst of a war you had nothing to do with!"

Filled with rage Ali longed to call upon the wrath of the Lord. Instead she sank to her knees and sobbed. "They were innocent children, God," her voice filled with misery. "Why does this happen in your world?" She blew her nose and stared up at Cliff through watery eyes. He sat beside her on the hearth and placing a warm hand on each cheek wiped the tears away with his thumbs.

"'Remember the alien amongst you for you also are sojourners in the land,'" Ali quoted softly as her sobs subsided. "Until today that commandment was just another one of those biblical mandates, a nice God-saying from the Old Testament and the alien was an impersonal nobody." She gently clasped Cliff's hands and kissed his fingers. "But now that impersonal nobody alien has a sweet, black face and a name and a personal story to tell." She turned and starred across the living room and out through the rain-streaked window into the black night. "Our national paranoia about foreigners feels so totally wrong headed and irrational to me now that we've been in the presence of a living, breathing beautiful child of God. Gideon's a real flesh and blood human being whom our God loves unconditionally. We gave him hospitality, served him a meal and ate together as family."

Cliff gently turned her around. His eyes full of compassion caressed her face. "You know those words Jesus spoke in Matthew where he says 'when you welcome the stranger you welcome me'? Well, tonight I am certain in the depth of my being that Jesus was thinking of our Gideon." Ruthalice's heart was so full of love for this wonderful man she felt it might burst. "There simply has got to be room in this enormous, prosperous country of ours for the Gideon Bosekas of this world! It's too depressing to think otherwise."

Cliff encircled her with his strong arms and drew her close.

"All I can say is thanks be to God for the Terrell Martins and Charles Hopkins and all people like them in this out-of-kilter world."

Ali nodded rubbing her damp cheek against his sweater. "They are living witnesses to God's command to love and to take care of the alien in your midst."

Chapter Seven – Monday Next

"Ok, that completes our survey of the Major Prophets. Are there any questions?" Ali dropped the chalk in the tray and fixed the class with her famous smile of encouragement. A student in the back row whose face was all but invisible under the White Sox cap, tentatively raised his hand.

"Yes, Brian."

"Do we have to know these guys by name?"

"Yes and you need to be able to tell me their basic message to the Hebrew people." Ruthalice lowered her head and fixed the class with an expectant look over the top of her glasses, *library matron style.* "And the Major Prophets are…" She paused waiting for responses from the floor.

"Isaiah, Jeremiah, Ezekiel," Amanda Coffin volunteered from the front row.

"Exactly." Professor Michels glanced at the clock then pointed at the chalk board. "Read the textbook plus these assigned scripture chapters in Amos, Micah, Hosea and Daniel for Wednesday."

The sound of zippers, cell phone tones and miscellaneous grumbling about too much reading, signaled the end of class. *I wish I had the nerve to play my air violin!* Ali mumbled to their retreating backsides.

"Ruthalice, I have a question."

"Of course, Amanda, let's go down to my office."

After dropping her books on the cluttered desk top, Ruthalice plugged the electric tea kettle into the wall socket in the middle of the bottom row of shelves. There was just enough room between the Bible Dictionary and the Concordance for the plug. Amanda set her back pack on the carpet, took a pen from her jacket pocket and selected the orange chair.

"I'm not sure I understand the differences between Jeremiah and Isaiah well enough to talk intelligently about them." She flipped open a college-lined spiral notebook. "Do you have time to help me?"

"Sure," Ali responded enthusiastically and for the next half hour the two women sipped tea and discussed biblical justice and prophesy.

"By the way," Amanda cocked her head to one side and slipped a strand of auburn hair behind her ear. "What does it mean to love my neighbor as myself?" She frowned. "I guess what I'm really asking is what is it I'm supposed to actually *do*?" She paused, a mischievous twinkle in her eyes. "I don't suppose it means I can hop in bed with all the good looking ones. I'm pretty sure Jesus didn't have that in mind."

"Good heavens!" Ruthalice raised her eyebrows in mock horror, "I should say not. But your question is an age-old one and a good one at that." Ali picked up her Bible. "What does Isaiah have to say about how we are to take care of each other?"

Amanda starred intently at her instructor. "Well, you said that Isaiah said that God says." Her laugh interrupted her recitation. "That's getting to be awfully third hand information, Ruthalice!"

Ali shrugged, her "what are you going to do?" look resting lightly on her face.

"Anyway, God says in chapter fifty-eight he's through with burnt offerings, doesn't need them anymore and God wants us to do things in a different way from now on. No more charred sheep and goats." She wrinkled her nose.

"You've got it." Ruthalice leaned forward encouragingly. "God is really gung-ho on justice as an acceptable sacrifice. Take another look at Chapter fifty-eight, Amanda. It's pretty heady stuff."

Amanda ran her eyes and her finger quickly down the onion skin page nodding vigorously as she read. "Let the oppressed go free, clothe the naked and feed them bread." She looked up her eyes shining. "I think I'm starting to get the answer to my original question."

"What does it mean to love thy neighbor – that one?"

She nodded and began collecting her books. "It's a do unto others kind of thing isn't it?"

Ali retrieved the pencil which had rolled across the table and landed on her boot. "I'll remove your yoke, if you'll remove mine."

Amanda stood up and stretched. "Thanks so much for the private tutorial lesson, Ruthalice" she said tucking the bottom of her shirt back into her pants. "My Johnny's been home with the measles since Thursday, and it seems like the only time I can study is at midnight."

"College is challenging enough when you're 19, single and supposedly without a care in the world. I don't know how you single moms do it!"

Amanda snorted dismissively. "I wouldn't know about that. By 19, I had two kids with another in the oven!" She paused at the doorway. "That was just about the time my no-good boyfriend decided to cut and run!"

"Are you still getting child support from him?"

"At least the son of a b," she stopped, blushing slightly. "Sorry, yes, but not every month. Mom helps out so there's enough to get by on with monthly assistance from my friends at the food pantry."

Ali smiled sympathetically. "Come back anytime, Amanda. You know my door's always open, and I'm always ready to listen."

"I know, and I will." She slipped in behind two parents and their daughter who were dutifully following the Admissions Office guide down the hallway.

"We just passed the Office of Campus Ministry on our right," the student intoned in a cheerful voice. "The Quaker meetingroom at the end of the hall is where Oakes Grove Friends Meeting holds unprogrammed worship. That means they don't have a pastor," she clarified as the little group shuffled on past and out of ear shot.

Back at her desk Ali began replaying her conversations with Cliff over the weekend. *Thankfully we've honed in on a cigarette as the culprit thus ruling out Gideon's lantern.* She picked up the faculty/staff directory and began idly thumbing through the bright orange pages picturing each face in her mind trying to recall which ones she'd ever seen smoking a cigarette.

Two hours earlier, Bev Lawson watched Richard wander slowly up the corridor and drape his wet coat over the wooden wall peg in her outer office. Waiting until he'd run down through the raft of message and appointment slips on his desk, she came to stand quietly beside him.

"Richard, Angus Bailey wants a word. He says he found something you ought to know about. This fire story's full of disclosures, isn't it?" she observed calmly as the President fingered her note from the fire chief. "It feels like there's no satisfactory end in sight."

"You're referring to the much sought after and highly prized 'light at the end of the tunnel' are you, Beverly?" *I just pray we aren't sitting on a bombshell that's about to explode.* Richard reminded himself that acceptance of the inevitable came with the job description. "Send Angus in, and get me a fresh cup of coffee while you're at it, will you please?" Watching as his secretary unceremoniously dumped the cold dregs into his prize spider plant, he cringed. "And you're sure acid's good for that plant?"

"Absolutely. They say it's good for the soil."

"Ah yes, the all knowing 'they'." Richard scratched his eyebrow with a long, well-manicured index finger. "When do I have to leave for my meeting in Columbus by the way?"

"Your appointment's at one so I'd say, what, eleven thirty? I'll ask Evelyn to come by the office."

Angus Bailey waiting impatiently in the outer office for Bev's ok, marched through the door and closed it firmly behind him. "Take a look at this, Richard," he instructed thrusting a large brown envelope at the president.

"What is it?" Richard asked unwinding the string from around two red cardboard clasps. He lifted the flap and pulled out a black flip-flop. "Good heavens, Angus, where did you get this?" He sniffed the rubber sole then sneezed. "Whew, it's smoky."

"Bingo!" Without waiting for an invitation, Angus took a seat in the conversation circle and sat back, a look of supreme satisfaction on his face. "One of my student crew members found it yesterday afternoon when they were cleaning up the Pennington cellar. After they'd hauled out all that scorched furniture, they swept the floor and discovered the flip flop under a pile of old rags in the coal bin at the southeast corner of the building."

"What coal bin?"

"Remember the original furnace?" The president nodded. "Well there's a small room in that corner of the basement with a wall, I'd say's probably six feet high, between the old furnace, which is still there by the way, and the coal bin. You gain access to the bin through a three-foot wide opening in that partial wall. The flip flop was stuffed in a corner of that little room." Angus paused. "We find the owner of this and," he snapped his fingers, "bingo, we've got the person responsible for the fire."

"What brings you to that conclusion, Angus?" The president held the sandal up then turned it over. "Just look at the cracks. I'd say it's too old to be wearable. Probably dates back to the days when student club meetings were held down there and since no one missed it, it's just stayed put." He handed the shoe back to his physical plant director than wiped his hands on the white handkerchief he pulled from his pant's pocket. "I suspect nobody's worn it for years."

Angus shook his head. "I disagree. Barbara told me this morning that clubs haven't met in Pennington since the early 70s, and there's no way that flip flop is thirty odd years old."

Angus shifted his weight and crossed his legs. The two men exchanged an uneasy stare. Richard sat down behind his desk and removed his glasses.

"Indulge me a bit here, Angus." Sticking one stem into his mouth, he began rubbing it lightly against his teeth. "Check your duty roster and see if any of your personnel might have been down there sometime earlier last week."

Angus extracted his cell phone from its belt case. "Judy, get the duty roster out for last Monday and Tuesday nights. No, I'll wait." He watched Richard replace his glasses and begin tapping a pencil on the smooth mahogany surface of his executive desk. "Oh really? Doesn't tell us a whole heck of a lot though does it?" Angus snapped his phone shut.

"Well?"

"Ira Ish was assigned the fall inspection of the furnaces on Tuesday. He clocked out at 9pm that night indicating he'd completed the work in both Fox and Penn so that doesn't get us anywhere."

A look of concern slipped across Angus' narrow face as his dark brown eyes traced the pattern on the Persian rug under their feet.

"Mind sharing what's got you puzzled over there?"

"I hate saying anything bad about one of my people." Richard set his pencil down. "I know that Ira has a lot on his plate these days what with his wife's sickly condition. You do know about Nora's condition?" Richard nodded. "I tend to look the other way when he comes in late of a morning and when he uses the shop phone to call Nora at home four or five times a day, but…" Angus cleared his throat.

"But, Ira isn't carrying his own weight anymore?" Richard suggested gently.

"That's it in a nutshell. He's put on a good 30 pounds over the past few years and lately he hasn't been applying himself enough to finish his assignments on time. Over the past six months I've been giving him verbal warnings, but a week ago Friday I finally wrote out a formal written grievance. Another sloppy job or one left undone, and I'll be forced to let him go."

Both men keenly aware of the emotional pain involved in firing an employee exchanged a sympathetic look.

"This is never easy, is it Angus especially in a case like this when we're talking about a man with enormous demands and burdens at home." Richard looked at his hands. "It almost feels like cruel and unusual punishment."

They sat in silence listening to the phone ringing in the outer office.

"And a man who's been serving Emerick College for nearly thirty years." Angus got to his feet. "I don't think Ira's got anything to do with this fire, Richard. He signed out at 9pm and went home. End of story as far as I'm concerned."

"The time card confirms he signed out at nine," Richard agreed solemnly, "but until one of us talks with him, we can't be 100 percent sure he went directly home."

Angus froze half way to the door. "But why wouldn't he, go straight home I mean? He hates to leave Nora alone especially at night." Their eyes met. "I hope to God I'm right but I'll call him in and talk to him directly." Angus paused. "Do you want to keep that flip flop?" he asked half-heartedly almost as an afterthought. "Maybe the police will want it."

"Yes, I'll keep it and inform Chief Turner," Richard replied absently, his concern still with the old handy man. "Does Ira have any family care or sick leave left?"

"Personnel's been more than generous in this case, but, to answer your question, no. Ira used up all his sick and vacation days and then some."

"I was afraid of that." Richard rose and came around the desk. "I know you'll handle this difficult situation." He opened the door then patted Angus on the right shoulder. "If I can be of any help, let me know."

The president glanced at the wall clock, picked up the phone and dialed.

"I'll tell Chief about the flip flop, sir," the female voice at the other end replied courteously. "I'm sure he'll want to follow up with you."

Twenty minutes later Dean Evelyn Feller arrived in the outer office looking just a little 'last year' in a knee length plaid coat. President Willson collected his briefcase. "Off to Columbus," he informed his secretary as they passed on the steps. "I should be back in the office by eleven tomorrow morning."

A drippy gloom enveloped the campus when Ira Ish arrived in his battered Ford pickup and logged in at nine thirty. What remained of the red and orange leaves hung limp and soggy as if the energy to wave and dance had been driven out of them by the cold persistent rain. As he headed for the college maintenance van his supervisor flagged him from across the parking lot. The ensuing conversation left him troubled and uneasy. Twenty windows in Douglas Residence Hall had still required caulking, but now with the last window prepared for winter, Ira tossed the empty cardboard tubes into the dumpster and suddenly felt like a ship come unanchored.

As he stepped around a shallow muddy puddle nestled in a low spot in the sidewalk, Ira spotted the Campus Minister striding down Wood Avenue. He watched as she chatted briefly with two students busily shoveling leaves out of the street drains. He watched her hold out a hand to check for rain drops then lower the polka dot umbrella, give it a shake and telescope the silver handle into itself. As he continued watching, Ruthalice bent over and picked up a bright red leaf before stepping spryly onto the wooden porch. Giving the umbrella another vigorous shake, she opened the door and disappeared inside the meetinghouse.

"You must speak with someone at the college, brother Ira," Father Paul had advised on Sunday, his heavy breathing penetrating the screen which separated the two men. "You cannot carry the burden of your fear alone." Father coughed lightly. "The weight of a secret grows lighter when shared."

In the ensuing silence, Ira clutched the rosary between the thumb and forefinger of both hands as if it were possible to squeeze courage from the sacred beads.

"Is there someone there you can confide in, someone who will listen without judgment?"

I know who to talk with, Father Paul, Ira thought checking his watch. *I will take my one hour lunch right now.* Quickly returning the tools to their proper places in the shed, he phoned Nora from Judy's desk, and at 1:30pm arrived outside the Office of Campus Ministry. He drew a deep prayerful breath and knocked.

"Come on in, it's not locked." Ruthalice swiveled her desk chair around then got to her feet. "Ira Ish, long time no see!" she exclaimed joyfully. Shaking his hand, she drew him inside and closed the door. "Do have a seat. Do you want something to drink?"

"No thank you. I just ate," he lied. *I'm getting good at prefabricating as Nora calls it.*

As she watched Ira sit down Ruthalice thought his body appeared uncharacteristically rigid. "I'm guessing something specific brought you here today, Ira. What's on your mind?"

She crossed her legs at the ankles and waited content for her visitor to take the next step. Ira watched his fingers compulsively curling and uncurling in his lap then cleared his throat. "There is something weighing heavy on my mind. You are the one I feel most comfortable telling it to since you're a minister and all."

Ira raised his head and began to speak in a soft, surprisingly clear voice, though he kept his eyes focused on the top of her boots. "Angus Bailey called me into the office this morning and asked me about signing out Tuesday night." He frowned. "Angus has never questioned my time card before or my movements, so I couldn't for the life of me figure out why he was asking me if I'd gone straight home. Anyhow I told him yes, of course I went home. 'You know how sick and frail my Nora is,' I reminded him. Angus just stared at me and didn't say nothing, didn't question me or nothing. After that he said I could go on my assignments for the day and dismissed me." Ira's eyes moved to her face. They brightened as if something had just shifted inside. "But I didn't go right home Tuesday night, Ruthalice, I went to Pennington Place."

"You were in Penn Tuesday night? " Ali struggled to keep the growing apprehension out of her voice. "Why was that?"

"My work assignment was to clean and inspect the furnaces, the old one in Fox Hall and the newer one in Pennington Place before going home. However since the one in Fox needed a lot of work, I had to pick up replacement parts and didn't get done until nearly nine o'clock. It didn't feel right claiming overtime for work I should've finished on my shift, so I clocked out at 9:10 and went to Subway for supper. I came back to campus and went straight to Penn."

"What time was that, Ira?" Ali asked reminding herself she was a pastor and not a police woman from Scotland Yard.

"I guess it was close to ten. The job took an hour or so because I was home by midnight. Nora was still awake listening to hymns on the Christian radio station."

Ira's fingers squeezed the fabric of his green work pants.

"Ruthalice, I am afraid I will lose my job." An agonized look began to creep across his face. His short powerful hands ceased moving. "I started the fire."

Ali's stomach churned as she seesawed between curiosity and disbelief. Ignoring his first comment, she asked, "What do you mean, Ira? How could you have started the fire? It began in the newspaper in the cubbyhole. That's no where near the furnace."

Ira's entire body sagged as he shifted in his chair. "I went to confession yesterday, Ruthalice," he began in a low voice. "I went to confession because I have fallen back into the sin of smoking cigarettes – again." Lifting his right hand, he waved off the empathy he sensed rising to Ali's lips. "I smoked while I serviced the furnace," he stated simply, his voice growing stronger. "I was afraid security might catch me if I left the building with a cigarette in my mouth, so I tossed the burning butt into that cubbyhole halfway up the steps. I thought it was empty!" His eyes never wavered from her face. "That's why I'm responsible for starting the fire which burned Pennington Place."

Ruthalice had been privy to the lifting of burdens before when folks had finally shared their hidden secrets, but the transformation Ira experienced was more profound than any she had ever witnessed. His eyes were no longer clouded by doubt and shame. The dumpy little handyman sat comfortably erect, his restless hands calmly folded in his lap. His face radiated an inner tranquility, and Ali felt bathed in light and peace.

"I want us to pray together, Ira. Is that all right with you?"

"I'd like that very much." He clasped his hands to his chest and bowed his head.

Ruthalice finished her prayer with words from the 23rd Psalm. "Even though I walk through the valley of death, I will fear no evil because you, oh Lord are with me, your rod and your staff they comfort me. Amen."

Ira crossed himself then kissed his fingertips. "God has forgiven my weakness for smoking. Now *I* must accept the consequences of my carelessness." Ira's eyes held no trace of fear. "Will you come with me to the President's Office, Ruthalice?"

"Of course I will Ira." She reached behind her for the desk phone. "When do you want to talk with Richard?"

"As soon as possible. I want to get this off my conscience."

After speaking briefly with Beverly, she hung up. "Richard's out of town for the rest of the day, but he can see us tomorrow morning at 11:30. Does that work for you?"

"I will be there."

Struggling to his feet, Ira stood awkwardly beside the orange arm chair then stepped forward and enveloped Ruthalice in an enormous bear hug. Mortified by what he'd just done, Ira dropped both arms. His face turned a deep red. Before he could utter a word, Ruthalice exclaimed, "Why thank you, Ira, there's nothing like a good hug to make a girl feel special!"

Standing in the doorway Ruthalice watched the sturdy little man shuffle down the long narrow hallway, then waved goodbye as the outer door swung shut behind him. "God bless and keep you, Ira Ish. May God give you continued courage and strength as you speak your truth tomorrow morning." She moved back into her office. "And please guide Richard into a place of wisdom, compassion and forgiveness."

Chapter Eight – Tuesday Next

"You're awfully quiet this morning."

Cliff leaned against the kitchen sink as the fresh morning sunshine streamed across the linoleum floor highlighting dozens of dust bunnies who suddenly appeared out of nowhere.

"Ira Ish started the fire, Cliff," she said matter-of-factly as she closed the refrigerator door. He stiffened watching her intently. "Are you sure?"

"Ira came to tell me he was in the basement Tuesday night servicing the furnace for winter." She joined Cliff at the kitchen window and slipped her hands into his. "He asked me to go with him this morning when he informs Richard." She bit her lower lip and sighed. "He says he tossed a lighted cigarette butt into the cubbyhole on his way out."

"Our mystery smoker." Cliff's jaw tightened.

"Yes, our mystery smoker."

"What else starts a fire?" he asked tenderly "besides lightening or a short?"

Looking over the top of his shoulder, Ali watched a red-bellied woodpecker work its way tail-first down the tree trunk poking its peak into the rough surface as it hunted for bugs. "He's going to be fired, Cliff. Richard will have no other choice." The woodpecker flew away chattering noisily. "Not only has Ira violated the no smoking on campus ordinance, but this isn't the first time he's misrepresented himself on the time sheet."

"And," but the words stuck in his throat.

Ali looked up alarmed. "And, what?" she asked sharply. Cliff's palms felt damp and sticky. "What, Clifford, what are you thinking?"

"It's conceivable he's committed a crime. I just hope to God he's not charged with arson."

"But Ira didn't know the cubbyhole was stuffed with combustibles!" Even as she protested Ali felt the utter futility of doing so. "Ira's a victim of this awful fire just like Gideon! The cement hole in the wall was empty for all he knew!" Ali suddenly felt queasy. "Who makes the 'arson' call? That's up to the authorities to determine not the college, right?"

"Right."

Reading each other's mind they turned and began rinsing the dishes, grateful for at least one activity over which they had some control. Cliff accepted the plates from Ali's wet hands and placed them on the bottom rack of the dishwasher.

"Richard will be reasonable in his decision regarding Ira, but Angus…" Cliff's voice trailed off as he pictured the volatile Director of Facilities.

"…will be fit to be tied," Ali added resigned to the fact that Ira's supervisor carried around a short fuse which seemed to be awfully easy to light sometimes.

A large Blue Jay chased two gold finches away from their breakfast as it bullied its way across the feeder strewn with black sunflower seeds. *There's plenty of seed for every single one of you, you know. You don't have to be such a jerk.*

"This is going to be a no good, rotten, lousy very bad day," Ruthalice announced. "I'm going to need a first-class attitude adjustment before taking on Suzy Henson's *Daughters* at 4:30."

Clifford, lost in his own train of thought, placed the black and white cow cream pitcher into the dishwasher and raised the door with his foot.

"Do you know how old Ira is?"

"I'd guess 62, but it's only a guess. Both of their girls are grown, and I know they have at least one grandson."

By unspoken agreement the M&Ms stopped talking. They'd done as much as they could for the time being. Cliff grabbed his leather satchel off the boot box in the mudroom as Ali lifted her woolen shawl from its peg just inside the kitchen door.

"I'll probably be late tonight, sweetheart," she said following him into the garage. "Weeks ago I let Suzy Henson rope me into speaking to her *Daughters of Sarah* group at 4:30. She made a shameless appeal to my vanity by informing me she'd already told her group quote Ruthalice's take on the wives of David is the best I've ever heard by anyone, anytime, any place unquote." Ali rolled her eyes in mock dread. "By the time Suzy serves high tea and the ladies do their round-the-horn 'what's your favorite woman in the Bible?' introductions, it will be after five before I get my 15 minutes of fame."

"Oh, the sacrifices you pastors have to endure!" Cliff swung open the door to his truck and tossed his briefcase onto the seat. "Makes me glad I'm a simple malacologist stuck at a little denominational college in the middle of southwest Ohio who gets to indulge his passion for clams and mussels by teaching invertebrate zoology a measly two weeks out of every four semesters!"

Ali grinned and batted her eye lashes. "Not a bad price to pay for being able to stay put on your ancestral family farm with an adoring wife added in to sweeten the bargain!"

He chuckled. "On a more practical note, are you saying I may or may not be called upon to make supper tonight?"

"Well put my dear, Clifford that may well be the case." She hoisted her canvas bag through the window of her little yellow car. "You're on standby." She came around to the open truck window. "I need to get going. I've got some calls to make before Ira shows up." They exchanged a perfunctory goodbye kiss and headed into town. Once in the parking lot, Ali sat for a moment collecting her thoughts, then closed her meditation with her daily morning prayer: "May I serve your purposes in everything I say and do this day and everyday. Thank you, God. Amen."

Ira knocked on the half-open door at 11:15 sporting a brand new Kelly-plaid flannel shirt tucked snuggly into navy-blue Carhartts, a black belt holding everything securely in place.

"May we pray before going over to Fox Hall?" he asked hopefully.

Ali smiled and without speaking took his calloused hand in hers. Keeping his eyes on the floor, Ira crossed himself when she had finished and released her hand.

"Thank you, Ruthalice. I'm ready now."

Ira followed Ruthalice into the corridor. Neither one spoke as they crossed the parking lot and climbed the stairs to President Willson's corner office. Richard looked up from his desk and spotted them standing side by side in the outer office.

"Come in, Ruthalice, Ira. I'll be with you shortly."

Ira waited until Ruthalice chose a seat then sat down to her left. The president laid his fountain pen on top of the yellow pad, closed the office door and joined the circle.

"What is it you wish to talk with me about?" he asked kindly skipping the usual perfunctory opening chit-chat. "I understand this has something to do with the recent fire in Pennington Place." Focusing his complete attention on Ira, Richard was prepared to hear whatever the old handy man had to say.

Twenty minutes later Ira followed his campus minister down the stairs and back across the parking lot to Frame Meetinghouse. Without speaking they entered the worship room at the far end of the building then sat side by side on the first bench inside the door.

"It could have been worse," Ira began rubbing both palms on his thighs. "With six months severance pay and Social Security starting on my birthday in April, plus Nora's disability payments, we can make it ok." He glanced sideways at Ruthalice. "It was awful nice having someone else in the room. Thank you for coming with me," he added shyly a thin smile playing at the corner of his lips.

"I am grateful you confided in me, Ira." She returned his smile. "Is there anything else I can do to be supportive of you and Nora at this time?"

"Could you come by and visit her, maybe later this week?"

"Of course," Ali replied immediately, "and I will hold both you and Nora in the Light of Christ," she added softly.

"Continue to pray for us." Leaning forward, Ira squeezed the edges of the bench and got to his feet. "I'll go empty my locker now."

Rising to stand beside him, Ruthalice extended her right hand. "You have been a good and faithful member of the maintenance team all these years." She swallowed the lump in her throat. "Go in God's peace, Ira Ish. I only wish you were leaving under different circumstances."

"Me too." He inhaled deeply then forced his breath out with a whoosh as if to expel all evil spirits that might linger inside and then squared his shoulders. "This afternoon I will meet with the police and fill out a written affidavit." His voice quivered and dropped to a whisper. "With God's help, Nora and I will walk through this dark valley before us as we have done so many times before." Pushing the meetingroom door open, he headed for the maintenance workshop and locker room for the last time.

Ruthalice sank heavily onto the padded bench. "Thank you, God; thank you, Richard; thank you, Angus for all your compassion and care under such emotionally charged circumstances."

Hearing the gentle swish as the heavy meetingroom door slid over the carpet she glanced over her right shoulder to see who had entered. Barbara Carroll looked quickly around the room. Spotting Ruthalice she walked over. "I was on my way to the library and thought I might find you in here." The dean of students smoothed her beige corduroy skirt over her elegant legs and gracefully sat down.

"Word travels fast."

"I got Richard's email at 11:53. Apparently he notified President's Council members the minute you two walked out the door." She paused. "We've been requested to keep this confidential until Angus informs the rest of the maintenance crew."

Babs fixed her gaze on the back of the bench directly in front of them. Rubbing its smooth surface with both hands, she turned to Ruthalice. "How is Ira taking his dismissal?"

"Pretty philosophically actually, and though I don't know Nora very well, she's always struck me as a woman with so much suffering in her life, she will absorb this as just one more burden to be born." Ali rubbed the crease on her forehead with her middle finger. "They are people of strong faith. When he was in my office yesterday he told me it was Nora who urged him to go to confession Sunday morning even though he hadn't told her the whole story. 'She can see into my soul' he said."

"Ira's lucky to have such support." Babs sounded wistful. "Something like this would have been Steve's excuse to cut and run. He never did care one whit about anybody but himself."

Ali remained silent allowing the twinge of regret over her minimal support during the Carroll's tumultuous divorce to run its course.

"Well, enough of the pity party!" The dean's hands dropped to her lap. "I came by to tell you something interesting, Ruthalice. Evelyn stopped by my office a few minutes ago and informed me that one of the students on the clean-up crew found a flip-flop in the basement of Penn."

Ali jerked to attention. "Really? Where was it?"

"Angus had a work crew down there Sunday afternoon, and one of the kids found it in the corner of the coal bin. I didn't even know there was a coal bin in the basement, did you?" With no response forthcoming, Barbara went on with her story. "Anyway, Richard informed the police who showed up about an hour ago to collect this new piece of evidence, but now that Ira's confessed to starting the fire, I'm not sure what a flip-flop has to do with the price of cheese." Babs chuckled and shook her head. "Surely our dear old Ira didn't clean the furnace in flip-flops, leaving one behind as he scampered up the stairs!"

Ali interlaced her fingers, slid her arms between her knees and leaned forward deep in thought. Dean Carroll gently placed a hand on her friend's back. "What's troubling you, Ruthalice?"

"Something's just occurred to me Babs, that's all. I need time to cogitate a bit longer if you don't mind."

Taking the hint Barbara rose to her feet. "Of course." She stopped at the door. "Oh there is one more thing, Ruthalice. When I called my RAs together last Friday night, I asked if they knew of any student celebrations planned for this fall. I thought somebody might have snuck fireworks in for something like that."

"Good thinking, Barbara. No wonder you're such an excellent dean of students!"

The trace of bruised feelings evaporated as the two women deliberately negotiated around the potential trap of professional territorial jealousy.

"Well, be that as it may, the students told me that the Delta Omega sorority is celebrating its 50th anniversary on campus on October 29th. They were also quite sure that if the men's soccer team manages to win the divisional championship, there will be a bonfire and much hoopdelah!" She grinned, "That's their word not mine."

"Thanks Babs, that's good information to have," *even if I'm not sure where it leaves us.* The dean allowed the door to close of its own weight behind her.

Outside on the sidewalk four male students, gym bags slung over their shoulders, playfully shoved each other as they sauntered to the athletic facility. Watching them pass through the tall, narrow meetinghouse window, Ali felt a surge of energy. *It's time to go find Charles,* she thought suddenly clear about what to do next. *He's going to hear about the flip flop any minute now, and I want to be the one to tell him.*

Taking the inside steps of Fox Hall as fast as she could, Ali was gasping for breath by the time she arrived at Curly's second floor office. The class schedule was scotch-taped to the door: "History Seminar, T/Th 2-3:15".

She scowled at her watch. "That's another forty-five minutes before he's finished." *Now what, Sherlock?* Walking to the copy room Ali found a discarded pad of sticky notes beside the paper clips. She tore off the top square and using the only pencil she could find wrote, "Call Me, ASAP, RaM" and stuck the note to Charles' office door. *That's the best you can do for now, kiddo, unless you're planning to barge into class.* Figuring that if she couldn't reach Charles without interrupting the history seminar then neither would anyone else, she headed back to her office.

Where the heck are you, Charles Ali wondered after her third attempt to reach him was to no avail. At 4:10, unable to sit still any longer, Ruthalice climbed the stairs to the second floor of Fox Hall one more time and pounded on the wooden door. She even stooped to rattling the door knob in the vain hope she might somehow be able to break in and discover her old friend asleep at his desk. No such luck.

Still hoping Curly would call, Ruthalice waited as long as she dared before walking the six blocks to the home of Suzanne Matilda Polk Henson, Ali's mother's oldest and dearest friend. Bible in hand Ali lifted the brass fleur-de-lys door knocker, let it drop and waited patiently on the sprawling front porch of the stately white colonial. Mums of every color humankind could cultivate were elegantly displayed in matching ceramic pots against the house. Water gurgled as it descended through a fountain of clay pots adding its voice to those of the potted chrysanthemums. Standing there Ruthalice was filled with joy. *Everything seems to be saying: WELCOME.*

Suddenly the door swung open. "My goodness, Ruthalice Michels you're actually five minutes early!" Suzy exclaimed delightedly before sweeping her into the brownie-scented interior. "Girls, girls, our speaker's here. Come and say hello."

With a bright smile plastered on her face, Ali accepted the rose-covered tea cup and joined eight women clustered around a flower-bedecked dining room table. *Only 90 minutes to go, girl. You can do this*! The group took their seats then spent the next 30 minutes introducing themselves. Finally it was Ali's turn. As she led the octet of elderly *Daughters* back to the royal court of King David and his many wives, Ruthalice lost tract of both time and the jumble of conflicting concerns she carried around since The Fire.

"We've got time for one more question," she said finally after a rapid fire glance at the mantle clock. "Yes, Mrs. Crimp, you're right. David took Abigail as his wife after as you so delicately put it, her nasty old husband Nahum died."

Suzy Henson took over. "Ok, girls, it's nearly 6 o'clock. Let's give Ali a nice round of applause, shall we?" Suzy led the applause then reached under her chair and extracted a large box wrapped in gold leaf paper with matching bow. "A little thank you from the *Daughters of Sarah* circle."

She beamed around the circle of perfumed seniors dressed in their casual best then placed the feather light box in Ali's hands. Ruthalice carefully untied the bow, slipped her fingers under the tape at each end and lifted the lid. Inside lay an exquisitely delicate turquoise and silver ball. Gently lifting it from the pale yellow tissue, Ali held it up for all to see. Light seemed to burst forth from the middle of the sphere as she held it by the stem and slowly rotated it. Fascinated by the changing patterns dancing inside, Ruthalice turned to her hostess.

"Where on earth did you find such a gorgeous thing?"

"You can thank Martha Jean." Suzy indicated the blue-haired lady beside Ruthalice. "She bought it on their recent trip to Venice."

"Gerald and I went to the glass-blowers the last day of our tour." The petite woman's voice was so wispy and soft Ruthalice had to lean sideways to catch her words. Cool bony fingers lightly patted the back of Ali's right hand. "I am so glad you like it dear," she continued in her breathy voice. "I have one just like it only mine's bright red." She looked vacantly at Ruthalice. "Actually," she added her voice suddenly loud enough for everyone in the room to hear, "I never liked that blue color, so when Suzanne asked me about a..."

"OK, gals," Suzy quickly broke in. "Don't forget the *Daughters* are at Jenny Feingold's next month, same time, different station," she added cheerfully.

Twenty minutes later Suzy handed Ali her wool wrap.

"You'll have to forgive Maggie my dear, she's a bit scatterbrained these days I'm afraid and doesn't really know what she's saying half the time. It's a shame really. Martha Jean Scattergood used to be Oakes Quarry's 'hostess with the mostest' but I'm afraid those days are well past."

"Good heavens, Suzy, don't worry about it," Ali assured her warmly. "The ornament is truly gorgeous. I'm going to hang it front and center on our Christmas tree."

"Oh, good. Did you see the shepherd and his two lambs inside?" Grinning at Ali's perplexed look, Suzy Henson gave her husky chuckle. "I didn't think so. Well, look more closely when you get home." She stepped onto the prickly welcome mat to stand beside Ruthalice. "Take my word for it, my dear. There's a young shepherd in there, I promise."

Ali started across the front porch carefully cradling the box with its delicate contents against her chest with her right arm, when Suzy tapped her on the shoulder. The touch of her fingers sent an electric shock through Ali's body. *Every cotton pickin' time you stop me like this you're about to get all conspiratorial and ask me something I don't want any part of.*

"OK, Ruthalice, I've been a good girl and behaved myself all afternoon, but now that all our little busy body friends have gone on home I want to know all about the recent incident." She fixed Ali with the LOOK, the one that rendered a rash of goose bumps when she was a little kid, and moved closer. "Give me the complete scoop, young lady," Suzanne demanded in a voice which matched the LOOK.

"The complete scoop on what exactly," Ruthalice asked playing the dumb card which had never worked very well. She was rapidly becoming annoyed which struck her as a more mature reaction to Suzy's badgering than panic, which was the other choice.

"On the fire in Pennington Place of course. Isn't the campus minister privy to all the secrets dirty or otherwise?"

"Good grief, Suzy," Ali retorted suddenly exhausted by her brazen attempt to pry information confidential or otherwise, out of her best friend's daughter. "Just read the Boone County paper and you'll know as much as I do." *Am I blushing with that little white lie I wonder?*

It sounded as thought Suzanne Henson had just harrumphed in annoyance. "You are stonewalling me aren't you, Ms. Michels just like your mom used to do when I got too close to the truth!" Suzy glowered at the nearest pot of mums and severed two dead heads from their stems with a pinch of forefinger and thumb. "You never were much good at gossip even as a teenager." She tossed the shriveled up blossoms over the porch rail. She peered at the tiny stain left by their resin. "Your mother raised you right, kiddo," she said gazing down the tree-lined street, "in spite of my attempts to the contrary.

What a meddling pain in the you-know-what I must have been."

Ali was about to offer a limp version of you-weren't-that-bad when Suzy abruptly changed the subject. "Thank you so much for coming this afternoon, Ali," she said briskly. "I know you have much more important things to do with your time and talent than speak to a group of little old ladies."

Will wonders never cease? Ali wondered as she carefully picked her way around globs of soggy leaves plopped about on the sidewalk as if by some unseen hand. *Just when I've given up on Duzy Suzy, she manages to come through with a surprising bit of insight.*

What would Suzy do if Gideon were suddenly dropped into her lap? Startled by the query's clarity, Ali stopped in her tracks. *Would she feed and clothe him as the stranger in our midst or lock the door in terror?*

"I don't really know," she whispered to the inner voice, "but I have a tough time imagining Suzy Henson slamming the door in Gideon's face or leaving him stranded on her front porch, be he a refugee or alien or undocumented worker or the man from Mars! Underneath that maddening contrary exterior beats a compassionate heart. Suzy would bring Gideon into her home and if she had any second thoughts, she'd simply deal with them afterwards."

For the first time in a long time Ali remembered why own her mother had loved Suzanne Polk Henson so much.

Back in her office Ali spotted the blinking red message light and snatched up the receiver. "Darn it Charles, I just missed you." She shrugged. "C'est la vie I guess," and hit the erase button. "I'll try again tomorrow."

The gentle niggling Ruthalice recognized as God's persistent tug at the edges of her heart remained with her all the way home. "All right, Lord," Ali said shutting off the car engine, "I'm open and I'm listening."

All of a sudden the skittish miscellaneous thoughts in her brain fell into place like once-jumbled jigsaw pieces, creating a complete picture. "Oh, my gosh!" Ali leapt out of the car. "Why didn't I see that before?" Dropping her bag on the cluttered countertop, she flung her shawl on the breakfast nook table and dashed into the living room.

"Cliff, Cliff, listen to this!" She threw herself onto the couch then tugged at his shirt sleeve like a spoiled child. He lowered the *Boone County Gazette,* and stared at his wife.

"You've discovered the formula for lasting world peace? Anything less can't possibly merit this much enthusiasm." He leaned over and kissed her on the left cheek. Catching her mood his voice became somber. "Tell me what's got you so revved up."

"I think I've figured out who put the fireworks in the basement." Cliff's right eyebrow shot up. "After Ira left the meetingroom this morning, Babs dropped in and related a conversation she'd had with her resident hall advisors last Friday night. The long and the short of that conversation is that the Delts are planning to celebrate the sorority's 50th anniversary on campus later this month. It isn't too much of a stretch to think that one of the sorority sisters planned to spice things up a with a fireworks display."

"That's illegal, you know," Cliff pointed out without thinking.

"That's beside the point, Clifford. Since when did that stop an 18 year old from doing anything?" Ali leaned forward. “Remember I told you about my meeting with Rani Brown, the Quaker student from Jamaica? Well, she’s been in my office a couple of times since then to tell me about conversations about fires and drawing attention to themselves etcetera that she’s overheard. At first I made the assumption the women were talking about the homecoming bonfire, but that wasn’t it at all.“ Ali made a crease in her skirt and began rubbing the raised material between her first and second fingers. “The point is Rani recognized one of the voices as Priscilla Brinkley’s. Then after the fire Rani told me that when she got up to go to the bathroom around 1:15 Wednesday morning she saw somebody running from behind Penn Place.”

“Gideon.”

“That’s my guess. But listen to this, Cliff.” He turned toward her resting his right arm on the back of the couch. “Remember that Rani overheard the girls bragging about how spectacular their little caper would be? I’ve been a bit slow on the uptake here, but I think I’ve finally put two and two together.” Ali stood up. Her pacing back and forth in front of the sofa reminded him of the murder mystery detectives on television who call the entire family together in the parlor to announce the killer. “Priscilla has access to the basement. She works upstairs in the Archives. I saw her name plate on the student worker’s desk. And Ernestine wouldn’t keep track of her comings and goings because Priscilla’s not part of the alumni office.”

“So she’s invisible and in plain sight,” Cliff added helpfully. “Whoa, slow down a minute.” He frowned uneasily. “If you’re headed where I think you are, you’re working up to a pretty serious charge, Ruthalice.”

Ignoring his word of caution, Ali plopped down beside him on the couch and continued to spin her theory. She had to put words to the jumble of emotions tossing about inside. "I know Priscilla's a Delt because her roommate told me so."

Cliff scratched the top of his head. "So your working hypothesis is that Priscilla has motive for buying fireworks i.e. the 50th celebration, and she has the means to keep their existence a secret because she has access to the Penn Place cubbyhole anytime she wants it."

Ali shifted uncomfortably. "It all feels way more real and a lot more serious now that we've put words on my hunch doesn't it?" She reached impulsively for his hand and gripped it tightly. "I guess I'm not ready to accuse Priscilla of blowing up Pennington Place and hauling her into court, but..."

"But, she could be our missing link and thereby be an accessory to a crime."

"At the very least she may have to take responsibility for the Delt's little surprise running seriously amok." Ali looked down at their clasped hand. "I've decided to visit Babs in the morning and find out more about this kid. I just know I'm onto something."

Chapter Nine – Wednesday Next

"Speaking of shoes, I knew there was something else I forgot to tell you last night!" Ali stopped at the red light. "One of the students on the clean-up crew found a flip-flop in the coal bin Sunday afternoon."

Cliff inhaled sharply. "Oh, God, Ali, have you told Charles?"

"I left him a message to call me before I went to Suzy's yesterday," she replied pulling into the Campus Minister's parking spot, "and I tried again last night after I got home, but there was no answer which is a bit disconcerting."

They sat in silence starring out the front window of Ali's lemon yellow Focus. Members of the cross-country team jogged across the campus green, their long thin legs moving so rhythmically they made running look easy. Watching as they rounded the corner of Harvey Library and disappear from sight, Ali let out an envious sigh. *I could run every day and never look like that.*

"This is disturbing news, Ali," Cliff said reaching behind him for his briefcase. "Anything which points to somebody besides Ira being in the basement recently means people will ask more questions. We're running an enormous risk here of exposing Gideon's presence." Cliff's voice trailed off as his gaze wandered up to the second floor of Fox Hall. "This discovery unfortunately raises the stakes considerably. Charles' involvement will eventually come to light." Cliff closed his eyes wondering how his dear colleague would hold up under the criticism which was sure to come his way from all quarters for his role in hiding an illegal alien.

"Unless."

"Unless what?" he asked opening the car door.

"Unless the powers that be are willing to accept Ira's cigarette as sole culprit and let it go at that. Then the investigation can stop." Ali pulled the keys out of the ignition and dropped them into her canvas bag

"You wish," Cliff replied gently. "I don't know if wishful thinking will make it so." He blew a kiss over the roof of the car and headed for Dalton Hall.

"I'll follow up with Charles, sweetheart," she called to his retreating back, "but he's in class right now and I teach Bible at ten, so I doubt I'll catch him much before noon." Grateful the heavy weigh of the past week hadn't crushed the joy out of the little pleasures of life, Ali stood enjoying the rear view of her husband's long, purposeful strides. "You go, guy!" she sighed happily. "Imbue those young minds with a passion for things biological!"

On the other side of campus at precisely 10:05am, Charles Eugene Hopkins clumped up the stairs of Dalton Hall, meandered down the second floor hallway and deposited himself in the wobbly visitor's chair.

"Good morning, Charles. You appear to be in fine fiddle this morning."

"It's a bugger of a good day, mate! A Brit like me perks up and comes to life when the temp's in the upper teens."

"We're talking centigrade here, right?"

"Of course, it's the measurement ordained by the Almighty."

Cliff felt a momentary measure of relief. The barometer for Charles' state of mind was his sardonic sense of humor. If sarcasm had not abandoned him, the burdens had not become too onerous to bear. Cliff took a deep breath suddenly felling like the specter of death standing at the parlor door with scythe in hand.

"Charles, there's been a new development." *I hope this latest bit of news isn't going to prove to be the proverbial last straw.*

A wary look replaced Curly's relaxed smile. Cliff lowered his voice.

"Ruthalice told me this morning that a flip flop turned up in the basement of Penn."

"Am I to surmise that's why your dear wife called me yesterday?"

Cliff nodded.

"The hounds are closing in, my friend. Your unwelcome news does indeed cast a shadow over the current state of affairs which I fear indicates urgency on my part in resolving this matter." *My God you've become verbose and tedious you old fool!* He gave his colleague an apologetic look. "Not sure I deserve the likes of you two, Clifford," he said ruefully, "you two M&Ms."

He watched the little black spider working her way down a thin thread of web into the safety of the hanging plant's foliage. *If only it were that simply to disappear from sight and be camouflaged by your surrounding.* Grasping the arm rests Charles suddenly pushed himself up and out of the chair. With surprising vigor and a dismissive "ta!," he disappeared down the corridor leaving Cliff in his wake feeling every bit the messenger who'd just been shot for delivering bad news.

As the last student packed his backpack, Ruthalice dropped her class notes on her desk, shut the office door and scurried across campus. She trotted up the steps of Fox Hall and at the gruff "present!" that greeted her knock, entered the spacious office. Charles raised his head, smiled weakly and motioned her to the only other chair.

"Hallo, Ruthalice." As she gently closed the door he added, "Looks like an official visit from our campus minister."

"I've come to tell you that maintenance"

"found a flip-flop in the basement of Pennington Place." Curly leaned his upper body against the edge of the desk. "Yes, Clifford informed me earlier this morning." He stared dolefully across the cluttered surface between them.

"It belongs to Gideon doesn't it, Charles?"

The senior member of Emerick's faculty looked around the office, his eyes passing slowly along rows of beloved texts and biographies lined up for inspection.

"I've got over eight hundred and fifty volumes in this room and an additional two hundred plus in my library at home." Curly articulated each word in his cultured British accent a habit he fell into when deeply troubled. "Gideon told me Sunday whilst we were dressing that he was unable to find his other flip-flop." Curly's eyes rested on a small pale-gray soap stone carving of an Inuit hunter, spear in hand. "Foolishly I dismissed it as a trivial point pompously pointing out that it was too bloody cold to wear sandals anyway and promising we'd stop and purchase proper footgear on our way to your abode."

Charles grit his teeth as the ponderous burden in his gut began to take on a life of its own.

"Gideon snuck out last night to go to work for God's sake!" The words spilled out in a torrent of bent-up frustration. "You know what he said to me when I chewed him out? 'I give my word to Miss Green. She count on me, Uncle Professor Curly. I must go to my job.' Bugger it all!"

A warm glow spread through Ali's chest.

"God love him," she said her voice thick with emotion. "Just think Charles how good it must feel for Gideon to know someone's counting on him, that he's needed somewhere."

"That's as it may be, but I feel like a damn greenhorn rookie cowboy trying to rein in a young stallion!" The old professor shook his head. "First Luther pops over, then he sneaks off to the warehouse and now the sandal!" He fixed her with a grim stare. "The stakes have been raised considerably, my dear. By now our president has informed the chief of police which means we're about to be overrun by a fleet of inspectors combing the campus for clues as to its ownership."

Half hidden beneath bushy black brows, Curly's eyes hardened along with his voice. "Our young friend has been flushed from his den like a fox. He may have managed his initial scamper without being spotted, but now I fear the authorities are closing in and an entirely new strategy is demanded."

Curly grasped his jacket lapels with both hands and tugged his coat until the collar stretched tightly across the back of his neck. Getting to his feet he turned to the east-facing window. Pennington Place her elegant façade streaked with black smoky smudges stared forlornly back at him.

"I'm not cut out for this, Ruthalice," he said his voice heavy with exhaustion. "I want to be done with this damnable interruption and the burden fate has dropped upon me. And yet," he paused, stuffed his hands into his trouser pockets and rocked back on his heels.

"And yet," Ali prompted gently, afraid of closing him up completely if she prodded or even moved a muscle.

"Indeed," he said as if in conclusion, seemingly oblivious to her presence. "There was this old soldier who kept babbling about mustard gas in the First War, how it burned and poisoned everything." Charles stared at the ground below. "What if the Germans use it again? what if I fall on the third rail of the train track and get electrocuted like my da said I would if I wasn't careful?" The old professor raised his head and gave his companion a melancholy smile. "As a lad I was terrified of everything hiding from the Blitzkrieg in the underground. *Everything*: the dark, the shadows, the unseen, creepy-crawlies." As the re-occurring childhood nightmare galloped across his mind, Charles felt his skin prickle and grow clammy.

"In spite of your fear you carry on," Ruthalice met his gaze with a warm smile, "like the good compatriot and friend you are."

"Yes, well." Charles coughed and turned back to the window. For a moment he seemed to be lost in a time warp of his own making. Suddenly he straightened up and squared his shoulders. "'It is the brain, the little gray cells on which one must rely'," he quoted slipping into an affected Belgian accent. "Yes, Miss Lemon, the hounds have caught the scent, but that kind of business does not succeed against Hercule Poirot!"

His laugh startled and alarmed her.

"*Dear Lord,*" Ali prayed silently, "*how desperately we need your wisdom and courage as panic seems to be taking over in spite of the bravado. Dear Jesus,* she pleaded, *please keep Gideon and Charles safe from all the hounds.*"

Ruthalice joined Curly at the window and laid her hand lightly on his shoulder.

"Lady Penn looks as though she's had a rough night out." Encouraged by the gruff chuckle, she added "Cliff and I will do all we can, Charles, and be assured we've told no one about Gideon."

"That never occurred to me. However my dear, the noose is tightening and constables are on the prowl." He spun around. "You and I will speak of this matter again in future." And without so much as a 'fare thee well', Professor Hopkins stepped around her and left the room.

Ruthalice waited while two faculty members walked by, pulled the office door closed behind her and hurried down the stairs. *I've no idea what Curly's planning to do, but it's time I acted on my hunch that Priscilla Brinkley is our fire-cracker stasher. Ira certainly contributed his part, but I'm convinced this is a case of where it takes two to tango!*

The Jones lobby was swarming with students. Ruthalice slipped into the dean's outer office and waited while Barbara Carroll finished her phone conversation. Replacing the receiver, Babs waved her on in and stood up.

"Can I get you a cup?" she asked brandishing her gold-trimmed white mug. "I need another shot before lunch."

"No, thanks, Babs, I'm floating as it is."

Ali remained in the doorway marveling again at how quickly the contrived casualness of the conversation circle across from the dean's desk made her uncomfortable.

Barbara Francelia Carroll was head and shoulders above the rest of her colleagues in the 'got class' department. Intricate lattice teak bookends supported a handful of colorfully bound books. Exquisitely-framed reproductions of Monet's lily pond and a Turner seascape balanced each other perfectly on opposite walls. A handsome octagonal Persian rug covering nearly every square inch of floor from desk to outer wall was to die for! *You just can't beat the combination of money and good taste,* Ali mused for the umpteenth time. *And just to prove you can't judge a book by its cover, you'd be hard pressed to find a more perceptive and refreshingly straight-forward Dean of Students! Nonetheless, every time I come in here I feel like I should check my skirt for cookie crumbs and my shoes for doggie doodoo or something else equally nasty before setting foot on the rug or sitting in one of those gorgeous pearl and peachy rose-covered upholstered chairs.*

"So business or pleasure?" Babs sat down.

"You said the Delts have an anniversary coming up."

"Their fiftieth is October 29th."

"I'm wondering if one or more of the sorority sisters decided fire crackers would add pizzazz to their celebration."

Babs stared thoughtfully into her cup. *This much acid can't be doing my stomach any favors* she reprimanded herself.

"Isn't Priscilla Ann Brinkley a Delt?"

"Yes, president actually." The dean raised her head and fixed Ruthalice with a no-nonsense stare. "She and Jen Blake, her roommate, live in Douglas Hall but spend a good deal of time at the chapter house on Mulligan Avenue, which, as you undoubtedly know just happens to be right next door to the Keefer place."

She picked a miniscule piece of lint off the left sleeve of her jacket and chuckled. "Bee Keefer's motto is *once a Delt always a Delt* which works to the college's advantage. Because in her day a Delt was a real lady and behaved accordingly, so Jack and Belinda keep a parental eye and tight rein on the comings and goings at the Delta Omega house."

"When I was up in the Quaker Archives the other day, I noticed the desk name plate. Priscilla is the student worker." *OK, get to the heart of this, Ruthalice, and quit pussyfooting around.* She shifted gears. "What's your professional take on Priscilla Ann?"

Gently setting her mug on the glass topped table, the dean placed her hands finger tip to finger tip and raised them to her lips. "A bit of a challenge. She's officially a sophomore but Emerick is the third college she's attended in as many years having flunked out of the first and despising the second." Babs squeezed her upper lip between her forefingers. "Papa Brinkley's paying the full ride, appears to be generous with his financial support, but the occasional Saks Fifth Avenue birthday present is the extent of his parental involvement. I've arrived at this conclusion from comments I've overheard here and there," she added dryly.

Ali merely nodded as the picture of a spoiled, lonely kid eager for attention began taking shape. "Out of sight, out of mind," she opined softly.

"There's a bit of the devil-may-care about her. Her RA has tangled with Priscilla Ann's expectation of getting her own way on more than one occasion."

"My way or the highway?"

"My way or just try and stop me!" The dean replied looking annoyed.

"I suspect she mastered the art of manipulation at a tender young age."

Babs lightly folded her arms and rested them against her chest.

"Her dad's a big wig CEO who apparently is on the road more than he's home. He did come to campus for Parent's Day which earned him a few brownie points in my book. Mama's a stay-at-home housewife who lives virtually alone on the Outer Banks. Does a lot of squabbling with her neighbors according to her daughter. Brings *Desperate Housewives* to mind, doesn't it?" she added humorlessly.

"The Brinkleys sent their daughter an awfully long way from home for her third attempt at school. At least they're not one of our 'helicopter parents' hovering overhead, ready to swoop in at the first sign of offspring angst." Ali fixed the dean with a puzzled look. "Does make me wonder though how they heard about Emerick. We're not exactly on the radar screen for the North Carolina surf and sun crowd."

A look of amusement scampered into Barbara's hazel eyes.

"An acquaintance of her mother's brother has a daughter who attended Emerick six yeas ago and loved it!" Barbara checked her watch. "Anything else on your mind today, Ruthalice? I've got an engagement at noon."

"Nope but this has been extremely helpful, Babs. Thanks." Ali got to her feet. "I'm working on a hunch."

"Please keep me in the loop," the dean replied then added almost as an afterthought, "Fire crackers would make for a rather spectacular 50th anniversary party. They are illegal by the way."

"So I'm told."

Stepping back into the sunshine and already formulating a course of action, Ruthalice headed straight for Pennington Place. *Why not? An unannounced pastoral visit from the campus minister might be just the thing!*

Upstairs a hand-lettered sign hung around the neck of a handsome iron horse statue on the student worker's desk. 'B back at 2' was penciled in bold script.

Phooey! well, that settles that. It's on to Plan B, and I do believe Plan B starts with lunch.

Having settled on her excuse for dropping by, Ruthalice returned to Penn Place at 2:15. Even though the windows were flung wide-open, the smell of smoke hovered in the open area at the top of the flight of stairs. The archival space with its picturesque view of Dalton Hall across the top of the porch roof had always been one of her favorite spots on campus. *The clutter is a bit off-putting right now,* Ali reflected skirting the boxes of books and file folders occupying the middle of the room. *But I do love it up here.*

Apparently unperturbed by the general chaos of her surroundings, Priscilla sat at the small student desk along the west wall casually flipping through a magazine.

"You've got quite a view from up here, Priscilla." Ruthalice noticed the sign had been removed from the horse's neck. "I'll bet this is a lovely place to work."

"It's ok." The smile was non-committal. "We're not really open," she added looking up and nonchalantly running her fingers through silky shoulder-length blue-black hair. "I'm just taking a break from the packing."

I'm dealing with a real pro here. She's got her who-gives-a-rip persona perfected to a 'T'. Ruthalice grinned deep inside knowing she was up for the challenge!

The young woman folded the corner to mark her place, closed the magazine and fixed her visitor with a sanguine smile. "You're the campus minister, right?"

Striking the most relaxed pose she could and still remain standing, Ruthalice lightly laid her right hand on the horse's head. Broadening her smile until her lips began to complain, she asked casually, "You a horse lover?"

"Have been all my life." Priscilla's eyes lit up. "Kelly, my dapple gray mare- I've got her boarded out at Candlewood Farm."

"So, do you get much opportunity to ride?"

"Couple times a week and for sure on the weekends." Priscilla glanced at her *Western Horse Woman* and began fiddling with a pencil. "Since I'm stuck on this campus every weekend, it gives me something fun to do."

"I've heard campus social life on the weekends leaves something to be desired."

"It stinks!" She dug an iPod out of her designer jeans pocket. Flipping it open she peered at the screen, shrugged her shoulders then snapped it shut. "Sorry about that. Did you need something in the archives?"

"Not really, I just came by to chat." Ali crossed her arms and leaned against the wall. "I understand the Delta Omega sorority is celebrating its 50th anniversary this month. You're a Delt aren't you, Priscilla?"

"President actually," she replied getting to her feet.

Shoving a cardboard box with her foot, she bent over and began haphazardly stuffing it with well-worn leather and cloth-bound volumes. Ali stifled the urge to grab the lovely old books out of her hands and lay them properly into their storage place thus affording them the respect they deserved as orphans from the fire.

"Got anything special planned?" she asked opting to keep the tone of curious and friendly campus minister, *though I'm beginning to feel more like Jessica what's her name on Murder She Wrote!*

"Oh the usual stuff." The young woman seemed to make an elaborate point of stifling a yawn. "Why do you ask?"

With precisely the opening she needed Ali dove in. "The fire marshal has determined that a cigarette tossed into that little recess in the wall partway down the basement steps is what caused the Penn fire." Priscilla paused in her packing. "Someone spent considerable time disguising the fact they were storing firecrackers there by crumbling up newspapers and stuffing them in front of an old cardboard box."

"Why would anybody do that?" Priscilla retorted reaching hard for a tone of indignation. Sitting back on her haunches she stared angrily up at Ruthalice who casually slipped both hands into her skirt pockets.

"Whoa, wait just a minute here! Are you implying something?"

"Just wondering what you make of my little theory?"

She glowered at Ali then returned to her haphazard packing. "What theory?"

"That fireworks would make a spectacular addition to the 50th anniversary celebration."

"That's ridiculous as hell!" Blushing slightly Priscilla soldiered on. "If one of the sisters is even thinking of a stunt like that it's news to me, and I outta know cause I'm totally in charge of the whole thing!"

"Would you be willing to ask around for me then, Priscilla? If I were president, I'd sure want to know if my sisters are planning something illegal behind my back, especially since it's a first-degree misdemeanor in the state of Ohio to own let alone discharge fireworks." Ali picked up the worn leather-bound copy of John Woolman's *Journal* patiently waiting to be packed away with the others lying by itself on the shelf beside her. She lovingly flipped through the book then gently laid it on top of the stack in the box. "The fine for first-time offenders is up to $1,000 with a possible six months in jail," she added casually watching the coed's reaction out of the corner of her eye. Nothing!

Boy you're good, or innocent argued the other adversarial voice inside. Realizing she'd come to the end of this little cat and mouse interrogation, Ruthalice lightly tapped the desktop with her knuckles and turned to leave.

"Can you imagine either Chief Turner or President Willson turning a blind eye to something as blatantly illegal as a fireworks display on the back lawn of a residential street?" She stopped at the top of the stairs. "I would guess a stunt like that at a minimum would bring years of probation as well as a heavy fine."

Moving quickly to the window, Priscilla Ann watched Ruthalice stride across the leaf-strewn lawn toward Frame Meetinghouse. Without a word she snatched the dark red leather shoulder bag her mother picked up at Coach as a going-back-to-college present and disappeared into the bathroom. Locking the door behind her, she gripped the sink loathing the look of panic reflected in the mirror.

"Geesh, I look like a deer caught in the headlights! Get a grip, girl. You can't walk across campus looking scared witless." Resisting the urge to scream in frustration, Priscilla slowly became aware of the click of approaching heels in the hallway and quickly turned both faucets on full blast. "Just a minute, Ernestine," she hollered over the rushing water. "I'm almost done in here."

"Take your time, dear," came the husky reply, "I can wait."

Pressing wet paper towel to her eyes, Priscilla took a deep breath, tossed the soggy paper in the basket and turned off the water. Pasting a look of distress on her face, she slowly opened the door.

"I'm so glad you're here, Ernestine, I'm suddenly feeling really, really sick." Priscilla wrapped both arms around her middle and looked up forlornly at the five-foot-eleven Director of Alumni Affairs. "Would you be awfully inconvenienced if I went home early?"

"Oh good heavens no, dear of course not. It's all this smoke, I'm certain of it! Go take care of yourself, Priscilla, you look pretty peaked. Go take a deep breath of fresh air. I can manage if anyone comes in which I doubt they will since the place looks disserted with all our first floor windows boarded up." Ms. Perkins exhaled deeply, a weary look of resignation on her thin face. "We're going to be packing things for awhile longer. You'll have no trouble making up your time."

As Ernestine pulled the bathroom door behind her, Priscilla hurried down the stairs before her supervisor could change her mind. *Maybe the old bat thinks I'm about to toss my cookies* she snickered making a beeline for Douglas Residence Hall. Once inside she ran down the hallway then burst through the door of her room startling her roommate curled up on the bed.

"Jen, we've got to talk!"

Priscilla locked the door behind her, spun the desk chair so its back faced the bed and dropped down straddling the seat. Fixing her roommate with the obstinate look her parents had come to dread she rested her crossed arms on the chair back.

"I've got a chem exam at eight tomorrow, Prissy. Can't whatever it is wait?"

"Now, Jen!" Priscilla was determined to squelch the sense of apprehension sneaking up on her by taking control of this conversation. "Believe me this is way more important than any chemistry exam."

Jen sighed and with a look of resignation on her face laid *The Principles of Organic Chemistry* face down on the bed beside her.

"Ruthalice Michels knows about the fireworks."

Jennifer Blake sat bolt upright and opened her mouth but before she could protest, Priscilla cut her off.

"Just listen to me ok," she hissed. "The cops figure the fire started when some dumb brained yoyo tossed a cigarette into the crevice where we stashed our fireworks. So duh of course they exploded!"

"Oh, no," Jen wailed sitting up so fast her chemistry text hit the floor with a thud.

"Jen, get a grip for pete's sake! Even if our smarty-pants campus minister with her let's-play-detective attitude thinks she's got it all figured out, there's no way she can prove anything. We bought 'em out of state, remember?"

"What are you saying, Prissy?" Jen swiped at her eyes with the back of her hand. "How can you be so sure they won't find out it was us?"

"Stop being so pathetic and just think about it for a minute, Jen." Her voice softened. "The fire burned up everything in the basement, right? And since it started in the newspaper there can't be anything left but ashes." Priscilla joined her roommate on the bed. "Look we've got nothing to worry about if we just act like normal people and keep our mouths shut. Trust me on this one, ok Jen?"

As tears trickled down her cheeks Jen squirmed uncomfortably then pressed her back against the solid pale-blue cement block wall.

"My parents are going to kill me if I get kicked out of school over this." Jen inhaled deeply then cleared her throat of the residue from her runny nose. "Mom didn't want me pledging in the first place. She'll have a fit!" Jen drew her knees up to her chest and buried her face in her arms.

Priscilla was momentarily speechless. Even though this was not the first time one of her brainstorms had gone awry and it was left to her to figure a way out of the ensuing mess, she was determined to swivel the spotlight of blame onto somebody else. *I'm not going down for this one. It wasn't us who ditched a fag in the basement now was it, officer? We don't even smoke, so how is this fire our fault?*

Priscilla inhaled deeply, counted to five then reached out and touched her roommate's head.

"Hey, Jenny-penny, it's going to turn out all right. We're sisters remember. We stick together through thick and thin!" Feeling her roommate relax Priscilla punched her playfully on the shoulder.

"Absolutely no one, no one but you and me know where those fireworks came from. Think about that. If we don't screw it up by getting hyper, this'll all blow over by Halloween."

Crossing her fingers behind her back, Priscilla silently offered her version of the Help Me, Lord fox-hole prayer and slid off the bed. Sniffling one last time Jen wiped her eyes on the bed spread and attempted a valiant smile.

"Mum's the word then, Prissy. The two musketeers stick together no matter what, right?"

"Right! "

Jen stood up, opened her arms and gave her roommate a damp hug.

"I guess I feel better already. I guess everything's going to work out ok. It's just..."

"Just what, Jen?" Priscilla tensed as her roommate's voice began to wobble again.

"It's just I feel awful knowing we're responsible for the fire in Pennington."

"We are? How do you figure we are? What planet are you on, Jennifer? Have you taken up smoking and become incredibly stupid at the same time?"

Priscilla began pacing from bed to desk and back.

"Fire crackers don't ignite on their own you know, Miss 'A' in Chemistry. There's no way in hell anybody can hang that fire on us! It's the idiot and his burning cigarette!" Priscilla's sense of self-righteousness was growing by leaps and bounds. "What an incredibly careless thing to do, toss a burning butt into newspapers. Give me a break already, will ya?"

"I suppose you're right as always." Jennifer dropped back onto the bed and starred glumly at her chipped red toenails. "I guess we'll find out who gets blamed won't we, one way or the other."

"Keep your mouth shut, Jen and tough this one out with me."

The two young women stared at each other across the room clinging to their resolve to stick together.

"Let's go eat. I'm starving." Priscilla grabbed a hair brush from her dresser top.

Jen shook her head and turned on the goose-neck lamp clamped to her headboard.

"Can't - I've got to study some more, remember?"

Priscilla rummaged through a stack of books on her desk then sank into the red beanbag chair in the opposite corner.

"Ok, I'll wait for you. I've got to read that chapter on respiratory diseases for Horsemanship tomorrow anyway."

Ruthalice spent what remained of the afternoon writing her bi-weekly "Friendly Musings" for the student newspaper. Satisfied with her essay on the role rumors play in campus life, Ali interlaced her fingers and stretched both arms above her head. *A quick trip to the potty and I'm outta here!* Her half-hearted search for any remaining dirty mugs to rinse out was interrupted by three raps on the door.

"I'm here," she responded automatically as she examined the *Support Your Local PBS Station* mug with a layer of cocoa in the bottom that had to be at least two days old.

"Hi, Ali with an 'i'". An imposing figure in her navy blue police uniform, Lieutenant Rosemarie Harris stood squarely in the middle of the doorway. "We need to talk, Ruthalice."

She stepped inside and closed the door.

"Sounds serious, Rosi, I'm all ears."

Ali motioned to an empty chair, but Rosi remained standing, hands on hips.

"There was just enough left of the original packaging for the fireworks so I was able to decipher three letters and figure out the name of the manufacturer." Lieutenant Harris's no-nonsense black eyes met Ali's inquisitive gaze. "With the help of my whiz-kid web dude son, we traced back to the company in Indiana that sells this particular brand of fireworks. Not bad for a lousy speller like me!" The hint of a self-congratulatory smile softened her face. "I played around with the letters UND until I came up with Thunder, googled it and bingo! there they are big as life: Thunder Mountain Fire Works. Their logo is 'Choose your Pyro-Power'. The owner wasn't real pleased to learn about the part they played in this particular caper."

"Whoa, I'm impressed, Rosi. We'll have to make you an honorary member of our *Puzzlers Are Us* club!"

The lieutenant chuckled. "Do I get a nice shiny plaque I can hang on my wall?"

They remained silent for a moment enjoying the lightness of a growing friendship.

"So where do we go from here?"

The smile disappeared. "Actually that's why I'm here. We know who bought the fireworks, Ruthalice. Thunder Mountain prides itself on keeping very good sales records."

Twenty minutes later Lt. Rosemarie Harris escorted Priscilla Ann Brinkley and Jennifer Elaine Blake to the Oakes Quarry police station in her black-and-white squad car. As Ali stood watching the tail lights disappear, the excitement she'd felt earlier in the day as she imagined herself right up there with Miss Marple and Jessisca-what's-her-name vanished leaving sadness in its wake.

God, please protect these impulsive children of yours as they enter their own valley of darkness. They desperately need your Love to sustain and guide them.

As she crossed the campus green, security lights came to life one by one. Ruthalice climbed the stairs to the third floor of Fox Hall.

"Beverly, I'm here to see Richard. It's vital that we talk immediately."

The president glanced up then motioned her in.

"There's something you should know, Richard," Ali said calmly and closed the door behind her.

"Want me to drive sweetheart? You look exhausted."

Ali leaned wearily against the car's head rest.

"In fact," he added as his wife closed her eyes. "How 'bout we eat at Louellens tonight?"

Driving home after two large servings of chicken and dumplings in the richest gravy in town, Cliff reached for Ali's hand.

"Want to talk?"

Ali turned and watched her husband's face flicker like an old silent movie as the city lights slipped by.

"Do you want the full story or the Reader's Digest expedited version?" she replied squeezing his hand.

"Whatever you're up for's fine with me. I'm your captive audience for the next 45 minutes."

"I tested my theory about Priscilla Brinkley and the Delt's 50th anniversary. Turns out Priscilla Ann's president of the sorority, but when I pressed her about the idea of setting off fireworks as part of the celebration she got indignant and insisted that no one was even thinking of such a stunt." Cliff hit the brake as two deer bounded across in front of them. "But she did and was."

"Did know and was involved?" Turning into the garage Cliff turned the engine off and swiveled in his seat. "And how did you learn that incriminating bit of information?"

"Lt. Harris came by the office around four to inform me she'd gotten enough of the manufacture's name from the burned packaging to enable her to track down the store. From there it was a piece of cake apparently for the sales clerk to trace the purchase directly to Priscilla Ann Brinkley, credit card and all."

"You're kidding! The kid used a credit card? What a twisted trail of innocent actions converging into a tangled web of intrigue resulting in one helluva mess, or something like that." Cliff was suddenly drained of words.

"You know about the flip-flop." Cliff nodded wearily. "Well, Richard told me the cops have it in their possession and are holding it as an item of relevance to the investigation. I don't know, maybe I'm getting a bit paranoid, but I swear Skip gave me a baffled look as if accusing me of knowing more than I'm letting on."

"Sweetheart, we're both in this now up to our eye balls, as you are wont to say, but we mustn't let our imaginations run away with our good sense." Now it was Clifford's turn to sigh uneasily. "It does feel like eons instead of just hours since I spoke with Curly, but his reaction immediately told me the flip flop belongs to Gideon. Charles is absolutely convinced that Gideon's about to be flushed out of the fox's den any minute by the INS."

The garage appeared to fill with water as Ali began to weep. *I seem to be doing an inordinate amount of crying these days.* She lowered her head and exhaled softly. "Cliff, he may be right."

"About deportation?"

"About being flushed out." Ali fished a wad of Kleenex out of her pocket. "Rosi asked me if there's another African student on campus."

"Another? Then she knows about Luther I take it."

"Yes. She told me the dispatcher reported that the 911 caller had a heavy accent that sounded African. So she followed up and asked Luther if he'd made the call, and he said 'no'." Ali blew her nose. "Now get this – Rosi said 'I stopped an African male one night in the parking lot of the Warehouse Store. He told me he lives on campus which satisfied me at the time so I didn't take his name.'"

"And you said?"

"That Luther is Emerick's only African student."

Cliff nodded and released her hand. "You know Ruthalice Michels, for a woman of the cloth you've become quite the detective, a veritable Rabbi Small in a skirt!"

"Wrong gender and wrong religious tradition," she chuckled, "but I appreciate the flattering comparison."

She kissed him firmly on the cheek then rubbed her cold nose against his warm scratchy face. Then suddenly from out of nowhere an enormous weight slammed into her chest.

"Cliff, I can hardly stand this any longer." She gasped for breath as if the wind had been knocked out of her lungs. "The poor man's simply traded one basement hideaway for another. It's just a matter of time before one of Curly's nosey neighbors spots him and calls the authorities. Sheppard Place is simply not a safe enough place for Gideon to hide. Besides, at some point dear old Curly's going to get worn out from sharing his bachelor pad week after week."

"You may be spot on with that one, dear heart." Cliff realized his wife's fear was contagious, and the more he thought about it the more legitimate it became. "At our weekly research confab yesterday Charles said, 'The Bishop of Swithum is relegated to the back seat these days whilst I attend to Gideon's predicament.' It was his way of justifying an entire weekend away from the library and his book research." Clifford felt an ache in his heart. It was an unfamiliar emotion he'd come to know of late.

Ali felt the strength of her husband's mixed feelings about this whole "Gideon Affair" as they'd begun calling it, and silently watched as the internal struggle played itself out on his handsome face.

"What are you afraid's going to happen" he asked finally, his voice back to normal. "That Immigration will swoop in unannounced deportation papers in hand and summarily stick Gideon on a plane bound for Somalia?"

"That's exactly what I'm afraid of, Cliff. I witnessed that very thing in Gatwick Airport outside London, and I'll never ever forget it. The poor man lay on the floor crying and hugging his brown paper bag pleading with the circle of Bobbies to let him stay in England, and of course there was nothing I could do. What can any of us do really in the face of these laws?" She pulled her heavy braid over her shoulder and rubbed its soft tip against her cheek. "I'm haunted by the image of Gideon, handcuffed to a burly INS agent, being dragged onto a plane bound for Mogadishu where he'll be summarily dumped back on the streets. It's a terrifying scenario, and I feel totally unable to prevent it."

"It isn't much of a life is it, being constantly afraid to answer the door or telephone, spending the bulk of your days in hiding, sneaking out three times a week to go to work for a few hours." Cliff rubbed his eyes. "My God, the man earned his Bachelor's degree fair and square. Circumstances have been unkind to Gideon which doesn't alter the fact that he deserves a real job and a new beginning."

"We are to treat the orphan, the widow, the poor and the alien amongst us as one of our own, for we also are sojourners in this land," Ali paraphrased softly. "Gideon Boseka orphan, poor, driven out of hiding by a fire not of his own making… He is the true alien among us. And, you know what I think, Cliff?" She paused. "I think that our little Emerick College campus right here in Oakes Quarry, Ohio *is* the land upon which we, you and I and

Gideon and Charles and the rest of us, are sojourning just like the Bible says."

"Sounds like the Old Testament equivalent of the golden rule to me."

"'Do unto others as you'd have them do unto you.' Yes, it's definitely like that."

In unspoken agreement the M&Ms left the day's accumulation of papers, notebooks and other academic paraphernalia on the back seat of the car and walked around the side of the house. Hand in hand they crossed the damp lawn to the front porch. Ali rested her arms on the porch railing. "The earth is the Lord's and the fullness thereof,'" she recited to the star-filled sky, just as a great-horned owl hooted from the woods. She turned and leaned her back against the oak rail.

"It's pretty amazing really. All Rosi had to go on were the letters UND on a one inch scrap of singed cardboard. Her son did an on-line search for fireworks manufacturers and found a Thunder Mountain somewhere out west. She contacted them and was told they have a distributor in Richmond, Indiana and the rest as they say is history."

His arm firmly around her shoulders, Cliff guided Ali through the front door, down the hall and into the master bedroom. Cliff dropped his jeans on the floor. Clad only in t-shirt and shorts, he slipped between the sheets. "What was the girls' reaction when you confronted them?" he asked pulling the blanket to his chin.

"Jennifer's initial response was complete hysteria. She collapsed on the bed sobbing, 'I told you they'd find out, Prissy!' After that little dead give-away performance, it was pretty anti-climatic. Turns out that Priscilla had smuggled the packages into Penn a few weeks ago, then stayed late one afternoon claiming she still had reshelving to do and offered to lock up. Nothing suspicious about that so of course Ernestine agreed." Ali disappeared into the closet re-emerging in an ankle-length orange flannel nightie. "And the motivation for this bit of theater - to up stage last spring's fraternity anniversary party. Those two women became obsessed with outdoing the Gammas by setting off a display of rockets and other what-have-yous that would blow everyone's socks off. They were aiming for the most spectacular fireworks show Oakes Quarry had ever seen!"

Ali unbraided her hair, brushed it with a few vigorous strokes and climbed into bed.

"When Jennifer finally got a grip on herself her only concern seemed to be whether the cops had to tell her mother. Rosi informed her that since she's 20 and therefore an adult her parents won't be notified unless she wants them to be. That bit of assurance seemed to allay her fears. The last I saw of them they were in the back seat of Lt. Harris' squad car on their way to the station to give their statements."

Cliff scooted over and kissed her forehead. "So what happens next?"

"I met with Richard right away of course. The usual procedure is for Babs to convene a judicial hearing, and then the college's wheels of justice will begin to roll. I suppose for starters Priscilla and Jen will be placed on probation, maybe even the whole sorority house. I have no clue what the police will do. At this point all I know for sure is that Ohio law is mighty strict when it comes to the possession of fire works."

Ali took his head in both hands and kissed his mouth.

"I've got it!" Cliff exclaimed through their pressed lips. "I finally remember the full quote I couldn't come up with before, 'what a tangled web we weave when first we practice to deceive.'"

"Ah, Sir Walter," Ali breathed into Cliff's ear as he stroked her bare hip. "He had such a way with words!"

Chapter Ten – Thursday Next

By three o'clock Thursday afternoon, Ali had wrestled with her urge to 'do something about Gideon' and pondered her options until her brain hurt. Though the bare branches still dripped and dark gray clouds loomed on the horizon threatening at any moment to engulf the sky again, the cold morning rain had quit. Periodically the sun peeked weakly through the clouds taunting her to come outside. Restlessness gained the upper hand. Ruthalice snatched her red polka dot umbrella, hiked the six blocks to 534 Sheppard Place and pounded on the kitchen door.

Dummy! Charles is on campus. Gideon's not going to answer the door.

She punched three numbers in her cell phone before it dawned on her that Gideon wouldn't answer the phone either. Thoroughly exasperated, she leaned her half-collapsed umbrella against the wall, jerked the door open and stomped into Curly's cozy kitchen. *Gideon's going to have a heart attack whether I storm the fortress or tippy-toe in, so let's just go for loud!*

"Gideon, it's me Ruthalice Michels." Her voice seemed to echo down the hallway and bounce back to the kitchen. Hearing nothing but her own breathing, Ali headed for the living room calling as she went. Opening the basement door she hollered down the steps. "Gideon, it's Ruthalice. I've come over for a visit."

Hearing the whispery sound of bare feet sliding across carpet, Ruthalice stopped moving. Gideon, his face barely visible in the dim light leaking around the window curtain, materialized in front of the loveseat.

"I am here, Ruthalice ma'am," he announced faintly. Ali strained to catch the words. "I am frightened when I hear someone knocking on the door. I hide behind the chair." He moved silently into the center of the room. "Now, you are my guest and are welcome in my new home." He bowed from the waist, his face glowing. "I get you something to drink, Miss Ruthalice. You sit here, please," he added pointing at the wing back chair.

Gideon padded into the kitchen and rummaged around in the refrigerator. "Here," he said proudly reappearing in front of her chair. He handed her one of Curly's mismatched glasses. "I take the strips, you are the flowers!"

Sipping their lemonade they smiled at each other comfortable for the moment with the gentle silence. Ruthalice took the opportunity to survey the modestly furnished living room with its jumble of bachelor paraphernalia accumulated over a lifetime of indifference to interior décor. The two wing-back chairs were a matched pair though hers was clearly Charles' favorite judging by the arm rest covers which were clearly a recent purchase of convenience since the fabric didn't agree with the rest of the chair. All that could be said for the frayed cotton drapes is they kept the light out while providing a modicum of privacy. The single well turned-out piece of furniture in the otherwise shabby living room was the delicate, meticulously polished harpsichord tucked safely into the corner. Rumor had it that Charles Eugene Hopkins, an accomplished piano player in his day, built the instrument himself because the ones on offer were not up to snuff.

"Gideon," she said setting her empty glass on the table, "I want to know something. Are you happy here?" His eyes darted around the room before coming to rest on his lap. "I am worried about you always having to hide. That's why I am asking."

His long black fingers gently massaged his thighs as a look of resignation settled on his face. "I know how to hide. When I am little boy I am hiding from my drinking uncle who comes to my mother when my father is gone." He lifted his head and fixed Ruthalice with a dreadful stare. "I hear my mother crying no! no! but I can do nothing." The skin tightened over his clenched jaw. "I hide after my mother and my little sister get killed at the house of my grandmother in the bombing of Baidoa."

As hopelessness hovered around the edges of her spirit threatening to overwhelm her with despair, Ali's earlier determination to persuade Gideon he must return to Somalia began to waver. *Have you walked a mile in my shoes yet?* The unspoken query startled her, and she blushed. *No of course not,* her inner voice replied. *Then do not rush to judgment.*

"There is too much fighting in my town of Doolow. When I go to school sometimes we hide from the fighters because the teachers say the soldiers maybe kill us; I hide after I get no more green card; now I hide again in basement of my friend Professor Curly." He shrugged his narrow shoulders. "What does it matter where I hide? I am good hider." Gideon's uncomplaining smile contained a hint of pride.

Suddenly overwhelmed by sadness Ruthalice could think of nothing to say. Words of advice, even expressions of comfort which came to mind sounded like tired platitudes to her embattled heart. Finding herself torn between the longing to embrace this resilient young man and cradle him in her arms and her penchant for offering practical suggestions, Ruthalice was trapped in the ages-old theological conundrum: what does God's love-in-action look like? *Indeed, Amanda, how do we love our neighbor as ourselves? Am I to offer shelter and protection or should I urge him to turn himself in to the authorities?*

Ruthalice leaned forward resting her elbows on her knees. Gideon sat motionless watching her wrestle with her conscience.

"There is no real government in Somalia now," he began in that incredibly straightforward way of his, "no control over people in the north where my town is. Islamist terrorists declare allegiance to Al Qaeda and plot to overthrow Somalia transitional government. The US don't like Somalia because it is a safe place for terrorists."

Ruthalice listened as the litany of violence grew. *You sound so matter-of-fact dear Gideon as though speaking your lines for a performance. Perhaps it's the only way you can talk about the atrocity that is present day Somalia.*

"The United Nations tells the world Somalia is worst humanitarian crisis of any country in Africa. The World Food Program is accused to be anti-Islamic by Al Shabab, so now they stop aid from reaching anybody. So over one million of my people are starving. Many more will die."

"But Gideon, if you stay in the States you'll always be a fugitive running and hiding from the law." This was the scenario which troubled her most. "You do not dare let your guard down. You'll have to be watching your backside all the time." *God, this is all so hopeless!*

"If I go back to Somalia I must be careful all the time. No," he insisted adamantly shaking his head, "it is much better I stay in USA."

"But, you'll never be able to have a normal life here." The minute the words were out of her mouth, Ruthalice knew what was coming.

"What is normal life, Miss Ruthalice? In Somalia it is run, hide from soldiers, always run, always hide. But in America soldiers don't kill me. All they do is put me in detention." His eyes filled with resolve, and Ali understood there was no dissuading him. "Until INS deport me, I stay here. I stay here with my friend Professor Curly." His amazing smile returned without a trace of animosity. "Professor Curly promise I stay with him and we figure out what next to do."

The stab in her heart spread out and encompassed her entire body; even her soul felt worn out and disconsolate.

"Dear Gideon, I simply cannot bear the thought of you consigned to a life as a fugitive, always on the lam forced to take cover and hole up in some dirty, god-forsaken place." Ruthalice intertwined her fingers. "My prayer vision for you is that you be able to stand in the sunshine as a free man." Her voice wavered. "And unafraid, dear God above all else unafraid."

"Where I do that, Ms. Ruthalice?" he asked wistfully. Gideon paused and lightly touched her arm. "Not here in Oakes Quarry, not in Mogadishu, not in USA, not in Somalia. Where I stand in sunshine unafraid?" His gaze sought the photo of Mr. and Mrs. Hopkins sitting on top of the harpsichord in the corner of the room. "I do not know what unafraid feel like, except," his eyes softened and welled with tears, "except on my knees with Jesus. God is my rock and my salvation, always my help in times of trouble."

Ruthalice followed his gaze to the young couple celebrating their 10th wedding anniversary. "Tell me about Serita and you daughter, Gideon." He continued to stare at the photograph of Charles young parents. "She and the baby died in childbirth, is that right?" The only sound was a loud gulp as he swallowed. "Did you give the child a name before you buried her?" she asked kindly.

"Grace," he replied taking his eyes off the photo and looking at Ruthalice with a smile, "Grace Marie Boseka. Serita die in birth but Grace live for another week in incubator." His hands rested lightly in his lap. "They all die and leave me, my mother, my sister, my father, my wife and baby daughter – everybody leave me but Jesus. That is why I pray God do not cast me away, do not take your spirit from me or I will die also."

Ruthalice stared at him in awe. "You have the faith that moves mountains, Gideon Boseka. I have never known anyone with such strength."

"You not know very many Somalis, Ms. Ruthalice," he said kindly. "We learn to trust only God."

"Gideon, there is something else I've been wanting to ask you about. Were you able to hold a funeral for your mother and your sister after they died in the bombing?"

He nodded. "Yes, I bury my mother and my sister, my auntie and my grandmother in the family plot." He shuddered. "Then the soldiers come. They try and catch me to force me in their guerrilla band, but I escape and hide."

"They were going to kidnap you and force you to join them? Child soldiers. Lord, have mercy," Ali moaned closing her eyes as they filled yet again with tears.

"Do not cry, Miss Ruthalice. They not catch me! My Uncle Professor Curly is very smart man, and he tell me he knows how I can stay in America. So do not worry about me." Gideon placed his hand against his throat and lightly touched the cross with his fingertips. "I know also how to pray," he said his voice filling with confidence. "I am sometimes very afraid but I am not alone now. I have you and Clifford and Professor Hopkins." He sat up straight and beamed. "I hope someday I am husband again and have many children!"

Ruthalice felt as though a warm hand just opened her heart. "You have much to teach me about suffering and patience endurance, my friend, and even more about faithfulness and trust. Your faith is constantly being tested and you remain steadfast. What a precious, beloved child of God you are."

She rose and walked to the love seat where his well worn Bible lay. Opening to Psalm 51, her eyes met his. "I always pray this verse, Gideon, verse eleven: 'Create in me a clean heart, oh God and put a new and right spirit within me.'" Ali closed the Bible. "I came here this afternoon convinced I knew better than you did what you should do, and I learned that I know nothing because I have not walked in your shoes. The Spirit spoke to me this afternoon through you, Gideon, and my heart is contrite. You are the expert here, not me," she added with conviction.

Out of the blue Ruthalice started to giggle startling Gideon who gave her a questioning look. The tension unintentionally broken she burst into laughter. "Gideon," she gasped taking both of his hands in hers, "You know what *I'm* afraid of? Frogs!" His eyes widened in momentary disbelief.

"Really?"

She nodded emphatically. "And big black spiders and SHARKS!" It was down right therapeutic shouting her childhood long held secrets.

"Really?" Then he got it. Grinning from ear to ear he joined in. "I am afraid of little green men!"

"Why on earth are you afraid of little green men?"

"Because," he grinned mischievously enjoying the game of one-up-man-ship, "it mean I am on the moon!" And they laughed together until their sides hurt at the absurdity of it all.

As the conversation rested for a moment Ruthalice's face relaxed into a gentle smile. "You said Professor Curly will work something out. I know Charles to be a good man and a faithful friend. I'm sure he will do everything he can to help you, Gideon, and so will Cliff and I."

"You and Professor Clifford are my new best friends." His eyes lit up. "Maybe I come and work for you on your farm and make a big garden and grow many foods. Up on the hill in the woods no one know I am there," he added confidently. "People say it is mystery that the garden of the M&Ms grows so tall and strong!"

Ali burst out laughing and clasped her hands to her chest. "The M&M Magical Magnificent Monster Garden! I love it!" Suddenly aware of how late it had become, Ruthalice reached for her umbrella. "I must go now, Gideon. Is there anything you need I can get for you?"

"A new green card?" Gideon chuckled. "Yes, I think a new green card!"

"Don't I wish I could," Ali replied sincerely. She drew the wool cape over her shoulders. "But until we can get you a new green card, how about dinner with us again this Sunday?"

"I come and cook flat bread and make chicken small-small." Her perplexed look caused him to grin even more. "Chicken stew with lots of vegetables. Hmmmmmm!" He rubbed his stomach. "It is very good Somali dish!"

"Then it's a date. Clifford and I will expect you and Charles at one o'clock on Sunday afternoon. Have Charles call me, ok?"

"OK, I tell him call M&M," he laughed again as they walked as far as the kitchen door. His spirits soaring Gideon remained by the window watching Ruthalice walk down the driveway. "I make grocery list for Professor Curly," he murmured happily. "Then we cook chicken small-small!"

A police car, its motor idling, occupied the Campus Minister's parking space. The officer inside watched Ruthalice pause at the entrance to Frame Meetinghouse, consider for a moment then head her way. Placing the cap snuggly on top of her jet black curls, Rosemarie Harris climbed out of the squad car and waited, clipboard in hand. Her demeanor signaled a no nonsense exchange was about to take place. Suddenly wary, Ruthalice felt her palms grow sticky as she approached the lieutenant. The women greeted each other with a perfunctory nod. *What is going on here? No hi Ali with an 'i' this time 'round.*

"I've been mulling something over for the past few days," Lt. Harris began in a congenial enough tone of voice. Ruthalice let her guard down an inch or two.

"And now I'm confused." She looked down at her black leather boots. "I think I told you that I stopped an African male in the warehouse parking lot a few days ago, and he gave me to believe he was on campus. Then you told me Emerick's only African student is a man named Luther Mouana, right?" Her dark eyes hardened. Ruthalice met the stare with one of her own.

"Luther is a Somali, and is Emerick's only student from Africa." *Why do I feel as though I have to fight formality with formality here?* Refusing to soothe the tone of their chat, she leaned lightly against the squad car's back bumper content for the moment to be led.

"I met Luther this afternoon," Rosemarie said nonchalantly examining the fingernail polish on her right hand, "and he is a good six inches taller than the male I questioned." She gave Ruthalice a quizzical look. "So, who is this shorter African male, Ruthalice?" The silence between them became increasingly confrontational. "Perhaps I am being unfair here in assuming you know everyone on campus," the lieutenant amended brushing off a leaf which had landed on the shoulder of her navy-blue police jacket.

"Are you equating this man and the Pennington Place fire somehow?" she asked as calmly as possible given the electricity charging through her system. "Otherwise I don't understand your interest in him." *Please understand what I'm doing, here, Rosi,* Ruthalice implored silently.

A knowing smile tugged at the corners of the lieutenant's lips, and her eyes softened. "Just curious that's all." She paused. "But, to answer your question, no, I don't think there is any connection now that the arson investigation is complete."

Still you wonder about the flip-flop don't you and it's possible connection to this sorry affair. Ruthalice straightened up and extended her hand. "Rosemarie Harris, I can see you are a force to be reckoned with and a worthy adversary. I certainly want you on my side if I ever find myself in trouble with the law." They shook hands. As the lieutenant pulled her door open, Ruthalice called to her. "Thank you for trusting my professional judgment on this one, Rosemarie. I appreciate it enormously." Their eyes met.

"We both have a difficult job," she replied taking off her cap and tossing it onto the front seat. "Professional courtesy and respect are at the top of my list."

"Mine too," Ali whispered as the black and white moved into the street, "and discretion, don't forget personal discretion."

The International Student Club gathered around the big wooden table in the back corner of the Leaky Cup Café. Luther and Rani both bundled up against the damp wind, walked over together after supper. Arriving before the others Rani unwound the thick wool cherry red scarf Mary Scott gave her for Christmas. Luther, resembling a large turtle, remained hunched down inside the navy blue Emerick sweatshirt his roommate's mother bought him his first term on campus.

"Olga and Bodil are here!"

Rani smiled happily at the two Norwegian women. Olga set her shoulder bag on the seat beside Rani. Bodil unbuttoned the snowflake-covered ski sweater, opened her notebook and waved at Rene. The handsome Mexican student whistling under his breath as he made his way toward them, plopped his solid five-foot-four inch frame on the chair beside her.

"We're all here, so let's get started." Bodil dated the top of the page then slipped a loose strand of hair behind her ear. "OK, what do we want to do for Festival this year?"

Twenty minutes later the five students had finished their list of various tasks required to host an internationally-flavored meal and dance and settled into amiable chatter. Rani surreptitiously glanced at Luther and saw the anxiety in his eyes. She reached for his hand under the table. He tensed at the touch then relaxed, squeezed her fingers and looked around the little circle of friends.

"I have something very important to share with you tonight." The others, startled by his serious tone, immediately stopped talking.

"What is it, Luther? You look worried," Olga said gently. "Is something wrong?"

"This is all confidential, ok guys?" Luther leaned into the circle. "I mean really, REALLY confidential."

Four heads nodded their understanding. Bodil clicked her ballpoint pen and set it on her minute book signaling the end of any official minute keeping. "You can totally count on us, Luther," she said warmly.

"My cousin has been hiding in the basement of Pennington Place for the past few months." The students stared at Luther in astonishment. "The fire chased him out Tuesday night, so he escaped by running to Professor Charles Hopkins' house taking all his belongings with him wrapped up in a blanket."

Luther brought both hands up from under the table and laid them palms down on the surface in front of him. Rani stroking the fringe on her scarf began to speak.

"I assured Luther that if our club knew about the terrible danger his cousin is in, we would all want to help." Three heads nodded in agreement. "Because," she continued lowering her voice, "Luther's cousin has been in the US illegally since his student visa expired." She met the eyes of each student in turn. "I think it would be a worthy cause for our International Club to take up, don't you?"

The prospect of rescuing Luther's fugitive cousin struck a responsive cord with Rene, and he leaned forward eagerly. "My cousin is a coyote and a very good one. He runs dozens of Mexicans safely across the border every year. I know I can get him to take Gideon to Mexico really cheap!"

Luther starred at him in disbelief. "What on earth are you thinking, Rene? We are not taking my cousin to Mexico legally or illegally. What possible good would that do?"

Startled by the sharp rebuff, Rene slid back in his chair. "It would get him out of the country for one thing," he retorted, annoyed by the quick dismissal of his offer. "I think we should talk with Ruthalice Michels, our campus minister," Rani suggested. "She will give us some good advice."

"The campus minister?" Rene snorted. "I doubt she'll come up with anything we can't all by ourselves. Besides," he added shooting a challenging look at Luther, "I thought you said you don't want anyone else to know about your cousin."

"She already knows," Luther responded matter-of-factly. "She and Clifford Mowry ate dinner with me and Luther at Hopkins place Friday night." He smiled. "She knows all about my cousin." Relieved by the amusement she heard in Luther's voice, Rani relaxed for the first time all evening.

"I can speak with Ruthalice tomorrow after Bible class." Bodil looked around the table. "Can you meet in her office at noon if she's free?" All heads nodded. "Ok, let's plan to meet in Frame Meetinghouse at her office at noon."

The little collection of friends stood up. Rene, mollified now that a course of action had been agreed upon, helped Rani carry their mugs to the communal sink. They rinsed and dried each one before returning them to their respective hooks on the pegboard lining the wall beside the coffee bar. The last to leave Luther and Rani followed the others down the porch steps and crossed the street. When they reached the south side of Pennington Place Luther led her to the backside of the building. They stopped to stare at the coal bin door barely visible behind the bushes.

"I hope they keep their mouths shut, Rani."

"We can trust them, Luther," she replied with more confidence than she felt, "because each one of us knows a refugee or someone who is less fortunate with no home and no place to go, someone who must hide in order to stay alive." She hesitated then encompassed him with her radiant smile. "I can see the questions on your face. You are wondering why I am speaking this way aren't you, Luther?" She paused to collect her resolve then began to speak. "I will tell you something that no one else in Oakes Quarry knows about me." She hesitated for an instant then commenced telling her story. "My 15-year old mother abandoned me when I was five. When I was seven years old, Dorcus and Rufous Brown found me living with a small gang of street ruffians and orphans in the alleys of Kingston. The Browns raised me as their daughter, their only child, and named me Rani after mama's grandmother and Sequoia for papa's youngest sister who died from malaria when she was just an infant."

Luther gazed intently at the beautiful woman standing beside him and realized it didn't matter anymore that he had only known her a few months. The secrets they now shared with each other bound them intimately together, and as his heart began to pound he took her hand, and promised himself he would never let it go again.

Chapter Eleven – Friday Next

Bodil patiently waited just outside the circle of students surrounding Ruthalice until they had finished asking questions then caught her attention.

"I have a question, Ruthalice."

"Of course, Bodil"

"The International Club would like to meet with you this noon if that's okay with you."

"Let's go check my calendar." The two women walked into her office. "Looks fine to me. May I ask what this is about?" she inquired. Bodil Casper in her four years at Emerick College had never once graced the door of the Office of Campus Ministry so the possibilities seemed endless.

Glancing quickly out the window, Bodil squared her shoulders. "Something came up last night during our club meeting, and some of us think we should talk to you before doing anything about it."

"And some are not so sure?" Ruthalice smiled sympathetically. "So, let's see. That means you, Rene, Luther, Rani and Olga, right?" She nodded. "Okay, I'll see all of you at noon."

The young Norwegian extracted the cell phone from her sweater pocket and disappeared down the hall.

"I'd better hot foot it to the hospital right now then," Ruthalice decided grabbing her keys and hospital chaplain card. An hour later after paying a pastoral call on the two students struck by a car last Thursday night, she returned to find Emerick's five international students lingering outside her door. She flung the door open, snatched a yellow pad and rolled her desk chair beside the sofa as the students took seats around the coffee table.

"So, what's on your minds?"

The group's unspoken deferral to Luther gave Ruthalice time to focus her attention on the young man she'd seen more of in the last two days than she had since he arrived on campus over a year ago.

"I, Rani and I," he began cautiously, after checking Rani's face to make certain it was all right to include her. The nearly imperceptible nod assured him it was. "Last night Rani and I told the International Club about Gideon."

A look of alarm sped across Ali's face. *Oh golly, five more fingers stirring the pot! So much for keeping our secret a secret.*

"We want to take on Gideon's case as a group project," Rani explained quickly. "I mean, The International Club decided to help Gideon get legal status in the United States."

"We all think if we can sponsor my cousin somehow then the US Immigration service will let him stay."

In spite of the apprehension gripping every cell in her body, Ruthalice felt enormous affection for these eager young students. *We all want to help, don't we God, everyone who knows about Gideon, myself included. Until yesterday afternoon I was positive that the right thing to do was convince Gideon to return to Somalia.* But after her own epiphany she was considerably more cautious about rushing to his rescue without way more information and considerable prayer!

"That's not going to be possible, I'm afraid," she said regretfully. "I have read the Immigration and Naturalization Service rules and there simply isn't any wiggle room. Since 1996 the law states that anyone who has been in this country illegally for more than one year is barred from immigrating to the United States until they have first returned to their home country and lived there for 10 years."

"Ten years!" Olga wailed. "But everybody knows how dangerous and unsafe Somalia is. He'll surely be killed." Her voice, filled with indignation and fear seemed to speak for all of them. "That's just plain not fair," she added glaring at Ruthalice.

"Unfortunately it doesn't matter what we think, Bodil. Fair or not, it's the way things are these days, and we're stuck with it." Ali's face was grim. *And I hate it just like you do!* "My friends, we dare not call attention to Gideon's presence in our community, and we most assuredly cannot inform the INS or Gideon will be summarily deported." She felt miserable. "I don't know how to be anymore plain than that."

"So we just ignore this injustice and sit around doing nothing?" Spit and words tumbled out in an angry torrent.

"I didn't say that, Rene. What I *am* saying is that we don't dare rush into action until we have carefully considered all the consequences." She fixed each one with a no-nonsense stare. "Is that clear?" Five heads moved up and down reluctantly. "In the meantime, do not share this idea with any of your friends because remember the more people who find out about Gideon, the less safe he is. We must all be clear on that point."

"If we mess up," Luther said simply, "and my cousin ends up in shackles on a plane bound for Mogadishu because somebody reports him…" The sentiment hung menacingly in the air.

Though their eyes were grim and sullen, the students understood the danger.

"All right then." Ruthalice got to her feet. "I'm going to make a few phone calls so I should be better informed by Monday about what options we do have." Her voice softened. "And just remember, guys, Gideon is safe for the moment with Charles Hopkins as long as he stays put and," she added firmly "none of us says or does anything. So, keep a lid on it, ok?"

The students rose as one, collected backpacks, scarves and gloves and filed dejectedly down the corridor.

"By the way," Ruthalice said loud enough for Bodil, who was bringing up the rear to hear, "I happen to agree with what Ann Richards, the former governor of Texas said. 'Life isn't fair. I know life isn't fair, but government should be.'"

The look of relief that swept across Bodil's face warmed Ruthalice's heart.

"I didn't think you cared at all," she stated pausing in the doorway.

More than you'll ever know her heart replied silently. *I can scarcely think about anything else.*

Waiting by the door until they left the building Ruthalice sank heavily into the closest chair feeling completely drained. Her heart pounded as panic swept up from her stomach. Burying her face in her hands she quieted her breathing until the fear subsided and her mind became clear. Retrieving her wool cape from the clothes tree she strode to Fox Hall. *It is time to include Charles and bring him up to date.* Outside his office she rapped lightly on the wooden door frame.

"It's open." He looked up from his reading.

"Charles, I must tell you about a meeting I just had with the International Club students."

Laying his red pen down on the papers in front of him, Professor Hopkins removed his reading glasses and stared at Ali with bloodshot eyes.

"All five of them know about Gideon." His jaw tightened. "The club believes that if they sponsor him and convince the INS it's too dangerous for him to return to Somalia, they will permit him to remain in this country."

Charles stared at her in utter disbelief. "Not possible."

"You and I know that, Charles," Ali replied, "but they're young and idealistic. I did manage to hold them off temporarily by informing them in no uncertain terms that any action on their part compromises Gideon's safety and promised to make some phone calls. For the time being they have pledged themselves to secrecy, but to be perfectly honest, I don't know how long that will last." She starred somberly across the desk. "These kids are full of self-righteous indignation and imagine themselves bona fide crusaders for a just and worthy cause! It's all quite poignant really, their sense of loyalty and compassion for a fellow alien." She gazed forlornly at his flushed face and added wistfully, "These young people just want this story to end happily. They're determined to rescue him. I only wish it were possible," she added lamely.

Wordlessly, Charles stood up and walked to the door. "I am going home now, Ruthalice. A young man's life is at stake here." He pulled on his cap. "Thank you for stopping by to alert me."

"Charles," she asked hopefully, turning to face him. "Do you think there's any point in going to the Immigration service?"

"Good God, no!" he responded curtly. "This is hardly the time for wishful thinking." Shaking his head in dismay, Charles marched down the corridor and disappeared.

As she headed back to her office a burden of despair settled upon Ruthalice. *I guess I was expecting a miracle and hoping Charles would provide the answer so that everything would work out for the best.* Ignoring the blinking message light on her answering machine, Ali collected her canvas bag and Bible, and walked to her car. She drove Lemon Drop to the long abandoned Oakes Quarry gravel pit three miles from campus and wandered along Quarryman Trail. Her favorite bench stood tucked under a drooping weeping willow tree beside the lake. Sweeping the leaves off the seat, she lay on her back and gazed pensively at the deep blue sky then closed her eyes and began reciting the 23rd Psalm. As she whispered, "You spread a table before me in the presence of mine enemies," tears filled her eyes and ran slowly down her cheeks into her ears.

Who are your enemies, dear Gideon Boseka, the renegade terrorists and armed soldiers in your home town, our country's immigration laws or your own decisions and nightmares? She sniffled and sat up just as a Great Blue Heron alighted and stood motionless in the shallow water. Ali gazed out over the placid surface.

"I have not walked even a block in Gideon's moccasins let alone a mile! I don't know any more what

I'm supposed to do so please instruct and guide me, God. I will obey to the best of my ability."

The heron squawked then lifted heavily into flight, and Ali felt her spirit rising with it on its graceful journey home. She reached under the bench and collected her Bible and bag. "Let your spirit fall on Gideon Boseka, dear God and refresh again that dear young man. If he is given his voice back he has much to teach the rest of us about suffering and endurance." Ruthalice smiled as the image of Gideon speaking truth to power came to her. "A messenger of peace – an ambassador for love and understanding – that's who our Gideon will become when he is finally walking in the sunshine and out of hiding once and for all!"

Enjoying the crunch of chipped bark under her feet as she walked the trail back to the parking lot, Ruthalice began to fume again. *There's got to be something useful I can do.* "I've got it!" she exclaimed slamming the car door. "I'll call my seminary buddy at the justice center in Phoenix and pick his brains." With a course of action in hand, Ali's juices were flowing. "Joseph was an attorney in his first life. He's perfect!"

Charles Hopkins strode purposefully across the parking lot, started the cantankerous little VW and narrowly missed turning into a red pickup truck barreling down the street. Horn blaring, the driver swerved and gave him the finger. Dutifully chastised Curly drove carefully as he began mentally charting his course of action. "First stop Wal-Mart to purchase a suitcase. The lad needs a winter coat, gloves, wool cap, and he can't keep wearing those same three shirts."

As the steps fell into place, Charles began to relax. The shopping completed he tossed two large shopping bags and a plaid, soft-sided suitcase on the back seat and drove to Sheppard Place. "Gideon," he called walking rapidly into the living room. Discovering his guest in his usual spot on the love seat, Curly dropped the plastic bags on the floor in front of him. "Gideon my boy, we've been cooped up in this house long enough so we're taking a trip this weekend." Charles ploughed on without waiting for a reply. "I called our friend Terrell Martin, and he's invited us up to Toledo for a visit."

Gideon's face broke into a delighted grin. "A trip adventure, Uncle Professor Curly." His face suddenly clouded. "But, I tell the M&Ms we come for dinner on Sunday. I promise to cook."

Charles replied airily, "Oh, that's all right. I informed Ruthalice this afternoon that we would be out of town this weekend. She said to come out some other time." He pointed to the suitcase by the basement door. "Gideon, I have a new suitcase for you to pack and a few new shirts, a sweater and winter outer garments are in the plastic bags."

"My goodness, Professor Curly, I take all that to Toledo?"

"It's much colder that far north," Charles insisted firmly. "Now, go and pack all your things, including your Bible and anything else you brought to my house." Seeing the puzzled look on Gideon's face, he added, "Martin indicated he wants you to stay with him for a few weeks until I can spring free down here and get back up to collect you."

Evidently satisfied Gideon picked up the plastic bags and suitcase and disappeared into the basement. A half hour later he reappeared in the kitchen his new coat draped over his right arm. “I ready to go to Toledo! You are taking not much Professor Curly?” he asked, indicating the small brown valise resting by the back door.

“A fellow my age travels light, my dear chap! Oh, by the way, do you happen to have your uncle’s phone number in Minnesota? I thought it would be jolly good fun to give him a ring whilst we’re in Toledo.”

“Call my uncle? I not talk with my uncle for months!” Digging in his pocket, Gideon extracted a small notebook. “I have it here,” he said turning the worn pages. “Yes, it is here, Professor Curly.”

“Jolly good. Now be a good lad and go double check your room to be sure you have everything. I’ll carry our cases to the car.”

Charles took the new Gore Tex jacket from Gideon’s arm and slipped two one hundred dollars bills into the inner pocket before pressing the Velcro strip sealing them safely inside. He placed the suitcases in the trunk of the rental car, slammed the lid shut with a thud, climbed into the driver’s seat and waited impatiently, drumming his fingers on the steering wheel. Gideon slipped into the passenger sea and buckled his seat belt.

“We take an adventure trip in a fine new car!” he said beaming eagerly at his benefactor. “I never go to Toledo. When I come to Emerick College, Dr. Martin live in Oakes Quarry.” He shook his head. “That was a very long time ago.”

“A lot of water’s gone under the bridge, hasn’t it my young friend?” Charles backed out of the driveway, turned on the headlights and headed north out of town.

"It's a long trip, Gideon," he warned. "Why don't you try to sleep a little?"

"No, no" he laughed lightly. "I want to watch. I like to see all the lights. In Somalia it is very dark at night. We do not have so many lights as here." He paused staring intently out the window. "I stay awake and keep you company, Professor Curly then we sleep at Dr. Martin's house." Gideon continued to gaze out the window into the night. "I like lights, Professor Curly," he added solemnly, "because then I see next what is going to happen."

Chapter Twelve – The Final Weekend

"My gosh, 8:30 already?" Cliff slid his feet around on the carpet, located his slippers with his right heel then padded into the living room. Bending over he kissed the top of Ali's head. "How long you been up?"

"Since about 5. After a good case of the 'four o'clock wobblies' I finally just gave up and came out here. There's plenty of coffee in the thermos," she added closing her Bible and patting the cushion beside her on the comfy green couch. "Come sit."

"So, fires and refugees got you all stirred up?" he inquired, his gray-green eyes full of concern.

"The worst thing about this whole darn episode is this fire never should have happened," Ali replied wearily. "If Priscilla had simply stashed her fireworks in the Delta house or dear old Ira crushed his cigarette out in the coal bin…" Her voice trailed off. "It's just all so darn coincidental and innocent really." She frowned. "The whole can't exist if one of its parts is missing or something like that." Cliff silently refilled her mug and smiled gently as Ali inhaled the steamy coffee smell managing to fog up her glasses in the process. "I guess all's I'm really trying to say is everyone's innocent and everyone's guilty all at the same time." She turned sideways on the couch, brought her right leg up and tucked her toe under her left knee to hold everything in place. "Take Priscilla and Jen for example," she began looking at her husband over the top of her ceramic mug. "What they did was incredibly stupid,"

"and illegal." Cliff rested his feet on the coffee table. "You're not even allowed to keep fireworks in this state for more than two days."

"Ok, and illegal, but remember the girls never shot them off." Ali pressed her back into the couch. "Then there's Ira. He's sure paid one heckuva stiff price for the 'sin of smoking' as he so quaintly put it."

"Bailey gave him a pretty generous severance package though don't you agree?"

Unwilling to be deflected from her litany of disrupted lives, Ruthalice merely nodded.

"Then there's our dear old hide-bound Curly Hopkins. His comfortable, predictable bachelor life has gotten seriously derailed big time and promises to remain so for the foreseeable future."

"Bishop Swithum's had to take some time off," Cliff opined scratching his chin.

"Who knows what the penalties are for harboring an undocumented alien these days," Ali added fretfully.

Suddenly restless Ruthalice jumped up from the couch and crossing to the other side of the living room flung open the heavy muslin drapes. "And then there's Richard." She paused as she watched the progress of three turkeys across the back yard. "He's devoted oodles of hours to the investigation to say nothing of the sleep he's lost, attended countless meetings, issued press releases in adnauseam."

Cliff slipped silently to the window, placed both hands on his wife's shoulders and turned her around. "And then there's the campus minister who's running herself ragged, hasn't had a decent night's sleep in a week..." He gently kissed her forehead then pulled her tight against him.

"I can't stop worrying about Gideon, Cliff." She leaned back slightly so she could see his face. "Whenever I think about him I want to rail against the INS and write my congressman about their inhumane regulations or go find a corner and bawl my head off, neither of which is particularly useful. I just feel so pathetically useless!"

The pastor and the professor clung to each other, her arms around his waist, his protectively around her shoulder. Cliff pressed his left cheek against her soft hair.

"There is one real victim in this whole sorry affair," he said finally relaxing his embrace. "Gideon." He smiled into his wife's upturned face. "I've come to think of him as Gideon the Innocent."

"He told me he's been running all his life and can't even imagine what being safe would feel like." Ruthalice took Cliff's hand and interlocked fingers. "Do you suppose our Gideon has seen the angel of the Lord face to face the way his biblical namesake did?"

"Something has carried him through the countless ordeals of passage into manhood." Cliff paused, a worried look creeping into his eyes. "Ali, have you decided what you're going to do now that the international students have gotten into the act further complicating an already difficult situation?"

"When I marched over to Curly's house on Thursday, I was dead certain the best solution for Gideon was to voluntarily turn himself in and go back to Somalia. I came away equally certain that returning was pure suicide and the worst possible thing he could do. Now I honestly don't know. I'm just plain stymied." Ali suddenly stopped talking and a warm smile began to spread across her face. "Actually, that's not entirely true. I'm going to continue praying for a solution and if I'm to be part of said solution then God needs to indicate loud and clear what I'm supposed to do."

"What about giving Terrell Martin a call, sweetheart? Not only has he got a vested interest in Gideon but he worked for the State Department after leaving Mogadishu so there's a good chance he knows somebody at INS. Maybe he'd have a suggestion or two."

"Maybe so." Ali touched the window glass. "I know he had a strong tie to Gideon at one time," she said watching her palm print evaporate. "But for now I'm going to heed my own advice and not rush into anything. If calling Martin feels like way forward I'll try him before we go to worship tomorrow morning."

The remainder of Saturday morning Ruthalice moved restlessly from one task to another, but even scrubbing the kitchen floor and kneading a loaf of bread didn't take her mind off Gideon Boseka. *You've got to engage your brain!* Scolding herself for ignoring the obvious, Ali opened the mudroom door and walked across the garage floor. From the back seat of her car she retrieved a cardboard box still smelling faintly of smoke and carried it to the breakfast nook. Inside was a hodgepodge of old photographs and hand-written programs from the earliest years of the college when it was still the Emerick Normal School for Women.

There must be tons of information in here I can use for my speech to the Women's Auxiliary of the Historical Society Tuesday night. Ali rummaged through the accumulated memorabilia. *I'm willing to bet that one of those dear ladies of the Auxiliary is a great-great granddaughter or niece or some such of one of these gals in that first graduating class.*

A brown-tinted photograph caught her eye. An elegant young woman wearing a plain white floor length dress gazed intently back at her. Turning the photo over Ali squinted at the faded writing, "*To my dearest Theodore, upon the occasion of my graduation from ENS4W. Love always, Molly Jean.*"

Digging deeper Ali uncovered the embossed program from the first graduation ceremony. On the back page was a brief biographical sketch on each of the five graduates. "*Molly Jean Monroe married Theodore Cope during her second term of school. The young couple took up housekeeping on the Cope Family Farm located on Hidden River, Boone County while she completed her education.*"

"Cliff, listen to this," Ali exclaimed excitedly as he stomped into the kitchen carrying a wire basket full of chicken eggs. "I'm working on my talk to the auxiliary, ok and came on the name Molly Jean Cope. She was in that first graduating class. I'm just about willing to bet the farm that she's related to our recalcitrant soccer player!" Her eyes glowing with enthusiasm, Ruthalice stated boldly, "In fact, I'll wager that Molly Jean is Ted's great-great-great grandmother!"

"And this gets us where?" Cliff set the basket on the counter and began placing each light brown egg into the pocket of a store-bought styrofoam carton.

"Remember my saying that Ted's father is of the opinion that college is a total waste of time and money? Well what if Roger Cope has no idea that his own great-great-grandma is a member of the first class to graduate from what is now Emerick College? Who knows? It might just give him a whole different perspective on a college education."

"Hoping to change poppa's mind?"

"Well, at least give him some family history to chew on," she replied stuffing photos and papers back into the carton.

"Say, Ms. Michels, I've got an idea. It's awfully nice outside, so how 'bout we go to the men's soccer match then hit Damon's for supper? We should be able to see most of the game if we leave right away."

Ten minutes into the first half, the M&Ms joined a handful of faculty and students seated on gray wooden bleachers at mid-field.

"Number 22, Jason Baxter is substituting in for Emerick," a voice announced through the loudspeaker.

Startled, Ruthalice swiveled around and stared intently into the glass enclosed press box behind them. "That's Ted Cope, Cliff. Look," she insisted resisting the urge to point. "I recognize his voice. By golly I'll bettcha Bob Stevens has made him team statistician and PA announcer for the remainder of the season. Way to go, Bob!"

Cliff nudged her and nodded at a heavyset man with a navy Emerick College scarf slung casually over his shoulders sitting two rows over. They watched in amazement as the dreaded Sidney Cope stood and gave a two-handed thumb's up toward the press box. From the booth his nephew returned both the gesture and the grin.

As the waitress led them to their table, Cliff grabbed a discarded *Oakes Quarry Gazette* from the hostess table and hurried to catch up with his wife. While they waited for menus he turned to the sports section leaving Ruthalice with the rest of the paper. He was in the middle of an article on the floundering high school football team when Ali clenched his arm.

"Oh God no! This can't be happening!"

Clifford looked up in alarm. "Read it to me, Ruthalice."

"The FBI has contacted the Oakes Quarry police department with information concerning the hiring practices of Smart Outlet Warehouses, Inc. Due to the large number of illegal aliens employed by the chain nation-wide (some estimates as high as 750 individuals), all locations have come under close scrutiny. The local store on McKaig Avenue issued a statement late yesterday afternoon indicating that they do not employ undocumented workers. An investigation of regional employee records commences on Monday. '"

Dropping a five dollar bill on the table beside their untouched water glasses, the M&Ms left the restaurant and without a word drove straight to Sheppard Place. Clifford jabbed the front bell as Ruthalice pounded on the kitchen door, but neither one got an answer. Ali scribbled 'call us ASAP' on her soccer program then slipped it under the back door. They stood for a moment in the side yard.

"This is so darned frustrating!" Ali railed at the empty street. "Where in the heck are you, Charles?"

"Maybe they went to Cincinnati for the day," Cliff offered hoping he sounded more optimistic than he felt.

"Let's go home, honey," he added dejectedly. "There's nothing we can do until Curly calls."

Sunday Morning

Hearing the light tap on her door, Rani pulled a sweater over her head, wound the cherry red scarf around her neck, and stuffed the room key into her jeans pocket. "I'm ready," she smiled as they stepped into the Sunday morning sunshine. Striding purposefully down Wood Avenue they arrived ten minutes later at 534 Sheppard Place. Luther pulled off his glove and rang the front door bell, waited a few minutes then rang again.

"I'll see if there's a car in the garage." Rani walked around the side of the house and peered through the dirty pane of glass. "His car's here, Luther."

"I'll try my cell phone," Luther said digging into his jacket pocket. They could hear the muffled ringing inside the house. Cupping her hands around her face, Rani peered through the kitchen window.

"Doesn't look like anybody's home."

"Come on, let's try the door." Without waiting for a reply, Luther giggled the knob and leaned against the back door which opened without a hitch. The two friends exchanged a nervous glance and stepped quickly inside.

"Yo, Gideon, are you here? It's me and Rani."

The no-sound of an empty space filled the house. Luther flipped the light switch at the top of the stairs then trotted down into the basement. Rumpled sheets strewn across the cot were the only indication someone had slept there. He spun around and bounded back up the stairs.

"Gideon's stuff's gone," he gasped leaning against the door jam. "His clothes, his blanket parcel, everything's just gone!"

Rani stared in disbelief. "But, where can they have gone, Luther? I looked in the bedroom," she added blushing slightly, "and Professor Curly's bed is made. I don't think he slept here last night."

"I think they're in trouble, Rani. Maybe Immigration found out about my cousin. Maybe one of our so-called friends couldn't keep their mouth shut!"

"Call Ruthalice Michels." Her voice was so uncharacteristically firm that Luther winced as if she'd struck him. "Call Ruthalice, Luther Mouana."

Rani listened intently as Luther explained where they were and what they had discovered. After a few minutes his face began to relax. "Thank you, Ruthalice. You have made me feel much better." Luther stuffed the cell phone back into his jacket pocket.

"What did she say?"

"She said not to worry yet. She's expecting the professor and my cousin at their house for dinner at one o'clock." He grinned sheepishly. "Gideon's fixing one of my favorite Somali dishes, chicken small-small."

Ignoring his editorial comment, Rani got straight to the point. "But that doesn't explain why all Gideon's belongings are gone, Luther! Even if they are doing laundry, his Bible should still be here."

"Unless…"

"Unless what?"

"What if Professor Hopkins has moved Gideon to a safer place and the professor is out taking a walk by himself!"

"That would be good." Rani still looked dubious. "But what can we do in the meantime?"

"Worry!"

She squeezed his hand. "You worry, and I'll pray, ok?"

"Who was that?" Cliff asked loosening his tie.

"Luther Mouana. He and Rani went to Curly's for a visit, and when no one answered the door or phone, they let themselves in." She shook her head a self-deprecating smile on her face. "I guess I never tried the door knob," she added sheepishly. "Anyway, Luther said Gideon's room looks cleaned out. I shared my hunch that Curly's got cabin fever, but that really doesn't explain the empty bedroom." She gave Clifford a baffled look. "I don't have a good feeling about any of this right now though."

Cliff watched her from the bedroom doorway, tie in hand. "Charles is a grown-up, Ali, and as long as I've known him he's made informed decisions. I can't fathom why all Gideon's stuff's gone either, but I trust Curly's judgment."

"You don't think he'd panic with the FBI snooping about?"

"Hopkins doesn't panic, my dear, even assuming he knows about the impending investigation of our local warehouse store."

"The two of them are due here for dinner any time now so I guess we're going to find out soon enough. Gideon's cooking chicken small-small," she reminded him grinning happily, "so I suspect we won't actually be eating for quite awhile. He insisted on buying all the ingredients by the way."

"Sounds intriguing," Cliff replied from the closet. "I'm changing into something more comfortable than this suit."

"Good heavens we're popular today," Ali muttered as the phone rang. As she listened a growing uneasiness started to creep into her stomach. The black cat kitchen clock, its long curved tail swinging mechanically back and forth, stared into the room with unseeing eyes. The bright red hands rested nearly upright at one o'clock.

"Babs Carroll wanted me to know the college judicial review board met for two hours yesterday afternoon and placed Priscilla and Jennifer on probation until they graduate," Ali announced joining Cliff in the bedroom and slipping out of her skirt. "Another infraction and those two are suspended from Emerick. They're also required to give written apology to the Board of Trustees as well as to the fire and police departments."

"Ah, the old kitchen sink treatment! The administration must have decided to nip this kind of extracurricular activity in the bud." Cliff buttoned his cardigan. "What are they doing vis-à-vis Ohio statutes on fireworks?"

"All Barbara said was the authorities are taking the necessary steps required under state law."

"Egad, that sounds ominous!"

"I doubt anyone's amused by this expensive little caper. It'll serve as an example for years to come of the importance of weighing risks, learning to anticipate unexpected consequences, etc. etc." Ali rolled her eyes.

"I wonder if Priscilla Ann will buckle down now and get serious about school," Cliff added. "If not we've got the classic 'three strikes and you're out'."

"We'll see." Ali pulled a red and white striped sweater over her head. "Be a dear and lay another fire, would you, Cliff?" She peered at her watch. "Something's not right, I can feel it in my gut. Shoot, it's already 1:45. I'm gonna go sit in the living room and worry until Gideon and Charles appear on our door step."

Sunday Night

At half past ten Charles Hopkins closed the garage door and carried his little brown valise into the kitchen. Dropping it on the floor, he shrugged out of his coat, went to the phone and dialed.

"Charles here," he responded as the receiver was picked up. "Yes everything's fine, Ruthalice. I am calling to apologize for missing dinner this afternoon. I'm frightfully sorry." Charles took a deep breath before plunging ahead. "After our little chat on Friday I came to the conclusion that Oakes Quarry was no longer a safe haven for Gideon, so I called Terrell Martin. You remember him I'm sure." He listened patiently to Ali's assurance that of course she remembers Dr. Martin's role in bringing Gideon to Emerick College. "Martin insisted I bring Gideon up to his place in Toledo whilst we figure out the best course of action. So I've done just that."

Charles pulled a rumpled handkerchief from his pants pocket and wiped his eyes before softly blowing his nose.

"Sorry, Ruthalice," he said apologetically. "I felt a sneeze coming on."

The phone conversation completed, the old professor dropped onto the nearest kitchen chair and buried his face in his hands. The tea kettle's insistent whistle finally forced him to his feet. Cradling his hot mug of tea with both hands, he wandered into the living room and sank into his easy chair without bothering to turn on the light. *You're just plum worn out, old chap; a bit long in the tooth to be driving cross country in the middle of the night.*

He starred at the delicate harpsichord in the corner of the room and wrestled with his conscience. *You know damn well that's not the issue here, you old fool. Lying to two dear friends whom you trust with your life, that's what's got your backside in a bind. I'm not really lying,* that contrary voice argued back, *I'm just not telling the entire truth that's all.*

"Oh, shut up!" he snapped out loud. "What's the bloody difference?"

Swamped by fatigue Charles closed his eyes. As images of the joy-filled reunion filled his head, an enormous sense of satisfaction settled in his heart. When Gideon awoke early Saturday morning asking if they were in Toledo yet, Charles had answered simply, "No, my young friend. We are in the Twin Cities." The shock on Gideon's face had been its own reward, "I have brought you to your uncle's house," he added easily, and with the speaking of those eight words, Professor Hopkins understood that in a lifetime of consequential decision-making, this had been his finest hour. The entire rag-tag clan swarmed onto the front porch of a dilapidated frame house filled to overflowing with Somali refugees. The gray-haired patriarch warmly welcomed him as the guardian who'd brought their countryman safely back into the bosom of his extended family.

"You are safe, nephew," his uncle had whispered huskily, clapping Gideon on the back before giving him an enormous bear hug. "Welcome home."

Now in the solitude of his little bungalow the memory of men embracing and weeping raised a lump in Curly's throat which threatened to choke him. Just as unexpected was the sense of utter peace which slowly encompassed him. As tension released its grip, Charles' face softened into a gentle smile. *There's one more call to make,* he reminded himself struggling to his feet. Charles made his way back to the black wall phone hanging above the kitchen counter, dialed eleven numbers and waited. After a few rings a sleepy male voice said, "Terrell Martin, here."

"Hopkins here…Yes my friend, it has been a long time…I'm doing as well as can be expected for an old man." He chuckled at the response. "Listen, I rang you, yes I know it's late, because I think you will be interested in the happenings this past fortnight here at dear old EC. They involve our mutual acquaintance Gideon Boseka."

Charles hung up and headed down the hallway. An unanticipated wave of loneliness crashed over him. A sense of having been summarily abandoned propelled him down the basement stairs. The cherished solitude he had jealously guarded for decades glared glumly back at him. Not sure why, he gathered up the crumpled sheets and lumbered back upstairs. The shabby little love seat where Gideon sat and read his Bible seemed to anticipate the return of an intimate friend. No longer would the occasional tea mug be forgotten and left on the coffee table until someone remembered to rinse it out. Listening in vain for the soft sound of whistling, Charles wondered, *was it truly only twelve days ago you took flight and landed on my door step?*

Clutching his soft bundle of bedding still smelling of Gideon's soap-clean scent, Charles solemnly closed the door to the basement. *You've been plum deserted, old boy,* he thought as he shuffled down the hallway. Reaching his bedroom, Curly dropped the sheets onto a pile of dirty laundry and collapsed into bed. *On the morrow I shall confide in my trusted and worthy friends, but tonight I have not the courage to do so. May they forgive my transgression of being economical with the truth.*

As the old professor pulled the duvet over his shoulders, resignation settled down beside exhaustion. "For so the game is ended that should not have begun," he quoted wearily and dropped off to sleep.

Made in the USA
Charleston, SC
01 September 2011